Mickey Doc

BY FINTAN HARVEY

Mickey Doc

ABOUT THE AUTHOR:

Fintan Harvey lives in Claudy, Co Derry, Northern Ireland. Fintan has written and performed stand-up comedy for 5 years, and has performed in many venues throughout Ireland. This is Fintan's first novel.

A massive thank you to all my friends and family for all your love and support. And to Sean Keddy for the amazing artwork. Cheers, son.

Websites and info. www.facebook.com/MickeyDocNo1

Design and Cover by. Sean Keddy (C) 2018.

By Fintan Harvey

For:

My nieces and nephews- Ruairi, Odhran, Dara, Caitlin, Sean, Eabha and Chloe.

Follow your dreams.

Mickey Doc

CHAPTER 1.

'Do ye have your lunch with ye?'

'Aye, I have it here!'

I hold up a plastic bag that has my lunch inside wrapped up in tinfoil. Ham sandwiches again. The dog is lying in the corner of the kitchen, just staring at me. I swear to God that mutt gets fed better than I do. I came in from work last night and noticed it was munching away on pork chops while I had to make do with fish fingers and chips. He kept looking over at me too, as if to say: 'I'm fucking better than you, Mickey.'

Aye, we'll see who's better.

I give it the middle finger as I walk out into the hall, then I shout up the stairs:

'Right, I'm away here Ma, I'll see ye later!'

'Remember to get next Friday booked off, and don't be leaving it 'til the last minute like you always do!'

'I will, aye!'

Just as I'm about to leave, I hear the shower go on. It's weird to know that your ma has been shouting down the stairs to you when she's in the nip. I just hope she had a towel on. She's on to me about getting next Friday off work for a job interview in a call centre. Half of Derry works in those places and they reckon it's easy to get in, just as long as I say the right things, which can be a bit hard for me at times because, as anybody will tell you, I'm not exactly the sharpest tool in the bed.

Anyway, it's 8 o'clock on Tuesday morning and I'm walking down to the bus stop, which is about ten minutes away from my house. The rain is absolutely pissing down and my fingers are froze! It's January now and it still feels like winter, which is weird if you think about it. I mean, everybody is talking about 'global warming' and crap like that, but how can it be global warming if the place is getting colder? Shouldn't it be 'global colding'? It's those kinds of things that make me not watch the news or have anything to do with current affairs. Well, that and the fact it's boring as fuck. I'm more of a music sort of person myself. I'm walking along with my iPod blasting out the tunes, Little Mix on repeat, and I can blank out the shit weather. You see, that's what I want to be: a serious musician, like the Little Mix girls. I want it all, I want the fame, the glamour, the signing autographs, the interviews, the paparazzi. My ma says I have the voice of an angel, and she's probably right. Actually, there's no probably in it, she's definitely right. I just need to get my big break. She reckons if I can get on the X-Factor I'll be a star. My da said it's a load of shite and it's ruining the music industry! What the fuck? It IS the music industry! He's just bitter, though. He always wanted me to follow in his shoes or boots or whatever, and play football. I fucking hate football, I was never any good at it and never wanted to be any good at it – mostly just to piss off my da. He played for Finn Harps and had trials for Everton when he was 19. He only lasted four weeks in England, though, and he had to come home 'cause he missed Derry too much. He should have stuck it out. Now he's a taxi driver and works most nights. He chooses to work all the time, but still complains about the people in his car. But at least they get to see him.

There's only about four or five people at the bus stop and they all look as fucked off as me. There's no way anybody could be happy standing at a bus stop in the pissing rain at this time on a Tuesday morning, not even the two men polishing off a bottle of cider and shouting at cars. I usually throw them a pound, or whatever change I have, but today's dole day so they're both flush, and so pissed they don't even see me. Fuck, its cold this morning. My mate Stevie was supposed to lift me but he's got a hangover again. Ever since his ma and da split up he's gone a wee bit off the rails. His new favourite word is 'YOLO', which means You Only Live Once. He says it ALL the time now. I got a text from him this morning saying:

Still going strong, there'll be no work today! YOLO!!

It's a good thing he works with his da or he'd have been sacked long ago. His oul' boy is still feeling guilty about the whole marriage break-up, so he's saying fuck all. Apparently he was caught with the secretary and she's an absolute cracker, too.

So aye, it's the bus again this morning!

I reply back to him:

Keep Her lit big man!! ☺

Had a Snapchat, too, from Marty. He was out with Stevie last night, obviously 'cause Stevie was buying – that's the only time you'd see Marty out on a Monday night. The only time you'd see him out at all, actually. Marty hasn't worked since he did ballboy at the Brandywell when Derry City played Barcelona when we were 12. He says he can't work because Barcelona Football Club are using him as their main tactical advisor, signed him up straight after the match cause they could see something in him, that he was gifted. Fucking touched more like. You see, that's the thing about Marty, he's a compulsive liar. Not bad lies, just shit like the time he told us he got asked to be Tom Cruise's stunt double in Mission Impossible 2, but he couldn't do it because Tom wanted him to get into Scientology. Nothing to do with the fact that Marty looks like a greyhound that learned to walk on two legs. Like I said, he's a moon man. His da is the same, actually. If Jeremy Kyle knew those two existed. he'd be throwing money at them to get them on the show.

His Snapchat was just of him taking a selfie with a bottle of wine. He actually gets uglier when he's drunk. Shaven head, one eye looking at you and the other looking for you, and teeth that are shades of yellow and stained purple from the wine. I send him a text:

You luk like an alco ebola victim last nite. And that's a improvement.

He's still one of my best friends though.

I arrive at work with two minutes to spare: some prick of a lorry driver had blocked the Strand Road and wasn't going anywhere, so I had to run the last bit. (Actually it was more of a fast walk: I'd be mortified to be seen running through town.) My dick of a manager is waiting for me at the front door:

'You're late, Mr Doherty!'

'It's 8.28 by me, I'm two minutes early!'

'I think you'll find in the Valuesaver employee handbook that all staff MUST be on the shop floor and ready to work five minutes before their shift starts.'

I just ignore him and walk on. Again, he's a dick. He looks like a dick, acts like a dick: therefore, he is a dick. He's probably the most annoying person I know. His name is Barry Templeton. He looks like a skinny mouse with a moustache and glasses and always wears a suit that's two sizes too big for him. Probably gets them in the second-hand shop. His pointy face always brings out the worst in me. He's worked here for 15 years as a department manager and it's his whole life. I swear to God he'd live here if they'd allow him. He has it in for me big time. I've been here for five years and he has hated me from the start. Mostly because I spend my days trying hard to do fuck all, which can be a stressful job in itself. Problem for him is, he just can't catch me out, and it wrecks his head.

I throw my stuff in my locker, then fix my hair. Looking good, even if I do say so myself. 8.32am. That gives me time to catch up on what's happening on Facebook, then I head down the stairs and onto the shop floor. As soon as I open the door, there's a customer standing there looking lost:

'Excuse me, do you have any LOW FAT breakfast bars?'

'Sorry?'

'Do you'se have any LOW FAT breakfast bars at all, love?'

She's making a point of making sure everybody hears her saying LOW FAT. She's about 40 or so, with a big mop of black hair, and she's wearing a pair of leggings that are far too small for her.

'Aye, we do, just straight down that aisle past the normal cereals, they're at the far side of the shop.'

I always say your first customer sets a marker for what kind of a day you're going to have…

'Could you grab me a box of them, I'm just in a while hurry to get to the gym for my spinning class …'

Nope, you're just too lazy to go get them yourself and you think muggins here should do it. I obviously don't say that though:

'I'll drop them up to the tills for ye.'

She has one of those annoying voices that just goes through your head:

'Make sure they're LOW FAT now!'

'What flavour?'

'Chocolate chip… just make sure they're LOW FAT!'

Of course it's chocolate chip.

Behind me I can hear her telling a woman she has just met how many calories are in the scones she just picked up. I'm going to take my time getting these, make her wait for a while. You see, when I started working here I actually liked people. I was a pleasant sort of a bloke, even a bit shy if I'm honest. But it's only when you work in a shop that you realise that most of the public just come into the shop to do your head in. It's like we're the stress ball they need to squeeze every once in a while. I've had everything from getting screamed at for not knowing the origin of the Golden Delicious apples (apparently, 'a tree' wasn't an acceptable answer) to having to clean up after a dog that got into the shop, ate half a pound of ham, then made its way around the shop recoating the floor with explosive diarrhoea. That was our good ham, too. People tried to catch it but couldn't get close enough without being hit by the mess. This in turn scared him some more which meant he spread it all over the place. He eventually crawled out of the shop like a wrung-out dishcloth, probably vowing never to wander in there again. Who was given a mop and brush to clean it up? Yep, Mickey Doc. That's another reason why I hate Barry Templeton.

I take a good 20 minutes, then I bring the breakfast bars to the till. She isn't even there yet, so much for her being in a hurry. Jenny is on the till, she's in her early 40s and I think she fancies me. She's a good-looking woman too, and although I'm only 25, I think I have a chance. She has long blond hair and blue eyes, and she always seems to have a tan – but I never hear of her going on holidays. Nice body on her too. Definite MILF material. I'd say she was some cracker when she was younger.

'Alright Mickey, what's the craic hi?'

'Not a while pile, Jenny! You're looking well today as always!'

I'm leaning up against the till looking cool as fuck.

'Go on you, ye wee skitter ye!''

She says it in a flirty way. I can tell. Next staff night out I'm definitely making my move.

'What time ye on to today?'

'Just till 2 o'clock, Mickey, then the real work starts when I pick the wains up from school!'

She has two wains at primary school. Don't think the da is still around.

'Hold on to those breakfast bars for a woman there. She asked me to go and get them for her 'cause she's too lazy to get them herself. No wonder she needs LOW FAT versions!'

Jenny smiles, I'm obviously impressing her here so I keep going…

'She kept asking for LOW FAT in a really loud and annoying voice, so everyone could know she's on a diet! Then she asked for chocolate chip, just can't stay away from that chocolate taste!'

She's still smiling, although a little weirdly this time. She's nodding slightly too, must be enjoying the craic – or turned on. Not sure which so I just keep acting the big man:

'I was going to give her half a pound of ham if she's that desperate to lose weight. Within ten minutes she'd be emptying herself out all over the place, like that oul' stray dog we had in here that time. That's bound to lose her a stone or two! But there's not a hope in hell I'd be cleaning up *that* mess!'

She's stone-cold still now and glancing over my shoulder. The realisation hits me that the LOW FAT woman is behind me. I'm thick as fuck sometimes. I can feel my face starting to burn when I hear her annoying voice:

'Do you have a problem young fella?'

'Erm… no?'

Fuck, my face is on fire now.

'Well get the hell out of my way then, ye little dickhead ye. You're lucky I'm in a hurry or I'd be reporting you to the manager. What's your name, anyway?'

I'm just standing there with my mouth wide open.

'Mickey.'

Can't lie, I have a name badge on. Of all days I decide to wear it. Jenny is looking really uncomfortable too, as she scans the items.

'Well, listen you to me, Mickey, your manager could be getting a wee phone call this afternoon to tell them what sort of a cheeky wee prick they employ!'

Then she just storms out after making sure to be extra nice to Jenny and throwing me a dirty look.

'Jesus, Mickey, that was embarrassing. Barry will kill you if he finds out!'

I'm still shaking and a wee bit nervous that the woman is going to come back in, so I keep looking at the entrance door.

'I know. Fuck it, I'll hopefully be handing in my notice here after Friday anyway.'

'Awk aye, that's the big interview! What time on Friday?'

'11 o'clock.'

I can feel my face starting to cool down a bit now.

'Well good luck anyway. So you think you'll get it?'

'It's a cert, Jenny. We'll have to have leaving drinks too. You'd better come!'

I give her a little wink, just to show her that I'm not annoyed about what just happened, even though I am. Sometimes I try to act the big-man to get girls to like me and most of the time it doesn't end well. Actually, it never ends well.

'Aye I'll come along, as long as I can get a babysitter. It'll be strange not having you about the place.'

'So you'll miss me then?'

'Awk aye, we'll definitely miss the craic with ye, Mickey!'

I'm so in there.

The rest of the day goes by very slow, as usual. It gets to 5.30pm and I assume the LOW FAT woman hasn't rung in, 'cause if she did, Barry would have me up in the office and fired before she had hung up the phone. I see him as I'm leaving. She definitely didn't ring 'cause he has a smile on his face.

'Make sure you're early tomorrow morning.'

'I will, aye. Hi that reminds me, I need Friday off for an interview.'

'It's Monday evening and you're only deciding to tell me now? You know the rules and regulations about booking days off – at least two weeks' notice AND it has to be signed by a manager.'

Dick, dick, dick, dick, dick, dick, DICK!

'I only found out about it. It's for a call centre!'

'Sitting on your arse all day, sounds like your perfect job…'

He means that as an insult, but it's the main reason I want the job, sitting on my arse all day, so the joke's on him.

'… I'll sign it off, Mickey, but just make sure you get the job won't ye?'

'Thanks. Barry!'

I say it with a huge over-the-top smile on my face. As I said, he's a dick!

Friday comes and my alarm goes off at 9am in the morning, although there was no need for it as I've been up half the night with a dodgy tummy. I woke at 2am and had to sprint to the toilet and pretty much spent the entire night there. After what happened with me yesterday with the low-fat woman, I suppose some people would call that korma? At one stage, my da came in from work and didn't know I was in the toilet. Their bedroom is next to the bathroom. I heard him use the words that no child should hear their parents say:

'Wake up, Mary, I fancy a ride the-night!'

To which my mother replied:

'Fuck off, John, ye got wan this month already…'

He continued with the pleading until he got his own way, like he always does, while I just sat there emptying out my insides. At this point I put my earphones in and listened to Sam Smith. He sounds a wee bit like me but obviously he's had work done in the studio, whereas my voice is the real McCoy's. I must have nodded off on the toilet 'cause I woke up at 6am and my legs were completely numb from sitting on the bog for four hours.

The smell of bacon coming from the kitchen makes my stomach turn again, even though nothing has come out the past hour or so.

'I don't want any bacon Ma, I have a bit of an upset stomach.'

'Aw well that's grand, there wasn't any for you anyway, I just had enough for your da. He's wrecked after a hard night so he'll need a good breakfast.''

I fucking bet he does. I also notice the dog is munching on some bacon. I throw him a dirty look, but he just keeps on munching away like he fucking owns the place. I'll get him one day, you just wait and see. Then my da comes bumbling down the stairs like he's a teenager again. He actually tries to high five me, but I just roll my eyes and put some bread in the toaster.

'What time's your interview at, Mickey?'

'11 o'clock'

'Do you want me to run you down?'

'Naw it's alright, Decky's dropping me down.'

'Ah, happy days, is he coming in? I need to talk to him about the match on Saturday.'

Ye see, my mate Decky's a brilliant footballer and my da looks at him as the son he never had. Out of my three mates, Decky is by far the most level-headed and the only one who knows where he's going in life. (Although I do know where I'm going in the music industry, I just don't know how I'm getting there yet.) Marty lives in the fucking clouds and Stevie is more often drunk now, than he's sober, but Decky has always been a grown-up. Even when we were all kids and everybody was drinking and smoking down the fields, Decky never tok part. He would come down all right but he'd always stand back and watch or laugh at the rest of us for being mental. Seriously sound bloke, though.

Decky rattles the horn outside as I'm buttering my toast so I just bring it with me. My ma wishes me good luck but all my da can say is:

'Make sure to tell Decky I said he needs to start tracking back more now he's playing in his new role. Tell him I said that, won't ye?'

I just walk on out without saying a word to him. The dog is waiting at the door, so I give him a wee sneaky kick on the way out. It wasn't even a proper kick, more like a wee tap with my foot, but the fucking thing lets a yelp out like he's just been shot. As I close the door I peak in and point my finger at the little fucker and make a throat-slitting sign with my finger for being a tout.

I run outside, jump the gate, then hop into the passenger seat of Decky's car and we make our way down the Buncrana Road.

'My Da said some crap to me, to tell you about the match on Saturday, but I won't even bore ye with it.'

'Aye, I seen him last week and he questioned me on the training I'm getting at Harps. He even offered to train me himself a couple of times a week!'

'Jesus Christ! What did you say to him?'

'I just told him I'm grand and if I need any tips I'll give him a shout. He seemed happy enough with that.'

'He's an embarrassment!'

'He knows his stuff about football though, ye have to give him that. Hi, what about Stevie? That man seems to be drunk every night now.'

'Aye, he was at a party in town last night and he didn't have a clue whose house it was. He texted me this morning to see if my da was working to pick him up.'

'Aye sure, he rang me too, I picked him up. He slept the whole way back to his house and I had while bother trying to get him wakened. His ma came out and slapped him around the head a few times to waken him. Man, she's got rough looking. Have you seen her lately?'

'Naw I haven't but I heard she's taking the break-up pretty bad too.'

'Aye, she looked like she had been crying. She doesn't take any care of herself anymore, just walks around in her housecoat all day and hardly leaves the house.'

There was a time I definitely would have given Stevie's ma one. Probably still would.

'Poor fucker. Sure, give me a shout later and we'll arrange to meet up to see what we're gonna do about him.'

'Aye, no bother, and text me after the interview to let me know how you get on.'

We pull up outside the call centre and I immediately get the feeling in my stomach that I need a toilet again – and quickly. Fuck! I grab my bag from the back seat with my Valuesaver uniform in it, and tell Decky I'll chat to him later. He beeps the horn and shouts good luck out the window. It's not luck I need right now, it's a toilet.

I go through the main doors and into the reception area, scanning the place for a toilet sign. There's a sexy wee receptionist sitting behind a desk which overlooks an open-plan office. She sees me looking lost and says:

'Are you okay there, love? Can I help you with anything?'

'Aye I'm here for an interview, Michael Doherty.''

She scans through a list, and as I'm about to tell her I need to use the bogs she tells me they're ready to see me now. Fuck!

She shows me through to a big office, the whole time I'm clenching my arse with all the power I've got. She tells me to take a seat and Ms Anderson and Mr Kelly will be with me right away. I have my back to the door. As I'm sitting I have a quick scan of the office, mostly to take my mind off what's going on with my insides, but there's nothing good to even look at. I'm starting to sweat now and I can feel tears in my eyes. After I'm sitting there for what feels like hours, the two interviewers come into the office, so I stand up to shake hands. As I turn around I realise I know the woman, and by the look on her face, I know that she recognises me.

It's the low-fat woman customer from work.

The shock hits me like a bus, which causes me to lose my grip on my arse, and the next thing I know I literally explode inside my trousers like a tin of beans in the microwave. The whole time I'm still standing there looking at the woman with a look of shock on my face. The both of them immediately know what just happened, mostly due to the foul smell and the horrible noises I was producing. Everything else seems to happen in slow motion. I can't even speak. The two interviewers just walk back out of the office and send in the receptionist girl. She has a towel covering her face and shouts at me like she's a cop or something:

'Follow me to the bathroom, we'll get you something to put on!'

I can't even look her in the eyes as she goes running out the door, even though that's the only part I can see now past the towel she's wearing. I just sort of waddle after her with my uniform in my hand. She keeps waiting on me and waving me on like some sort of office hero. The air seems to be changing colour and I feel like I'm in a war movie. I finally make my way to the toilets at the far end of the offices. Some bloke is coming out as I'm going in. He says hello, but I can see him getting sick a bit in his mouth when he gets a blast of the smell. I waddle over to a cubicle and spend a good twenty minutes wiping and cleaning, I get my Valuesaver uniform on and walk back out through the open-plan office with a bag of shitty clothes in my hand. This is by far the most embarrassing day of my life. I think I'm in shock 'cause I can't speak, I just want to get out as quickly as I can. The people that work there look really pissed off, probably because of the smell that's taken over their office. A few drama queens have their heads stuck out the windows for fresh air and I think I seen a woman crying. Nobody even bothers to speak to me until the wee receptionist girl comes over to tell me that they'll be in touch. She's still wearing the towel around her face. Just as I'm about to go out the door I can hear the low-fat woman say loudly:

'There's no way I'll be cleaning up after that!'

Korma is definitely a bitch!

CHAPTER 2.

It's a half past nine on a Saturday morning and I'm out of my bed and hangover-free for a change. This really is a fucking first. The lads, Decky, Stevie and Marty, were all heading out in town last night, but after what happened yesterday at the interview, I decided not to bother going out. All evening I had to listen to my ma go on and on about the interview – 'What sort of questions did they ask you?' and 'Did you answer out loud and not mumble like you always do?' I told her I absolutely nailed the interview and that I'll review what kind of packaging they come back to me with. Hopefully, they don't come back with a cleaning bill. I told the lads the interview went well and that I couldn't go out because I had a date with a girl I met on Tinder at the last minute. I don't think Decky believed me, but he didn't say anything. He's good like that. He usually knows when I'm lying. It's like he has a third sense or something? Marty gave me some advice: he told me the last person he met on Tinder turned out to be a famous Hollywood actress who was out looking for a bit of rough. Actually, it wasn't really advice, more just the ramblings of a mad man. He wouldn't tell me who she was though. He said it would put my life at risk, which was nice of him I suppose. Stevie rang me when he was pissed and I swear to God in our two-minute conversation he must have used the word 'YOLO' about 20 times. I'm starting to get a bit pissed off hearing that word so I wasn't too bothered when Decky rang me this morning to come out for breakfast with him and Marty to talk about what's going on with Stevie. Next of all I hear the horn of

Decky's car so I run out and jump in the front seat. There's no sign of Marty:

'I thought you were picking Marty up first?'

Decky points his thumb behind him. I look around to see Marty out for the count on the back seat, obviously still dressed in last night's clothes.

'I called around to his house and his ma said he was on the sofa, didn't make it as far as his bed last night. He got up, walked out to the car with me without saying a word, then got into the back and fell asleep.'

I give Marty a clash on the head but it doesn't wake him. I try a harder one but as the car moves forward I miss and my hand lands on the pool of drool that has gathered at the side of his mouth.

'Ah, for fuck sake, I've got his drool on my hand!'

I wipe the drool on Marty's shirt.

'Ah man, is he drooling on my seats again? Here, stick that magazine under his head.'

I carefully lift his head and put the magazine under. All of a sudden, Marty's eyes open wide and he tries to bite my hand but only manages to clamp on to my shirt sleeve with his teeth.

'Get the fuck off me, ye prick!'

He's locked on to my shirt sleeve now and he's shaking his head from side to side and making growling noises like a dog! I'm starting to panic but Decky rolls up the magazine and smacks him on the nose with it which makes him release me and fall back onto the seat. I swear to God, he's like a wild animal sometimes.

'What the fuck are you doing, ye dickhead, ye?? You tried to fucking eat me!!'

I'm illiterally shaking!

'Jesus, sorry man! I was having a fucked-up dream that I was a koala bear getting attacked by a load of Mexicans. I woke up and you scared the shite out of me!'

'I scared the shite out of you!? Jesus Christ, if you've given me rabies or some other sort of Ballymac disease, I swear to God I'll get you put down!'

'Sorry man, relax!'

'And my shirt sleeve is fucking soaked!'

'It'll dry up.'

'I'll dry you up if you ever try to bite …'

Decky interrupts:

'Right, lads, relax for fuck's sake.'

I give Marty a bit of a death stare, just to let him know he can't be trying to bite people whenever he feels like it. He stares out the window the rest of the journey, like a wounded dog. I'll make it up to him when we get there, because beneath all the madness, he's an innocent sort of fucker.

We go into McDonald's and I order three sausage and egg McMuffin meals. I buy Marty his, just to let him know there's no hard feelings or anything. We sit in the corner and the lads tell me the craic from last night. Well, up to a point. Decky left at midnight because of his match today, and Marty can't remember past 11pm. They tell me that Laura

Dillon was pissed off that I wasn't there and she tried to get off with Stevie to make me jealous. You see, Laura Dillon is a girl I went with last year, and when I say 'went with' I mean we did it, as in the dirty deed if you know what I mean? We had sex. I went out with her a few times after that until I realised she was actually nuts, when she appeared everywhere I was. She told me that she has a feeling something bad is going to happen to me and she has to be there to protect me. I must have some sort of a scent that attracts psychos. Kinda like the Lynx ad that attracts hot women, I attract nut-jobs.

Decky does a pretty good impression of her, I must say/ He opens his eyes really wide and talks with a really deep voice:

'Tell Mickey Doc that I won't be waiting around for him forever, I've already given the best years of my life to him and this is the thanks I get! (Screams) I'M BETTER THAN THAT!!'

Me and Marty are in stitches laughing, then Marty goes:

'You better like rabbit stew cause she's boiling up the ingredients!'

The two of them laugh their heads off, but I just pretend to laugh 'cause I don't really get it. That happens more often than you'd think.

I need to change the subject, because when I was seeing Laura Dillon for those couple of weeks I might have told her some stuff I'd never told my mates, like about me wanting to be a singer and that. I'd dedicate my first number one to her, blah, blah, blah. She always tries to push me about going on the X-Factor. It's kinda nice that she believes in me, even though she is off her rocker.

I ask them:

'What's the craic about Stevie now, then?'

Marty seems pleased that somebody is almost worse than he is:

'He threw up all over the place in the Metro last night, and he looks like shite, man'

And that's coming from Marty …

He continues: 'I know we all love our drink and all, but Stevie isn't Stevie these days. I don't even know what he's going on about anymore, he just fucking waffles half the time about nothing.'

Again, this is coming from Marty of all people!

'He's obviously not dealing well with his parents breaking up. His da being his first role model, the guy who he looked up to his whole life ends up breaking the heart of his mother, who is of course the first woman that Stevie ever love.'

You see, sometimes this mad fucker can totally surprise you and come out with stuff that's deep and meaningful. Me and Decky are listening to him with our mouths open.

'He probably feels lonely and, understandably, disillusioned about life, and I'm pretty sure he is somehow blaming himself for what's happened.'

But we both know these moments of clarity don't last long.

'I think we need to take him to the woman who lives at the bottom of my street. She does exorcisms, kinda like witch-doctor stuff, I'm sure she could reprogram Stevie and get him back. We could even add in a few martial arts moves like the way they did in The Matrix.'

And he's back. Told ye, doesn't last long. I knew he spent too much time with the witch at the bottom of his road. I'm not saying she's a real witch like, but she definitely gives me the creeps.

Mickey Doc

Decky takes over:

'Aye, some good points there Marty…'

Marty looks chuffed, it isn't too often he gets praise.

'…but I think we need to talk to his ma and da. Neither of them wants to give out to Stevie, obviously – they're both feeling guilty and are trying to keep him onside. They just need to sit him down and chat with him, tell him everything is going to be alright and reassure him they're both still there for him.'

This is why Decky is the brains of the operation.

'Now, what do you say about calling up to his da first and see what he has to say?'

Fuck, Stevie's da has never really liked me: at least I don't think he does. Stevie always said he was just winding me up, but I can never tell. As I said, I had a bit of a thing for Stevie's ma and his da caught on to it. He always slags me about it and tells me he'll knock my head in if I try anything, then laughs. It's hard to know if he's serious or not, though.

I go 'maybe you two should go up on your own? That apartment he lives in now can't be too big. It's bound to be crowded with all of us there?'

Decky knows I'm lying as usual. He's like:

'You just don't want to go, Mickey,' cause his oul' boy always winds you up and you always take the bait. He's a wind-up merchant. He just picks on you 'cause you take it all to heart.'

'I'm not afraid of him, I just wouldn't hit somebody twice my age!'

'You'll be hitting nobody. Look, I'll pick ye both up about 4 o'clock when I get back from my match. Marty, you get yourself a few hours kip, man, 'cause you look like shit, no offence: and, Mickey you just calm yourself, his oul' boy is pretty sound really.'

We get up to leave and Marty whispers to me:

'If you need a few martial arts moves yourself I could get Mrs O'Hagan to say a few spells over you. I'll get it at mate's rates and all.'

I just shake my head at Marty, but I must remember to Google later if witches are actually real?

Decky drops me home first. My ma and da are just putting their coats on before they go out:

'Where are you two going?'

'I'm dropping your ma up the town, meeting the lads in the bookie's, then I'm going to the match. What sort of form is Decky in anyway?'

'Same form he's always in! He's grand.'

It's turning into a fucking obsession.

'Did you tell him what I told ye to tell him, about tracking back more?'

'He already has a fucking coach. I don't think he needs another one.'

'A few tips from an old pro never hurt anyone, and you watch your mouth, boy.'

My ma opens the front door and it's pissing from the heavens.

'Aw for Jesus sake, John, it's lashing out there!'

'Well, I can't control the fucking weather ye know!'

'Aye, but you've the car parked halfway down the bloody road, I'll get drenched!'

'It's not my fault that Polish fella next door has all his mates round and takes up all the spaces! Give me the umbrella and I'll go down and get the car, bring it up and collect you.'

'Naw! I'm going to need the umbrella to get from the front door to the car! Do you know how long it took me to get this hair right? And you said you were going to talk to next door about leaving a space for us! You would nearly think you're afraid of them or something.'

'I'm hardly! I just wouldn't go hitting boys half my age.'

He can be pathetic sometimes. He throws his jacket over his head then runs down the road to get the car. A few minutes later he's back and my ma puts up the umbrella and manages to nearly take my eye out.

'Right, I'm away, so make sure if you go out that everything's switched off and all the doors are locked. I came back last week and the place was lit up like Altnagelvin Hospital, and nobody in. And make sure you let the dog out to go to the toilet after the rain stops.'

The mutt. We wouldn't let her pride and joy to get wet now, would we?

My ma walks to the car, holding on to the umbrella for dear life. I go into the kitchen to make myself a bite to eat and the first thing I see is the dog staring up at me. It isn't wagging its tail, or anything, like it does around everybody else. It's just standing there staring at me, with its tail in the air. I stare back at it. There's no way I'm going to get beat in a staring contest by this little fucker. We're staring for at least a minute and neither of us has blinked. I can feel my eyes starting to get itchy. He starts to growl: he must be feeling it too. After another 30 seconds he blinks:

'You fucking loser!!'

I do a victory dance around the kitchen while making an L sign for loser on my forehead. It might seem a bit extreme but fuck it, he deserves it. He just remains there looking at me until I finish, then, while still looking straight into my eyes, he just lifts his left leg and pisses on the kitchen floor.

'You little bastard, you done that on purpose!'

I go to grab him but he runs under the table. He's a Yorkshire terrier so he's small and fast. Now he's barking like fuck. I chase him out into the open floor with a brush, then catch him: making sure to get a hold where he can't bite me.

I whisper in his ear:

'There was only going to be one winner here, sunshine, and it looks like today isn't your day!'

Then I open the back door and throw him out in the rain. It's still pissing it down and he's not used to the bad weather, so that should teach him a lesson. I clean up the piss then go to make a sandwich and stick on some One Direction. I'm belting out 'Best Song Ever' like a pro, when I look out the window and see the dog hunched under a tree, shivering, and with a look as if to say 'I'm sorry, you win'. But I'm not falling for it. I'll leave him there a bit longer. 'What Makes You Beautiful' comes on next. I swear to God I can sing it better than any of those boys. I do a version of it where I slow it right down and it's just me singing it with no music. Laura Dillon said it was the most amazing thing she'd ever heard, and that's not her being crazy. I sing for another half an hour or so, then flick the telly on and watch The Big Bang Theory. It's funny how smart those lads are, I just wish I could get more of the jokes. I must have fallen asleep because I'm woken by someone knocking at the front door and I notice I have six missed calls on my phone. I was having a nice dream, too, about Cheryl Cole singing to me while I'm in the bath. Fuck, that's why I'm pitching a tent. I walk to answer it and stand with my body behind the door and my head peeking out. It's Marty and he's looking a bit fresher now. He still looks like a little scumbag, though.

'Are ye ready or what?'

'Aye. hold on a minute till I get my shoes on.'

'Decky's team were beat 3-0 today, so don't be mentioning it to him.'

'Tubes.'

'Right, we'll be in the car. And brush you hair, it's sticking up everywhere!'

This coming from the fella who has had a number one all over since he was two, because his ma said it was the cheapest option and it's easier to catch the lice. I let out a roar to see if my ma and da are in but they're obviously not back yet. She's probably buying half of Derry. I throw my shoes on, then lock the front door. Fuck, it's still raining. I jump in the back of the car and we head towards Stevie's da's apartment. Decky plays some crap music in his car:

'What's that you're listening to now?'

'That's Bob Dylan, man'

'Who?'

'For somebody who likes to think of themselves as a bit of a singer, I can't believe you don't know who Bob Dylan is!'

'He sounds like something my da would listen to! Actually, is he anything to Bob Marley? My da listens to him sometimes, too. And who says I fancy myself as a bit of a singer?'

'We all know the craic, man, I don't know why you get so uptight about it.'

I get uptight.

'I'm not uptight about anything! I'm just not that comfortable singing in public, or talking about it for that matter. Now can we change the subject, like? Can we talk about those wile looking tracksuit bottoms that Marty is wearing?'

Decky laughs and catches my eye in the rear view mirror, and smiles. How the fuck does he know everything, even when it's just in your head?

'There's nothing wrong with my tracky bottoms. Dunnes Stores finest, I'll have ye know. Just because I don't leave the house like I'm in some sort of a fucking fashion parade like half the lads in Derry...'

'Marty, sometimes you simply just shouldn't leave the fucking house!'

The banter goes back and forth until we pull up outside Stevie's da's house. It's weird thinking that Stevie's da lives in this shitty wee apartment complex, on his own, now. He has always been a bit of a big time Charlie: flash car, dresses well, thinks he's the dog's bollocks, and now he's living on his own in this shithole, eating microwave dinners every night. That should bring him down a peg or two.

Mickey Doc

We ring the bell for him to buzz us up. Decky already got in contact with him to tell him we're calling over. He buzzes us up and we get to his apartment where he's there waiting for us at the front door. He invites us in and asks do we want a beer or anything. He seems like nothing has happened and he's still a cocky fucker with his designer shirt and his Rolex watch.

'There's the lads! And Mickey! How the hell are yez, anyway?'

Marty and Decky both say their grand, I just walk on in and ignore him.

'What about you Mickey? Did your balls drop yet?'

He bursts out laughing. He's one of those people that when he thinks he has said something funny, he looks at everybody else to make sure they laugh, which makes you feel uncomfortable until you pretend to laugh, because he'll keep on looking at you till you do.

'So what's the craic, then? I take it this isn't a social visit?'

Decky speaks first:

'We just wanted to see you, Jack, because of Stevie. We're not trying to pry into your business or anything, it's just we've noticed Stevie hasn't been the same since you and Donna broke up.'

Jack and Donna! That's their names! I was trying to remember there, in my head. They've always just been Stevie's ma and da to me. He doesn't look as cocky anymore as he walks over to the settee, and sits on the arm of it. Within about five seconds he has gone from being this larger-than-life character to a scared-looking old man. He fiddles with his wedding ring as he speaks:

'It's about him going out getting pissed all the time, isn't it?'

He has tears in his eyes and the colour has drained from his face. He looks smaller somehow. Fuck, I'm starting to feel sorry for him now.

Decky continues, as me and Marty keep our heads down:

'Aye, it is, Jack. It's been four months now and he has been drinking every night and most days. Everybody likes their pints and that, but he's getting carried away. We're just worried he won't stop until he's … well, until he can't.'

Stevie's da has tears in his eyes now and he looks around at all of us:

'Jesus Christ, you lads are good mates to him …'

I'm waiting for him to say 'except Mickey' but he doesn't.

'… I'm sure you all know I fucked up big time and that's why his ma chucked me out. I was feeling shit about getting older, and I let myself get carried away. That's no excuse, though. I let myself down and I let my family down and now my son is turning into an alco.'

Decky is the only one of us who can speak:

'You need to start getting tougher with him, Jack. If Stevie thinks he can get away with it, he'll keep going. He thinks he's punishing you as much as anything. You can't be held over your actions forever and he needs his da there for him. Talk to him.'

Stevie's da is literally crying now. I feel like I'm on an episode of Oprah. Everybody has tears in their eyes, me included.

'I will, lads, I will. I didn't want to believe things had got so bad. I just thought he went on a bit of a bender.'

'It is just a bender and he'll snap out of it. Just do your best, man, and if you need us or anything, you have my number now. We all care and we're here to help.'

He puffs out his chest again, wipes his eyes and stands up.

'Right, fuck that. It's time for me to get my son back into shape again and maybe try to get my family back together.'

'That's the spirit. All is not lost.'

Decky should have his own talk show. He's amazing with things like this.

 'Cheers lads, you're a good bunch, hi. Even you, Mickey.'

Stevie's da walks us down to the front gates and thanks us again. Marty, the little fucker, beats me to the front seat so I get in the back. As we pull away, I look back at Stevie's da and he gives me the middle finger. Then smiles. I just smile and give him the middle finger back. It's probably the nicest moment I've ever had with the man.

I arrive back at the house and tell the lads to text and let me know where we're heading tonight. I walk up the path to the house and I can see my ma and da are back. As soon as I get to the door, my ma opens it like a psycho, and asks me where the fuck I was!

Fuck, did I leave the lights on again?

'I was out with the lads! What's the big deal?'

'What's the big deal? What's the big deal?? The big deal is, sunshine, that you left that poor wee dog out in the rain and the freezing cold, while you were out with your mates! The poor thing almost died! We got home to find it lying under a bush, shaking and whimpering and soaked right through. I swear to God, if she catches pneumonia and dies, you may look for somewhere else to live!'

She? Fuck I always thought it was a 'he' dog! I look into the living room and it's wrapped in a towel in front of the fire, with my da sitting beside it, just staring at it. He doesn't even look up at me.

'Sorry! Look, I let it out for a piss when it stopped raining and it was running around enjoying itself so I just left it for a while, it seemed to be having fun. Then I forgot all about it and Decky called and I never even minded it was out there.'

'Jesus, Mickey! You know how much that thing cost and you know your ma would be gutted if anything happened to it! Just be more fucking careful in future, right?'

I start heading up the stairs and he shouts up behind me:

''Oh, and another thing, that wee girl Laura Dillon called a while ago and left you an envelope. It's sitting up on your bed.''

What the fuck? I thought she had stopped coming to the house! If this is another love letter, I swear to God I'm going to scream. I open the envelope and inside is a form with a huge X on the front. The hairs on the back of my neck and my arms stand up when I realise what the X is all about.

It's an X-Factor application form.

CHAPTER 3.

The application had been in my drawer for almost a week now, because I couldn't bring myself to fill it in. I stare at the form for ages. It has me captivated. I have so many things going through my head, and yet nothing at all. The bold text and the strong colours are jumping out at me, grabbing at me and pulling me in. I don't know how long I've been sitting staring at it, but my ma must have come in to close the curtains in my room at some stage. It's dark now and just my desk lamp lights up the form. The words they use are like hypnosis to me: Star quality. Fame. Likeability. All the words I have dreamt, over and over again, being directed at me. Even the texture of the paper grabs me. It's not the usual paper you get at work or in a newspaper. It's stronger and it has class written all over it. Not literally like, just … unliterally, if that's a word? Even the smell of it is like nothing I've ever smelt before. And I've smelt some bad things, as you know. Then I realise what the smell is. It's the sweet smell of success, and Mickey Doc has developed a taste for it.

I get a pen from the drawer to fill in the form.

Name: Michael Doherty.

Michael Doherty. It even sounds funny for me saying it. I've been Mickey Doc since as far back as I can remember. Apparently, I was Michael Doherty up until the day I was christened, then, from that day onwards I've been Mickey Doc. My christening day is always being retold at family get-togethers when everybody has had a few drinks. Of course, I don't remember that day, but apparently it's the first time I spent a night in a pub. After the christening in the chapel everybody went to the Delacroix for drinks and sandwiches. Of course, the party went on well into the night before my parents thought they had better get home. Unfortunately, there had been a mix-up along the way. They thought my Aunty Margaret was bringing me home and minding me till they got back. That wasn't the case at all. Apparently, after a few drinks, and with being in the company of a newborn baby, my still-single Aunty Margaret got broody and went home with the first bloke that smiled at her. My ma and da went home, stopping along the way for a fish supper and curry sauce between them, thinking my Aunty Margaret was in the spare room with me. It wasn't till the next morning when my da got up that he realised I wasn't there. My ma rang the police and told them I'd been kidnapped. Ten minutes later, three of the regulars from the pub came around the corner, pushing me in my pram. Alice, Joe and Tommy were three seriously hard-core alcoholics. But that didn't matter at the end of the night when they realised I was left in the corner on my own, not making a sound, just looking around and taking in my surroundings. They stayed with me that night, found a bottle in the bottom of the pram and fed me. Found nappies in a bag and changed me. Patted my back until I got my wind up and walked with me till I fell asleep. For years after, the three of them would visit me at home, bringing whatever sweets or small toys they could afford until, one by one, their illness ended them. That night of my christening in the Delacroix, Alice, Joe and Tommy started calling me Mickey Doc, and it has been that way ever since.

Date of Birth: 17/02/89. AGE: 25.

25 years old. I don't feel like I'm 25. I thought by this stage in my life I would be somebody. Ever since I was a wain I wanted to be a

performer. I used to set up a little stage in our living room and sing in front of my mother. My da liked it at the start, but as I got a bit older he got annoyed and would tell me I should be out playing football like all the other boys. He told my mother to stop letting me 'act like a girl' in future, but she carried on letting me perform for her, behind his back.

Around that time. I got a part in the school nativity play. I was desperate to show my da that I could do this and do it well. While all the other kids were learning their lines, I was practising being a tree, as this was the part I was given. Our teacher was very much into drama and told us about a thing called Method Acting. That is where you basically become the character that you are about to play. I wanted to be the best tree that the school had ever seen. Every evening when I got home from school I went out to the small forest behind our house and stood amongst the trees. I moved my arms like them when the wind blew their branches. I made the noises of the wind blowing through my leaves. 'Swwwwooooosshh, swwwooooosshh'. I stood in the one position for hours, even in the wind and rain and only went home when my arms and legs could take no more.

Finally, the big day came and I looked out from behind the curtain at a packed assembly hall. I could see my mother with my uncle, but I couldn't see my da. My Uncle Bob had brought his new video camera, so at least my da could see it later, he was probably working. Our drama teacher, Mrs O'Neill called me to one side and told me that Barry Devine was sick and couldn't perform so I would have to change parts. I was now an innkeeper and I was distraught. It wasn't that I couldn't do it, it was just that I had put in so much hard work into being a tree and I felt like I had nailed it. I now had a line to say:'We have no room in the inn for Mary and Joseph and baby Jesus (nod head) but we have a stable out the back.'. I tried my best to learn the line but the nerves took over and my mind was blank. Mrs O'Neill dressed me up in Barry's costume and told me I'd be great and that I should just say the line in a loud, clear voice when Mary and Joseph came to my door. I stood behind the cardboard door awaiting the knock from Mary and Joseph. I could hear them getting turned down by the other two innkeepers next door. Then, the door knocked. It was Mary and Joseph of Nazareth looking for a place to have their baby, the Son of God. Everything from then on happened in slow motion. I didn't open the door. After 30 seconds of not knowing what to do, Joseph opened the door wide himself and the spotlight was on me. For some reason I stepped out of the inn causing Mary and Joseph to step backwards. Unfortunately for Mary and Joseph, they were met by an innkeeper who thought he was a tree. I had my arms outstretched and moved them gently in the breeze. Mary and Joseph looked on in disbelief as I stood, feet together and arms outstretched. I had found a point at the back of the assembly hall that I stared at while I made the noise 'swwwooooshh, swwwooooshh…'. Nobody knew what to do. The entire audience was laughing but I didn't hear them. I was a magnificent tree, swaying in the breeze that blew through Bethlehem that day. 'swwwooooshh, swwwooooshh'. Just a pity the tree was blocking the front door of a popular inn and rewriting the nativity. After a few minutes the quick-thinking innkeeper next door saved the day when he shouted out the door:

'Hi Mary and Joseph! I just minded, I have a stable out the back where you can have your baby! You can use it if you want!'

The rest of the nativity play went on but nobody could hear anything over the laughter of the crowd. I stood through the whole thing, swaying in the breeze while the remainder of the nativity went on around me. People went to the payphone and rang people who weren't there to come see me. My mum had to pick me up afterwards, still standing like a tree, and carry me home. My da wasn't too impressed when he got home and heard about it. He said I embarrassed him and that he'd never hear the end of it from the lads in the pub. Ever since that day I never performed in front of anybody again, apart from my ma. And, on the odd occasion, the trees out the back.

ADDRESS: 32 Glen Park, Derry, N. Ireland.

That has always been my address. I'm proud to be from Derry, but I really want to get away from it and do something. My da had the chance when he was my age, but he came back after four weeks 'cause he missed it. I think if I left then I'd be gone for good. Of course, I'd visit and that, but I wouldn't live here. My da missed his family and he had just met my ma a few weeks before leaving ,so he came back for her, mostly. I went to school just down the road, and that's when I started hanging around with Decky, Marty and Stevie. On the first day of primary school we all sat at the same table and we stayed together since. None of our families really had much money so we never felt like we were missing out on anything. Marty was always that bit worse off than us, so we always made sure we had an extra snack with us during break to give to him. No words were said, the snacks were just passed to him. We had an understanding. Marty doesn't look much different now from when he was at school. Still the same haircut and that small and wiry body. I'd bet his uniform still fits him. Only thing is I remember him burning it in his back yard on the last day of school, only to find out his ma had meant for it to be passed down to his wee brother who was just over a year younger than him. He got in a lot of trouble for that. Stevie was always quiet as a wain. It wasn't until secondary school when he started to fill out that he came out of himself. Then, he became the life and soul of the party. He really is a funny fucker with the smart answers when he gets going. Most of the teachers hated him because he could always cut them off or twist their words. All the teachers loved Decky. He was smart, well-mannered and sporty. All the girls loved him, but I only ever remember him going with one girl and that was when he was 15. Decky was always just far too interested in football to have a girlfriend. Through the years we have always been close and always had each other's backs. Like the time of our formal. when Stevie was caught kissing a girl who had a boyfriend that went to a different school. There must have been about 20 fellas looking to kick his head in at the end of the night. All the rest of our class stayed out of it because these other lads had a bit of a reputation. Stevie was scared, but he wasn't too bad when he realised that me, Decky and Marty were by his side. Marty said that if one of us gets a hiding, then we all get a hiding. And we did. But we never had any bother with anybody after that because people knew that if you hit one, then you hit the four of us.

OCCUPATION: Sales Assistant.

Sales assistant. Well, that's what it says on my contract anyway. I'd say that I don't assist in sales in any way, shape, form or fashion. If anything, I 'de-ssist' sales? If everybody in that shop was like me, then it would have gone out of business long ago. It's not that I'm lazy, it's just that I don't give a fuck and there is a difference. I started there when I was 20 after being on and off the dole for three years before that. That's another thing about Derry, there isn't much work about. So, when I got this job, I swore to myself that I would do the best I could to keep it. Then I met my department manager, Barry, and all that changed. He's one of those people who can just suck the life right out of you as soon as he walks into a room. The first time I met him he asked me if I was a team player. Now, I was understandably nervous, that being my first day and all, and I hold my hand up for being a wee bit thick from time to time. So, that question threw me because, with my da, any mention of a team/player was a reference to football, so I thought Barry was asking me do I play for any football team. I told him I don't play for any team and that my da has tried to push me for years to play for a team, but there's no way I ever will. I'm just not that into it, I told him. This obviously wasn't the answer he was looking for. His face went red and he said that he must find out how the hell I got through the interview. From then on in he gave me the crappiest jobs in the place. Anything that other staff didn't like doing became Mickey's job. Cleaning out the fridges – Mickeys job. Cleaning up spills – Mickey's job. Every day that I step into the place my insides go cold. I have to play little games just to make the day go in quicker. Like, when somebody leaves their basket or trolley unattended I would take things out or replace their goods with other stuff just to watch them get confused and think they're losing their marbles. I'd put a couple of Tampax boxes into a single man's trolley, or bury loads of condoms (extra large) at the bottom of a woman's trolley just to watch them get embarrassed when the get to the checkout. Most of my days were spent daydreaming though. Daydreaming about the X-Factor.

HAVE YOU AUDITIONED FOR THE X-FACTER BEFORE: No.

In my head, every day for the past five years.

ARE YOU A SOLO ARTIST OR GROUP? Solo.

Definitely a solo artist. I've never sung with anybody else before. I'm sure I could do it if I had to. Like, if Simon Cowell liked my performances so much that he asked me to join One Direction, I would have to say yes. Me, Marty, Decky and Stevie dressed up as The Backstreet Boys once for a charity fancy dress day at school. Nobody had a clue who we were 'cause we just dressed in jeans and t-shirts and Marty painted a goatee onto himself. Now, most people would have used face paint. Not Marty, though. Marty used a permanent marker and really put it on thick. For the remaining three months of school he looked like somebody who should be on a list and not allowed within 100 metres of a school. His school photograph for that year still sits on the mantelpiece at his home and it looks like somebody drew on it with a marker. The only other pictures they have in the house are of their dogs, so you can imagine what Marty's eight brothers/sisters look like.

DESCRIBE YOURSELF/GROUP IN TEN WORDS: Really talented, driven. Star about to be born. The best.

I only added 'the best' in at the end because I had to make it up to ten words, and it's really difficult to find a sentence that's only two words. Laura Dillon always called me the best. Like, anything I done, she would be like 'oh my God you're the best'. The lads don't know this but I still keep in touch with her from time to time, mainly because she is good for my confidence. I have told her a million times that I don't want to be her boyfriend and she says she has accepted that now, but she also says she still considers herself as my girlfriend, because I need her. She's probably right, I do need her in some ways. I wouldn't be sitting here filling out this form if it wasn't for her. She always seems to be where I am, too. It's like she's stalking me which is also good for the ego, although it does get a bit scary from time to time. Like, sometimes at work, I'd be standing with a brush in my hand, basically pretending to be doing something when I'd see her out of the side of my eye, just standing there, staring. Then when I turn around she's gone. I might see her nine or ten times at work in the same day, but she doesn't come over to me or anything. She just watches. A few weeks ago I was out for dinner with my family for my granny's birthday. I was sitting having my steak and chips and I could feel somebody staring at me. I looked around and there she was. standing outside the window looking in. This time, she didn't run away or duck. She just stood there and nodded, as if to say 'I'm here, don't worry about anything, just go back to eating your dinner'. She often sends me text messages saying:

'go follow your dreams ... but be careful. XXX'

At first, I didn't know if the '... but be careful' bit was a threat or just good advice. I'm still not 100% sure actually.

IF SUCCESSFUL, WHERE WOULD YOUR PREFFERRED AUDITION BE? Manchester.

They gave me a list of places and Belfast was one of them. It would obviously be the closest place for me, but there's no way I'd do it there because there's bound to be other people from Derry there. and the chances of me bumping into someone I know are high. I know it sounds stupid that I'm afraid of bumping into people I know when I'm going to be singing in front of a large audience and on TV. but I don't want anybody to know at first. I just want to get the auditions done and if they pick me then I'll know that I'm really good enough. I kinda know that I'm good enough already, but it would be nice having someone other than my ma or Laura Dillon say it. I'm not even going to tell the lads until I'm through. They'd probably give me loads of stick if I didn't.

I answer all the other questions and fill out the rest of the information they need. The next thing I need to do is record a video of me singing, and send it with the application. My ma and da have gone out. Every Thursday night they call around to my granny, so I have the house to myself. I set up the camera on my phone and position it on the dressing table so it takes in my whole body. I put on my favourite skinny jeans and put on my favourite T-shirt. I then do 40 press-ups to make sure my pecs are in good shape. This T-shirt always makes them look great anyway. After 20 minutes making sure my hair is right and ten minutes warming up my vocal chords, I'm ready to go. I don't have to think too much about what song I'm going to sing: ' What Makes You Beautiful' by One Direction.

It takes me 15 goes to get it right. A couple of times I messed up the words or lost a note, other times I just wasn't happy with the way I was standing. I ended up changing my jeans three times and done another 40 push-ups just to keep the pecs in tip-top shape. If anything, I'm a perfectionist.

Just as I get everything ready to be sent off, I get a phone call from Decky. I answer with:

'What's the craic in Iraq?'

'Grand, man, look Stevie's da rang me, he seems to have sorted things out with Stevie and he's back talking to Donna again which can only be good.'

'Fucking hell, me, you and Marty should start doing this for a living! Families eh – you break 'em, we fix 'em.'

Decky just carries on talking without even acknowledging that class line! Maybe he didn't hear me right…

'So he said the four of us can all use their holiday home in Bundoran for a week if Stevie proves he's sorted himself out. Could you get the time off work? Marty's up for it and I'm up for it and I texted Stevie and he's up for it although he said he's suffering from the worst hangover ever at the moment. But he's definitely in a much better place with himself. It's only five weeks away, what do you think?'

'Families eh- you break 'em, we fix 'em.'

'What the hell are you on about, man? Are you up for it or not?'

'Of course I'm up for it, I have days owed to me that need to be taken anyway. You never commented on the line. though.'

'What line?'

'For fuck sake, Decky, do you not even listen to me anymore? Families eh – you break 'em', we fix 'em.'

'Sorry, man, that was a cracker line, you should definitely write it down and use it again.'

'I'm putting it as my Facebook status this very minute …'

'Don't be doing that. Stevie is feeling bad enough at the minute without thinking we're gloating about helping out!'

'Alright, I'll just text it to Marty then. When the fuck did you start getting your period? You're going on like a woman who just found me pissing over the toilet seat!'

'Sorry, man, I just have a lot going on at the minute.'

'Like what?'

'Aw just football stuff and that, nothing to worry about. So, Metro tomorrow night then, or will we head to The Bentley for a change?'

'Aye, fuck it, we'll head to the Bentley for some fresh pickings!'

'Are you getting fed up getting turned down by all the same girls every week in the Metro?'

I laugh. 'Cheeky fucker. I have a much better scoring average than you and let's not forget it!'

Decky laughs: 'Good point. Right, man, I'll give you a shout tomorrow and make sure to get that booked off work and don't be leaving it till the last minute like you always do!'

I say cheerio and hang up. Then I text Stevie saying:

'Nice one about your da letting us use Bundoran! Give me a shout when you're feeling better ye bender!'

He texts back straight away:

'Happy days! Can't wait for it! Things can only get better! ☺'

It's the first time in months he hasn't said YOLO in a text! Thank fuck for that!

I then text Marty saying:

'We should sort out families for a living – Families eh? You break 'em, we fix 'em!'

Marty texts back:

'ROFL MAN! Cracker lines as always!! Lol ☺☺☺'

Mickey Doc

I go to bed feeling good, not just because of Marty's reply, although it did feel good for somebody to appreciate my line, but because when I post the application tomorrow it will be the start of the rest of my life.

CHAPTER 4.

'Has everybody on this fucking bus been knighted or something?'

Marty has his headphones on and he's sitting next to me. He's listening to Garth Brooks. I know this because every 30 seconds he'll shout out a random lyric.

'Where the whiskey drowns and the beer chases my bluuuuuues away, and I feel okay ..'

For fuck's sake! I turn around to Stevie and Decky who are sitting directly behind us:

'Has everybody on this bus been knighted or something? All I can hear is people calling each other sir!'

I then do a pretty good impression:

'Hi Sir, gone get your legs aff my side of the seat before I cut them aff ye!' – 'Get de fuck sir, you're sprawled out there like a big fucking heifer!'

Stevie and Decky both burst out laughing! Although Decky tells me to keep my voice down a bit because these country lads could turn on you very easily. They seem to use the word 'sir' all the time, all the 'culchies' do it, which is basically anybody that isn't from Derry city. It's a Saturday morning and we're on the bus to Bundoran. Things are going great for the four of us. Marty is a happy camper because he got Garth Brooks concert tickets last night as a present from his ma and da. Probably the first decent present they've ever given him. He's always been a huge fan of his and it turns out his ma won £900 at the bingo and bought tickets for herself, Marty and Marty's da. It was through his ma and da that he became a fan in the first place. It wouldn't be my cup of tea, but, sure, each to their own. Stevie is looking the best I've seen him in months, and I don't mean that in a gay way, just as a mate bigging up another mate. He's a great colour and he seems in much better shape and well spruced up. His ma and da are giving things another go, although his da still hasn't moved back in. Apparently, they're taking things slow and dating again which Stevie is over the fucking moon about.

'They're so hell-bent on giving, walking a wire, convinced it's not living if you stand outside the fire.'

Jesus Christ, we aren't even properly out of Derry yet. He sounds like a fucking cat giving birth. At least he's happy, though. Decky is also in great form. I mean, Decky is normally always in good form but today he just seems that bit happier, it's like he has a different look about him that I just can't put my finger on. I don't think he's seeing anybody 'cause he would definitely have said something, especially when I'm always slagging him about scoring more than he does. Maybe it's just because we're all going away for a week. It's the first time we have all got away together in a few years and it feels good. I feel good. Actually better than good – fucking class! Not just because of our wee holiday, but because I got a very important letter in the post on Tuesday – I've been cordially invited to take part in the judge's auditions of the X-Factor in three weeks! It will be recorded and I'll be on the TV. I'm finally going to be famous! I had planned not to tell the lads until after the actual auditions, but I'm not sure if I can keep it to myself that long! Like, the producers must have liked what they seen on my video if they cordially invited me to Manchester? I'm going to try to put it out of my mind as much as possible for the week, though, and just enjoy myself.

'Going round the world in a pick-up truuuucckk! Ain't going down till the sun comes up!'

I turn around to Stevie and Decky again:

'Gone somebody swap seats with me?'

Stevie laughs:

'I'm sure Marty felt the same way about sitting beside you – he's the smart one bringing his fucking iPod!'

Like I said before, he can be a smart fucker.

The country lads, who are taking up the entire bus, have been drinking since before we boarded and it's only 10.30 in the morning. There must be about 40 of them and it looks like they're going on a stag weekend. They're rowdy as fuck, but maybe I'm just jealous 'cause they're on the sauce and we aren't. We're not drinking because Decky reckons it's for the, best because of Stevie, blah blah blah. There's two lads sitting across from us that have started into a game of dead arm. Basically, they're both taking turns to punch each other on the arm and the first to quit is the loser. The bloke who's the stag is sleeping on the back seat and his mates have drawn a large cock on his forehead.

As usual, Decky is the man with the plan:

'Right, as soon as we get down there we'll go to the shops and get some food in. We'll just throw in a few quid each and get enough to do us for the week. I don't mind cooking the dinners, but the rest of you can look after breakfast and lunches.'

'We'll have to get some drink in, too …'

I said it before I even thought about Stevie. Decky gives me the eyes.

'Don't be thinking you can't drink just because of me lads, I'll be grand! I'll just stick to having beers and I'll be alright. It's not like I'm off it or anything. I'll just not be hitting the spirits or the shots! We're going to Bundoran for a good time, not a fucking pilgrimage to Lough Derg!'

You see, I knew he would be grand with it. Decky is just being Decky:

'Are you sure, man? You know I won't be drinking a while pile anyway?'

'He said he'll be grand, Decky, for fuck's sake! If he doesn't mind a few drinks in the house, then that's up to him.'

'Right, as long as you're sure, Stevie. We'll get some drink in too. As soon as we get off the bus we'll go get a bite to eat in a café or something, then hit the shops. Then, we'll see where to go tonight. Does that sound like a plan?'

Me and Stevie both agree. The two lads who were playing dead arm beside us decide to chat to us. One of them is wearing a Derry GAA jersey and the other is wearing a check shirt. They look like brothers, but I can't be too sure. Everybody out that way is related in some way.

'Where are you lads from, horse?'

Decky answers. He seems to understand their language a bit better:

'We're from the City. Just heading down to Bundoran for a wee week. Recharge the batteries and all that.'

I'll be fucked if I'll be recharging any batteries! I don't say anything. though…

'Quare job, sir! We're heading on the rip for the weekend for our boy's stag! Some craic!' He points at the fella with the cock on his head.

Decky sees the confused look on my face and tells me that 'our boy' means his brother.

'You see, I knew they were all related out that way!'

Stevie punches me on the shoulder.

'What? I said related NOT retarded!!'

Fuck, I said all of that out loud. Luckily, only Stevie and Decky heard it because at that moment, Marty started into his loudest bit of singing yet, and he's really getting carried away. He's like a child. I don't think he realises that everybody can actually hear him when he has the earphones in. I swear to God everybody has stopped talking and is listening to him. You could hear a pin drop, apart from the words that are coming out of his plaque-filled mouth:

'AND THE THUNDER ROLLS AND THE LIGHTENING STRIKES, ANOTHER LOVE GROWS CO-OLD ON A SLEEPLESS NI-IGHT, AND THE STORM MOVE'S ON OUT OF CONTROL …'

Then the weirdest thing happens, the entire bus sings the last bit in harmony:

'DEEP IN HER HEART, THE THUNDER ROLLS!'

Suddenly, the whole bus is cheering and shouting. Marty takes off his earphones and realises what's going on. He thinks he's a fucking superstar or something. Stevie and Decky are getting as carried away as the country lads with their shouting and roaring. Stevie holds Marty's arm up high, like he has just won something. All he did was sing really badly to a bunch of drunk culchies. Hardly a big achievement! I just clap for a few seconds, because at the end of the day, he is a mate and all that. Luckily, we arrive in Bundoran a few minutes later. People are high fiving Marty and slapping him on the back as we get our bags out of the boot of the bus. They're obviously big fans of Garth Brooks, too, by the way their talking, but that's hardly fucking surprising. There's a lad wearing a Liverpool jersey that Decky is deep in conversation with, he could talk about football for hours. Stevie is telling some of them the best pubs to go to and where is good for a lock-in. He knows Bundoran well after coming here for years with his ma and da. They seem like a sound bunch, except for the one who is talking the ears off me about his twin-cam. I wasn't even entirely sure what a twin-cam was when he started going on about it. I thought it was a type of camera that, like, records two things at once. Turns out it's a type of car.

'I swear to fuck sir, there wouldn't be another twin cam in the whole of North Derry that would get near this thing.'

I just nod politely. I'm not even really listening, I'm just thinking about what I could have for lunch 'cause I'm fucking starving. Doesn't matter anyway because the fella, I think his name's Keith, is just talking away about engines and exhausts. Finally, we get our bags out of the boot and say cheerio to the Dungiven lads. They head off up the road like a big bunch of cowboys from the wild-west, and we head off to a café that Stevie recommends.

'It's just up around the corner here. It's nothing five-star or anything, but you won't be hungry after it, I guarantee you that!'

Happy days. My kind of place. Stevie leads the way into the café and we all sit down at a table. The place is old-looking and it has loads of souvenir-type things on the walls, and loads of old-looking plates, saucers, pots and kettles hanging from every available space. As Stevie said, it's not five star, but I couldn't give a fuck as long as the food is dished out warm and quick.

Marty is looking around, taking it all in. Stevie says what I'm thinking:

'This is probably the classiest place you've ever eaten in, eh Marty?'

Marty just continues looking around and says:

'I'm not too keen on eating in these swanky-type places. I was in one once and you had to eat a pizza with a knife and fork. Who the fuck does that??'

We all burst out laughing. The waitress girl asks us if we're ready to order. Me, Marty and Stevie order the full Irish breakfast and Decky orders a chicken Caesar salad. He never eats crap, he's always all healthy and stuff.

Stevie starts talking about the difference between an Ulster fry and an Irish breakfast.

'Ye see an Ulster fry doesn't have anything in it that can't be cooked in bacon fat, whereas a full Irish has other things in it like baked beans and toast.'

'Isn't Donegal in Ulster, though? And we're in Donegal now, aren't we?'

It's not too often I have something worthwhile to say when it comes to conversations, so I'm delighted when Decky and Marty nod in agreement, and wait for Stevie's response.

'Aye, you're right, we are still in Ulster but the counties in the south will go with the full Irish as opposed to the Ulster fry. The Ulster fry is mostly associated with Northern Ireland.'

Mickey Doc

I'm pretty pleased with myself that I said something that was right and I was taking part in a proper conversation, but then Marty the dickhead goes and changes the subject:

'Hi, it's a pity Ireland didn't make it to the World Cup, we'd have some nights out for that. It just won't be the same without them being in it.'

'For fuck's sake, Marty, we're talking about the difference between Irish breakfasts and Ulster fries here. Nobody wants to talk about football.'

Turns out they do. The next 45 minutes are spent talking about the upcoming World Cup. A few times I tried to get us back to talking fries, but nobody takes me on so I just sit there with a head on me. Typical.

We finish our grub, then head to Lidl to get some food and drink for the house. Decky takes charge and budgets our money. He reckons 20 euro each will get us our food for the week and everybody just gets their own drink. Me and Marty let the other two handle the food shopping while we go to the off-licence for the booze. Stevie and Decky tell us what they want and that they'll sort us out after. They only want 24 cans of Heineken between them, which is fuck-all really for a week. We arrange to meet out the front afterwards, and get a taxi back to the house because of the amount of groceries, drink and luggage we have. There's no fucking way I'll be carrying all that.

Me and Marty go to get a shopping trolley then I realise I don't have a euro coin:

'No need, man.'

Marty pulls out a Swiss army knife and then shoves the blade into the place where the euro should go. He wiggles his hand a couple of times until the trolley is released from the rest.

'Hey presto.'

'How the fuck did you know how to do that?'

He winks as he puts the knife away. 'Just a wee trick I learned. I could start a car with this, too.'

Sometimes I think people from Ballymac are pre-programmed to be able to commit crimes. One time I got locked out of my house and Marty was with me. I rang my ma to see where they were at and before she even answered the phone, Marty was opening the front door from the inside. He had went around the back and got in through the bathroom window. They're even built for breaking and entering, 'cause it was the wee small window at the top and I still don't know to this day how the fuck he got up there and how he got through it.

We pick up the drink then meet Decky and Stevie out the front. We get a taxi pretty quickly and head to the house, which is about five minutes away. It's a really nice place and, luckily, doesn't have too much stuff that we could break. There's only two bedrooms. Stevie and Decky take one room and me and Marty take the other. I check the drawers in the room to see if Stevie's ma has left anything behind. Nope, empty. I warn Marty that if he snores, then he'll end up going out the window and he'll need more than a fucking Swiss army knife to get back in. We throw our stuff in our rooms then we all meet in the living room. Stevie puts on the radio and I think about having a can. It's only 3pm in the day and I don't know if the others will be starting so early. I decide to test the water:

'Jesus, my throat is dry. I hear you shouldn't drink the tap water on holidays either, 'cause there could be anything in it.'

Stevie laughs:

Jesus, Mickey, you're in Bundoran not fucking Africa!'

'I'm just saying, though, I don't know what the water is like here and I'm thirsty.'

'You have a shitload of beer there! Drink one of them!'

Thank fuck Stevie is cool with it. I knew he would have been. I look over at Decky to see what he says. I'm expecting at least a condensating look.

'If you're getting a beer, gone grab one for me.'

Thank fuck for that. Stevie and Marty both ask for one, too.

We all clink tins and cheers each other. Before we know it, the cans are going down well and the craic is good. We're all half-tanked and enjoying ourselves. At about 6 o'clock Decky says we should get a quick change and head down to the pub. He's changed his fucking tune, but I'm not complaining. We all go to get ready. Me and Marty are ready first, then Stevie joins us back in the living room. Stevie rings a taxi and it arrives just as Decky is ready. I was actually waiting for us all to be together in the living roomy to make an announcement about the X-Factor, but Decky took too fucking long and the moment passes.

We arrive at the pub and Decky pays the driver and tells us we can get the first rounds in. From outside the pub we can tell that the place is buzzing already. The first thing I hear when we get in is:

'There's the boys from Derry! Come on in to fuck, horse!'

It's the lads from Dungiven and they're well on at this stage. The stag still has the cock drawn on his forehead, but he's upright now and standing at the bar drinking shots. They all slap our backs and offer to buy us drinks. The twin-cam bloke drifts back over to me and starts talking about cars again, only this time he can't really hold a sentence together. He can barely stand up and every few minutes he gets confused about what he's saying and just lets a roar out of him:

'My brother, sir, has a GTI and I swear te fuck, sir, she's some weapon. He went down from Magherafelt one day and had her over a hundred, then they fucking- YEEEEEOOOOO! And we never even seen the fucking thing … but the fucking tail end of her was like this big red fucker then she just – AAARRGGGHH!! Come on te fuck ye mad hoors- YEEEEOOO!'

I honestly don't know what to be saying, so I just walk away from him and go over to Marty where he's talking to four lads about Garth Brooks':

'In Pieces was his best album, but it's hard to choose a favourite. Everything he does is just class.'

Fuck this, I'm pretty pissed now, and Garth Brook's just annoys me. I look over to Stevie and he's arm-wrestling a big farmer-looking bloke at the bar. He wins and the farmer bloke hands him a fiver and tells him he'll have a rematch later. Decky is at the end of the bar with the bloke in the Liverpool jersey and they're having a full-on conversation and laughing away. As I said, Decky could talk about football 24/7.

Before I know it, it's 11 o'clock and a band has started up in the corner. We are pissed as fuck now, and everybody is on the dance floor dancing and singing away and punching the air. The band seems pretty good but maybe that's because we're full. A few of the Dungiven lads have taken their tops off and are up on the stage. Before I know it, Stevie and Marty have their tops off, too, and have joined them. I notice two girls sitting just off the dance floor. They must have just come in cause nobody else has spotted them yet and I better get in there fast before anybody else gets there.

'What brings good-looking girls like you here?'

They both look at each other then burst out laughing.

'What the fuck are you laughing at?'

'We were just wondering how long it would be before one of you lot came over to our table. Two minutes and 35 seconds. You're a quick mover.'

'That's not all I'm quick at.'

They laugh again, then I realise what I just said. That sounded better in my head. Fuck this, I'm too drunk to be trying to make sense. I don't even say anything else, I just walk away. I go back to the bar and get another drink. I look back down at the girls a few minutes later, and I see the fucking twin-cam fella sitting with them and getting on great. They're hanging on his every word, and their not even laughing at him. This is a fucked-up town, if a boy like that can seem interesting. I should go back down and tell them I'm going to be on the X-Factor, but there's no way I could deal with getting rejected twice in the one night by the same birds. I don't remember much after that. Apparently, I threw up outside after smoking. I don't know why the fuck I even tried smoking as it always makes me sick. The next thing I remember is we're back at the house and most of the Dungiven lads are there, too.

Things are kinda hazy for the rest of the night. I remember the twin-cam lad had brought back the girls he met at the bar and there was no way he was for sharing. I decided to deal in the only kind of currency these people understand and offered him an arm-wrestle in exchange for one of the girls. I lost, and quickly, too. One of the girls shouted that I'm definitely quick at everything and they all burst out laughing. I fucking hate being the butt of a joke! I storm out of the kitchen to find my mates. Everyone is sitting in the living room, with Marty standing in the middle and he's singing Garth Brooks songs. Fucking singing! I'm meant to be the singer of the group! I'm meant to be the star attraction! I'm going to be on the X-Factor for fuck's sake! I try to push in and get people's attention to tell them that a real professional singer is here. The whole room suddenly turns on me before I can make my announcement, then I'm told to 'shut the fuck up, sir, before I put my fist down your throat.' Stevie is on the settee with a girl sitting on his knee. I think it's one of the girls the twin-cam fella brought back. Stevie must have beaten him in an arm-wrestle, the bastard. I tell Marty he's an arsehole and he just looks at me with a confused look on his face. Stevie asks me what's wrong and I give him the middle finger and call him a dick. Everybody seems to be against me and telling me to shut up, so I leave to find Decky. He isn't in the living room and he isn't in the kitchen, and there's no way he's in the bog that long. I hear a noise coming from the bedroom. There's no way he scored? I do a mental count in my head of the twin-cam girls. One in the kitchen, and one in the living room. I'm sure that's all the girls that came back. He must have hit the bed. I burst into the room and knock on the light and I get the biggest shock of my life. Decky is sitting on the bed, and he's kissing the fella that was wearing the Liverpool top. He's actually kissing another bloke. I stare for what seems like a lifetime and Decky stares back at me, both of us not knowing what to say. I call him a prick, then slam the door and run to my room. I'm in a bit of a state now, my head is spinning and I feel sick. I quickly pack my bag and as I'm going out the door, Decky is standing in front of me. He has tears in his eyes. I can't even look at him, so I push him out of the way and into the phone table. He falls hard. I run the rest of the way into town. I don't know where I'm running to but there's no way I'm going back to that house.

CHAPTER 5.

It's the start of May and a beautiful day. (I'm a poet and I didn't know!) It's also the day before I leave to go to Manchester, the biggest day of my life, and I feel great!

Well, apart from the sickening, empty feeling at the pit of my stomach after falling out with my best friends, and totally abandoning one of them for being gay. Fuck, it wasn't even because he's gay! It was a shock at first, I'll admit, but the thing that hurts me most is that he didn't even tell me. He's obviously known for a while and it probably explains why we ended up in Pepe's gay bar on a few occasions on nights out. It's funny how things only add up after they have happened. The main thing that annoyed me was that everybody seemed to have been stealing my thunder that night. Stevie sorting his life out, Marty thinking he was a singer and Decky coming out like that. It's the talk of the fucking town and everybody is saying how great it is that he's happy. Like he wasn't happy before? Stevie and Marty rang and texted me to try to sort things out with Decky, but I didn't answer or reply. I'm still pretty annoyed to be honest, even though it was over a month ago. I haven't heard a thing from Decky, I just spent my time practising singing and practising being a superstar. I have way too much ahead of me to be worrying about what they get up to. I'll just bury that empty feeling at the pit of my stomach and forget about them. I'm going to be a star.

My flight isn't until 8pm and I have everything packed and ready to go at 11am in the morning. The reason why I have everything done so early is because my ma and da are making me go to my cousin's tenth birthday party, then my da is going to bring me to the airport at 6.30pm. George's birthday party is the last place I want to be at the moment because he is, without doubt, the most annoying child I have ever met. Ever since he was four he has wanted to be a priest! A fucking priest!? Jesus Christ! Priests are something old people want to be! He even goes on like a fucking priest, which if you ask me is wile creepy. But oh no, you couldn't say anything like that around my ma or aunties. He's the golden boy and I'm pretty sure they're just looking for a free pass into heaven or something.

'Mickey are you ready yet? We'll be leaving in 10 minutes!'

'I'll be down now, Ma!'

'We don't want to be late, Father Kelly will be over to give a blessing at 12 o'clock and I don't want to be missing that!'

Yep, where most kids have a bouncy castle, this kid has a priest giving a blessing. I bet the other kids fucking love him. I dander down the stairs and my da is standing with his coat on, ready to go. He looks at me and shakes his head. I know he thinks the same about it as me.

'Could you not of got an earlier flight? Would have got me out of this crap.'

My fault, as usual…

My ma bursts out of the kitchen, dolled up to the nines and she's wearing enough perfume to knock out a donkey. I think in some twisted way, women of her age try to tempt priests. It's like some sick game they play – 'This is what you're missing' kind of a thing. The priests fucking love it, too.

'Right, are we all ready? Now, before we go I don't want any cheeky remarks or comments out of you two. This is a big day for wee George and for the family.'

My da is sort of staring into space and talking, sometimes he doesn't realise he's talking out loud. I definitely got the stupid genes from him:

'Wasn't like that in my day. It was the priests that wanted to be in kids, not the kids being into priests.'

This echoes around the hallway for a few seconds … My da realises it wasn't just said in his head, it was said outside his skull. He opens the front door wide, and steps into the porch. That was a quick move. He knows my ma won't scream at him where the neighbours can hear. Her face has turned red and I can see a wee vein on her forehead that looks like it's about to burst at any moment. She just leans in close to him and says:

'I swear to God, John Doherty, if I hear you coming out with anything like that today, I will personally rip your balls off, mash them up and feed them to ye with a spoon!!'

My da takes a reddner and walks on to the car. I can't help but laugh. She then turns to me:

'And that goes for you too, any lip today and you'll be able to hit higher notes than the Bee Gees on helium. Got it?'

This is going to be a long day, but fuck it, get through this and then it's Manchester time.

We arrive at my Aunty Margret's house and make our way to the front door. My ma has lost her aggression and is full of smiles and fake laughter. She can be such a fake bitch sometimes. George is waiting at the door, greeting guests as they come. He's dressed in black trousers and a black shirt with his hair combed to one side:

'Aunty Bridie, Uncle John, how nice of you to come and help me celebrate this day.'

My da just awkwardly shakes his hand and walks on in. My ma hugs George and kisses him on the forehead:

'Oh would ye look at you! Beautiful boy! Happy birthday my wee darlin'! Here's your present from the three of us.'

I knew fuck-all about any present. I don't even know what you would get him.

'Aunty Bridie you shouldn't have. As if God hasn't given me enough to be blessed with such a glorious family. But thank you.'

Seriously, ten years old?

He opens the wrapping paper without tearing it. Most kids would have used their hands AND teeth to tear it to shreds.

'A pair of rosary beads! Oh, how wonderful! Thank you so much Aunt Bridie!'

He leaves the present on the phone table with the rest of the rosary beads. There must be about 30 sets there, all different colours and probably different levels of holy powers. Obviously, nobody had a clue what to be getting him. In fairness, though, I'd say he goes through them pretty quickly. I'm up next:

'Cousin Michael ...'

Michael! Fuck! I can't stand the kid, but for some reason he makes me nervous. Like talking to the headmaster at school, even when you've done nothing wrong you still feel guilty.

'… thank you for coming and thank you for the lovely present.'

'No problem. I knew you would like them. I told my ma they would be the perfect thing for you. You must nearly have the whole set now?'

He looks at me like he already knows it's something stupid before he even asks.

'What set?'

'The power set of rosary beads.'

'Oh, I see you're still mixing up sci-fi with religion. Your mother spoke of that before. We had hoped you had grown out of it by now.'

What the fuck? I just stand there nodding. It's like he has an aura of holiness, if that's even a term.

'I haven't seen you at mass in a while, Michael. Are you having problems with your faith?'

'Am, no … I just must have been going to different ones than you. You know how it is with all these masses these day, you tend to miss people like?'

This little fucker can see straight through my lies. I'm physically shaking and I can't look him in the eye. He stares at me for about ten seconds, then smiles:

'Michael, everybody has a crisis of faith from time to time. It's nothing to be embarrassed about and it's healthy. Go enjoy yourself and I'll talk to you about it soon.'

Mickey Doc

'Thank you, George.'

Thank you!? I feel like I've just been told off by a priest. He's only turned ten and he has turned me into a mumbling dickhead. He shakes my hand, then tells me the rest of the guests are in the living room. I put my hands flat together then bow to him like an idiot. This kid needs brought down a peg or two, or nailed to a fucking cross where he belongs. I pull out my phone to text the lads that cracker line, then I remember we're not speaking and that makes my stomach hurt. Fuck.

The living room is huge. The whole house is fucking huge. Like me, George is an only child. At least I turned out normal, though. The suite of furniture has been pushed back and there are rows of plastic chairs lined along each side. There are only ten kids here and at least eight of those are related to him. The children and adults are sitting on the chairs, chatting to each other, drinking tea and eating buns. It feels like a bloody wake instead of a kid's party. I made my ma and da promise not to tell anybody about the X-Factor and, if anybody asked then, tell them I'm going to visit friends this evening.

'There he is, our wee superstar! Mickey Doc on the X-factor! Who would have believed it!?'

For fuck's sake, my Aunty May! My ma and her big mouth! If she knows, then everybody will know. She turns to a man and woman standing beside her:

'This is our Bridie's boy, he's heading to Manchester this evening to be on the X-Factor! We're all so proud!'

They look like they're part of the God brigade. The bloke, he's about 50-odd and is wearing corduroy trousers and a beige woollen jumper. He seems delighted to meet me in fairness to him:

'Oh, the X-Factor, how wonderful! Father Kelly was just saying last week during his sermon how he should…'

He starts laughing out loud:

'… how he should… ha ha ha ha, he should make his own version of the X-Factor for God. The God Factor!! Ha ha ha Oh, how we laughed didn't we, darling?'

She isn't laughing. She doesn't speak at all. It was a shit joke in fairness, even for a priest's standards.

He just continues talking:

'Yes, we did laugh. So, what time are you on at, we must make sure we're at home this evening to see you?'

'Well, I'm not on the telly tonight. I'm just going over there this evening then I'll be doing my audition tomorrow. It won't be shown for another couple of months, though.'

'How exciting! We'll make sure to say a prayer for you, won't we darling?'

She still doesn't flinch. He has probably killed her brain over the years. I can see her bra sticking out of the top of her blouse. I'd say she was a looker in her day, and I think she might have a thing for me. I still would.

He's still laughing at the God Factor thing, the fucking pleb:

'Ha ha ha we surely will. God Factor! Ha ha ha!'

I ditch the God squad and make my way over to my da who is chatting to my Uncle Peter. In the background, I can hear my Aunty Margaret telling other people about how I'm going to be on the X-Factor. I feel like a bit of a celebrity already, although this isn't the kind of party I'll be attending after tomorrow.

My Uncle Jim gets me in a headlock and rubs my head with his fist. The fucker always wrecks my hair – and my head.

'Here he is, the superstar is here!'

'My da shakes his head at him to tell him to keep his mouth shut, but it's too late.'

'Sorry son, it just slipped out!'

'It's alright, Da, Aunty Margret has told the whole place already. Good to see I can trust my family to keep a secret.'

'Wise up, Mickey, ye dickhead ye, your da just toul' us you're going to be on TV, hardly something you can keep a secret forever! So what's the craic with your mate Decky, then? I hear he's gay now?'

My da looks away. He still can't come to terms with the fact Decky is gay.

'Aye, he is, aye. I haven't been chatting to him in a while.'

'Is he still going to play football? He wasn't at the match on Saturday.'

"Am, I'm not sure, he probably will. Can't see why not.'

My da suddenly speaks, but he's just thinking out loud again:

'He was such a good talent. The best I'd seen in this town since Liam Coyle was that age. What a waste!' He shakes his head in disbelief.

'Fuck up, John, the young fella is gay, it's not like he murdered somebody!'

My da is still talking to himself out loud:

'He reminded me of a younger version of myself in my prime. Obviously, not in a gay way though!'

Then the room goes quiet. I swear to God the lights dimmed and it got darker outside when they appeared at the door. It's George and Father Kelly followed by three nuns. They're all moving like one big super-being. I'm not sure if it's just my eyes playing tricks, but I swear I can see smoke behind them. It's a seriously scary-looking sight. It's like everything is happening in slow motion. My ma and my aunts are bowing to them, and moving kids off seats for them to sit down. George's eyes have got bigger, it's like he can see everyone in the room at once, and is judging us all.

'In the name of the Father and of the Son and of the holy spirit, amen'

'AMEN'

Father Kelly remains standing and starts the blessing with that big priest voice of his. I feel like I'm in a horror movie.

'We are gathered here today to celebrate the birthday of our dedicated parishioner George McLaughlin. It delights me that someone so young could find themselves so involved in the church and his parish. He is an exceptional child and a source of pride for myself, his family and, of course, God our Father...'

For some reason I look to the door expecting God to actually walk in, sort of like a Surprise, Surprise moment. Thank fuck he doesn't.

'... Let us pray.'

Mickey Doc

The prayer seems to last for ages with loads of head bowing and blessings going on. Not once does the fucker say a prayer for me and my X-Factor audition. I can't help taking quick glances at the door for God, but, just as I thought, there's no sign of him. I ask my da which hand is over which for communion, but the dick just sticks out his tongue. I think he may have had a few wee sneaky drinks.

Turns out, George isn't important enough for communion, but up next is the cake. Everybody sings Happy Birthday, then the usual 'hip-hip-hooray'. George blows out the candles and his ma tells him to make a wish. I can hear my da saying that if Michelle Keegan isn't at least two of his wishes then they need to get the kid looked about. For once, I agree with him. Then my da catches my eye and taps his watch:

'We'd need to be away in the next five minutes, Mickey, to beat the traffic!'

'Just going for a piss first, Da.'

I head out to the downstairs toilet, but there's somebody in there and by the noises they're making there's no way I'm going in next. Sounds like a horse trying to push a car out of its arse. Father Kelly is standing nearby and he can obviously hear the noises 'cause he's staring at the door with a weird-looking half-smile on his face. I tell him that he may need to do an exorcism to help get that out, which is a cracker line, but he doesn't see the funny side of it, and he creeps me out a bit with his answer:

'How dare you talk about your mother like that! She is a beautiful woman!'

That's all down to her trying to seduce him, ye see, he looks like a bear trapped in the headlights. Sometimes I pray that I was adopted. I run up the stairs 'cause I'm absolutely bursting at this stage. I decide to have a sit-down pee because I just want to sit on my own for a few minutes, away from the craziness of downstairs, and think about the journey I'm about to go on. Not just the plane journey, but the life journey I'm about to begin. I always get psychological when I sit on the toilet. I look at my phone and there's a new message. It's from Marty:

'Gud luck 2moro Mickey'

At first, I feel happy, then sad and then angry. Then my belly hurts again. I pull up my cacks, then wash my hands and leave the bathroom. George must be waiting to use the bog 'cause he's standing waiting at his bedroom door.

'It's alright, George, you can go in, I was only doing a number one.'

He doesn't move, just stands there looking at me.

'Come in to my room for a minute for a chat, Michael.'

He doesn't even wait for an answer, and I follow him into his room without speaking. There is nothing in this room that would tell you a ten-year-old sleeps here. There's a few holy pictures on the walls and an old wooden desk with a wooden seat. He tells me to sit down there and I do it, again, without speaking. As I told you before, he has a sort of hold over me.

'Now,, Michael, I believe you're heading off on a new journey in your life.'

What the fuck?

'Can … can you read minds?'

'Read minds? Don't be silly Michael. This sci-fi/religion mix-up is getting out of hand. Your mother told me you're going to Manchester to be on the X Factor. It's a very exciting time for you. For all of us.'

'It is, I can't wait! It's everything I've ever dreamed of!'

'And yet, you look sad.'

'I'm in top form.'

'Your mum and dad are proud of you, ye know.'

'I know they are. I just … it's just sometimes I want to make them proud. Sometimes I think there's more in me than just Mickey Doc who works in Valuesaver and gets full every weekend and all the girls fancy and want to be with.'

He just nods, like he's taking it all in.

'I've always wanted to be somebody. Somebody who, when they're walking down the street, people will stop and go "there's yer man, Mickey Doc. He's class".'

'And what about your friends? I've heard you've had a falling out?'

I'm convinced he can read my mind. I'm going to Google it on the way to the airport.

'I think we've just grown apart. It happens when you get to our age.'

I get that pain in my belly again, and I wince.

'All I'm going to tell you, Michael, is that friendship is a very important part of what makes us human. I know you don't go to mass or anything, but that's your prerogative. Just be careful when you go away, it can be a lonely place, even when you're surrounded by lots of people.'

He lifts a pen and a piece of paper from the desk and writes on it.

'This is my number, Michael. Ring me if you ever need to chat or if things are getting too much for you.'

'Er, thanks.'

'Always remember, Mickey: people aren't always what they seem. Beware of the wolf in sheep's clothing.'

Wolf in sheep's clothing? The wee fucker must have been at the altar wine.

'Er … aye, I'll remember that, George.'

What the fuck?

A car horn beeps from outside and I know right away it's my da. I put the piece of paper in my back pocket and awkwardly shake George's hand. I think I might be crying a little bit. I wipe my eyes and make my way downstairs where it's all hugs and 'good luck' and my ma shouting out the door 'ring me when you get there'.

The 15-minute journey to the airport goes by in a blur. Me and my da are sitting in silence, but it isn't awkward, it's like we're both thinking about stuff. I check my phone and I have a few messages. Marty, Stevie and Decky have all text but I delete the messages before I even open them, because they seem to bring on the stomach pains. The other text is from Laura Dillon. She wishes me all the best of luck and other crazy stuff about how I'm the love of her life and the greatest person ever, which is all good stuff to hear in fairness. I text her back:

'Thanxs. Can't get on the internet. Can 10 year old priests read minds?'

I'm sitting on the plane and all sorts of things are racing through my mind. Tomorrow I will be standing in front of Simon, Louis and Cheryl. I have 'What Makes you Beautiful' by One Direction on repeat on my iPod 'cause that's the song I'll be singing. The words to the song are ingrained in my head and I know every single note I should be hitting, and every single move I should be making when I'm singing it:

Baby you light up my world like nobody else (raise right hand) *The way you flip your hair* (flip hair) *gets me overwhelmed* (raise arms) *But when you smile at the ground it ain't hard to tell* (look at ground) *You don't know- oh-oh* (clench fist) *You don't know you're beautiful* (raise right hand in the air).

This helps me a lot because it's actually the first time I've been away on my own. I've been on holidays abroad with my parents when I was younger, but this is the first time doing it all by myself. I wonder if Manchester is bigger than Derry? I wonder if I can understand the people? I'm staying in an Ibis hotel and my ma gave me the money for a taxi from the airport to the hotel. Apparently, where I'm staying is close to Old Trafford where the auditions are at. The audition letter said I have to be there no later than 9am in the morning so I'm planning to be there for 6 o'clock to get a good spot in the queue.

I get off the plane and go outside to the taxi rank. The place is full of all sorts of nationalities and languages. There's two guys standing next to me waiting on a taxi and I swear to God they're making up their own language. It just sounds like they're saying:

'He hang yaw, he heng ping wing ting…'

It's probably not what they're actually saying, but I've always been crap at languages. They're probably Chinese, or French or something. I get to the front of the queue without making eye contact with anybody, and the next thing I know a taxi pulls up and beeps his horn, even though I'm standing two feet away from him:

''You fookin' gettin' in or what mate?'

'Aye, can I throw my bag in the boot?'

'Ee are, it's a fookin' black taxi, mate. Just bring it in the back!'

I tell the driver where I want to go, then put in my earphones, I don't want to talk to him 'cause he seems like he wants to kill somebody. Any car that is within a four-foot distance from his car is being called a cunt. He actually gave the middle finger to an elderly woman and called her a cunt 'cause she took too long to cross at a zebra crossing. In fairness though, she gave him the middle finger back and made a wanker motion with her hand. I give him the £8 for the journey and he asks me am I here for the X-Factor. I ask him how he knew that, and was there something about me in the papers over here? He looks at me like he's trying to work out if I'm really that stupid, then he points across the road to a huge building with 'Old Trafford' written on it. My heart sinks when I see there's already at least 1,000 people in the queue and it's only 9 o'clock the night before auditions. Fuck.

CHAPTER 6.

I'm trying to run, but my legs just won't move as fast as I want them to, it's like they're made of stone or something. My heart is beating so fast I think it is going to burst out of my chest. The mob is gaining on me. Some of them are wearing T-shirts with my face on them and they're chanting my name. Others have weapons and they want to hurt me. I recognise a few of the mob: Stevie, Decky and Marty are there and they're throwing stones at me. Marty's head looks really big. I think I can see Po from the Teletubbies too, but that could be just a costume. I can see my ma up ahead, she's standing at a doorway calling my name, but she just seems to be getting further away and the mob is gaining on me. I trip and fall, and as the mob are about to pounce I hear a siren and hope it's the police. The siren is piercing through my ear. Then I wake up in a cold sweat and realise it's my alarm going off. I look at my phone and it's 4.15am.

Fuck. What the hell was that all about? I lay there for a minute, trying to get over my nightmare, then, I take in where I am and what I'm doing here. When I got to the hotel last night it was heaving with people, so I just went straight to bed and set my alarm for this ridiculous time. Two hours to get myself ready then I should be in the audition queue for half six. I do my usual getting-ready routine: a few push-ups, a long shower using French Connection UK body wash while singing, this is so I smell good AND get my voice muscles warmed up. I like the professional approach. I read somewhere that Whitney Houston used to do this before playing a concert. There was other stuff she done, too, pre-gig but that's not my cup of tea. After the shower I do 10 more push-ups and then get dressed. I spent a lot of time before packing, deciding on the perfect outfit. The kinda outfit that is going to make people think 'holy shit, this guy is not only a great singer, but he knows how to dress ... and he has a great body'. Then it's time for the hair. This takes me a good 45 minutes to get right. Although my hair isn't long, it has to be styled to perfection. A bit of hair sitting the wrong way could cost me getting through to the actual main show. I then do some poses in front of the full-length mirror on the wardrobe. I need to see myself from every angle and in every way of standing, just so I know the look is right. After a few tweaks to the hair and clothes, I'm finally ready to present myself to the world. World, I present to you ... Mickey Doc!

It's 6.45 by the time I'm making my way through the lobby of the hotel. The place is absolutely jammed with people coming and going. There is a weird mix of people and all the chat seems to be about the X-Factor. I grab a few slices of toast and a banana and make my way out the main door and head across to the audition queue. There must be thousands of people here already. I only thought there was weirdos in the hotel lobby! There's a man here who's at least 60 and looks like my old form teacher. Only difference is, Mr Hutton always wore a nice suit. This bloke is wearing a pair of bright blue cycling shorts, a blond wig, make-up and one of those wee dresses a ballerina wears. I think they're called a tom-tom. He is wearing nothing on his upper half apart from a really hairy chest and what looks like nipple clips. I dodge past him as he's practising his 'do-re-mi' like it's the most normal thing in the world. I honestly can't stop staring at people. Some of them look normal like me, but others are just pure fucking nuts. I'm walking along, staring, when all of a sudden I walk into a man wearing a hi-vis vest who has a clipboard. I'm not sure anymore who is normal and who is nuts, so I apologise and ask him if he's here for the auditions. He looks like a bouncer with his shaved head and big frame.

'You wot ,mate?'

'Are you here for the auditions?' I say it slowly and loudly this time, in case he's a looper and can't understand me.

'I'm fackin' security here. mate. Are you just gonna walk round with yer gob, open or are ya gonna join the fackin' queue?'

'Am … I'm going to join the queue, I just can't find the end of it!'

'Over there, mate, behind the geezer dressed as a cow.' He points over at a large middle-aged man who is wearing what looks like a giant cow onesie. Again, this all seems normal to people here.

It's kinda like what I imagine Strabane to be like, only without the violence. Marty and Stevie ended up going back with a girl to Strabane one night and were lucky to get out with their lives. They said they only went there 'cause Stevie was trying to get off with a girl and Marty tagged along with the promise of free drink. Turns out the house was owned by a local paramilitary family and the girl was the daughter of the 'main man' in Strabane, and still lived with her family. Three men (her da and two brothers) interrogated Marty and Stevie in the spare room for 45 minutes. Because it was 3 o'clock in the morning and the men had been woken out of bed, they didn't bother getting dressed and each of them just put on a balaclava while only wearing boxers and string vests. They would fit in nicely here, nobody would blink a fucking eyelid.

I walk over to the queue and stand behind the person dressed as a cow. I try not to make eye contact with him so I just look ahead. There's a girl in front of him, who looks seriously pissed off but she is kinda hot. I catch her looking at me a few times. She has long black hair with a bit of a red streak in it and she is wearing really tight jeans and a tight top which shows off her class boobs. She's wearing a pair of knee-high leather boots with huge big heels. Even the cow man has a few wee cheeky looks at her. Then the cow man turns to me and nods his approval. I try to look away, but before I know it he's talking to me in what turns out to be a very posh-sounding accent:

'So, young man, what has attracted one so young to such a place? Is it the promise of fame and fortune, or the animalistic lure of competition for a maiden like that which stands before you?'

'Eh?'

'Are you here to find love or something more?'

'I'm here for the X-Factor auditions, what are you here for?'

'Oh, now that is a question ... what are we here for indeed? Some of the greatest minds have pondered that very question over many, many millennia ...'

I hardly tok in a word of what he was saying, I didn't even bother to try 'cause I don't understand the words posh people say, but before he got to finish his sentence,e the girl with the red streak in her hair interrupted:

'Listen you fookin' twat, are we gonna have to listen to your shite all day, or am I gonna have to rip your udders off and shove them up your fookin arse? Eh?'

'There will be no need for such language or threats of violence, young lady, we are all ...'

She interrupts again, this girl doesn't take no shit:

'Listen, dickhead, if you keep talkin' then I'm gonna have to start shouting at the top of my lungs that you touched my arse and offered me money for sex. I'm sure the Irish lad here will back me up...'

She looks at me and I nod. I actually feel sorry for the man, but I don't want to get on the wrong side of her. As I said before, she's hot and is getting hotter by the second.

'Now, do us all a favour and fuck off ya twat!'

The cow man's face has turned red and I can see a bit of a tear in his eye. He looks at me with his bottom lip trembling, like he's about to burst out crying. My heart melts for him, but all of a sudden I find myself acting the big man in front of a girl again:

'You heard the lady, fuck off ye twat!'

He looks a sorry sight as he walks out past the people who have recently joined the queue. As if things weren't bad enough, the girl springs forward and kicks him up the arse as he's leaving. He doesn't even say a word. It's the first time I got a really good look at her body and it is amazing!

'Fookin' twat! So, Irish, do you have a name or are you just gonna stare at me all day?'

'The name's Mickey Doc and I'm from Derry. I like how you told that dickhead where to go!'

'This place is full of fookin' twats, you get into conversation with them and you're fooked. So, can you sing?'

'Aye, I wouldn't be here if I couldn't'

'That's good, my name's Mandy.'

She puts out her hand for me to shake it. Even her hands are beautiful.

'So are your hands always that sweaty, or is it just when you're nervous?'

'My hands get sweaty when I'm annoyed.' I can feel my cheeks going red.

'Loosen up, man, I'm not going to bite your head off … well not unless you want me to.'

She gives me a cheeky wink. Jesus, these jeans I'm wearing are getting tighter by the second.

'So, Derry is in Northern Ireland, right?'

'Aye it's in the north-west. Have you ever been there before?'

'In the past two years I've been to Paris, Barcelona, Ibiza, Rome and Los Angeles. Why the fook would I want to go to Derry?'

'Eh, 'cause Derry was the City of Culture last year and we had the biggest Fleadh ever, over 200,000 people in one week?'

'You're funny, wanna hang out while you're here?'

'Damn right I do! Where are you from?'

Mickey Doc

Jesus Christ!! I could actually score here! Not like that's a big shock or anything, of course …

'I'm from Rochdale, about 45 minutes from here. It's a fookin' shithole. I live with my mum and my stepfather who are both fookin' dickheads. The sooner I can get out of that place, the better.'

'Aye, I'm the same in Derry. My ma and da are dickheads, too. My mates have been acting dicks lately, too, so the sooner I get away the better.'

'Mates and family will only do one thing – let you down.'

'Aye, I kinda lost the head with my best mate, Decky, when I found out he's gay. He's a great bloke, too. Fell out with my other two best mates, too. Not even sure why, they must have been assholes.'

'Blah, blah , blah , blah, blah. That's all I'm fookin' hearing, Mickey! Every prick here has a fookin' sob story, don't you be one of them, too. If your mates are arseholes, forget about them. Now, how are we going to skip this fookin' queue?'

I want to tell her they're not arseholes, but she is hot.

'I was thinking we just wait for the people in front of us to go in, then we go?'

'And stand here waiting with these bunch of dicks? I'm jumping the queue, you in?'

Fuck, I really shouldn't.

'Aye, I'm up for that alright!'

Next thing she pulls out a voice recorder, a clipboard and two passes that go around your neck which say 'PRESS' in big letters. I'm pretty confused, but sure that's nothing new.

'Why do you need to press the passes?'

She looks at me like I'm stupid. I'm used to that look, though.

'What ya mean?'

'Where it says PRESS, what happens when we press it?'

She stands there staring at me for what seems like ages.

'You are as thick as dog-shit, Mickey, but in a cute way. PRESS means we're part of the press, like a reporter or a journalist!'

The penny drops. If there was to be a soundtrack to my life it would be the sound of pennies dropping.

'Aw, that kind of press. So what's the plan?'

She rolls her eyes like I'm the most stupid person she ever met. I'm definitely not the stupidest person I've ever met.

'This queue is gonna take fookin' ages, right? So we can speed things along and have some fun as we go. You just follow my lead. We're reporters from the Manchester Tribune, doing a report on the X-Factor auditions. These fookin' freaks would believe anything if they thought they would get their names in print, or their faces on TV.'

I put my pass around my neck, then she grabs me by the hand and pulls me along the queue. She's pushing people out of the way shouting:

'Press, coming through … right, who wants to be interviewed for the newspaper?'

Mickey Doc

Suddenly people in the queue jump into life when they hear the word 'interview'. It reminds me of my ma's dog when it hears the word 'walkies', he reacts like a fucking animal, too, the spoiled little prick.

Mandy whispers to me:

'Right Mickey, you record this and I'll ask the questions.'

I whisper back:

'But I don't know how to work this thing! Is there even a CD in it?'

'You don't have to know how to work the fookin' thing 'cause we don't work for a fookin' newspaper, and we don't give a fuck what these dicks have to say. Got it?'

She's right in my face when she's saying it and she looks angrier than my ma when I tell people her real age. But I still find her really sexy! Not my ma, Mandy! Jesus, I better not start mixing up those two thoughts!

I just nod at her like a lovesick puppy.

We push our way, up to a group of people who are around my age. I think they're from Scotland or Wales. I always mix those two up.

Mandy starts talking to them, and she sounds amazing, just like a professional. She even changes her voice, kinda takes the roughness off it. She's even smiling:

'Okay, guys, how are we all doin'? Can you spare a few minutes of your time for an interview for the Manchester Tribune?'

The four blokes at the front step forward. They're all taller than me, so I feel a bit 'insecure' if that's the right word? Mandy is talking to them with that big fucking smile she has got on her, and I immediately start to feel jealous. A lad with a big rugby-looking head answers:

'Ack aye, nae botha, love!'

'Brilliant, so where are you all from?'

'We're frae Scotland and we're here tae win the X-Factor!'

They all cheer.

I'm starting to get jealous of the way she's talking to them, and they're loving it.

'So, who are your biggest influences?'

She's definitely flirting with them. She has her hand on the arm of the bloke who's talking and keeps looking into his eyes.

'Wan Direction and Take That, two power-hooses in music. As ye can see, love, we're all good-lookin' lads who can sing. The X-Factor wouldnae know what hit it!'

'You are definitely good-looking alright!'

Fuck, they're going to steal my girl!

They all cheer again. Then all of a sudden, without warning, I just start shouting:

'YOU WON'T WIN THE THING 'CAUSE I'M MICKEY DOC AND I'M GOING TO WIN!'

I open my eyes and everybody is staring at me.

'Yer aboot te go on the X-Factor and yer a reporter tae?'

'I'M NOT A REPORTER, I'M MICKEY DOC AND I'M GOING TO WIN THE X-FACTOR!'

I may have said that too loud. Sometimes things just come out when I hold them in too much.

'So are ye two takin' the piss with this newspaper stuff?'

Mandy jumps in with that big fake smile still going. I can see that she's angry, though, and she wants to kill me:

'I'm sorry, you guys, but I should have explained earlier that my colleague here with us is "special".'

She puts her fingers up like rabbit ears when she says 'special'. I fucking hate that, mostly 'cause I don't know what the sign means? She keeps going:

'He's been with us for a few weeks, and my boss decided it would be a good idea to send him along with me for the day. Get him out and meeting people, you know? It's part of a care in the community programme.'

She sort of whispers that last bit to them, but says it loud enough for other people to hear. The lads nod as if they had an idea already. They didn't need much convincing. Suddenly people are patting my back. The big Scottish guys are gathering around me and talking to me like I'm five years old.

'Hey chum, you get in there and show Simon Cowell what ye got!'

Another one rubs my head:

'Aye: you show 'em you're a superstar, buddy.'

My face is still red and I'm about to tell them where to go, when Mandy jumps in again:

'Sorry guys, but Mickey here is starting to get a bit flustered and I've been told by my bosses to keep him happy or his seizures will start, so we're going to move on. Come along, Mickey.'

She takes my hand and leads me away. The Scottish wankers start high-fiving me and telling me I'm a superstar which does feel good, even though they think I'm mentally handicapped. Actually, I should have showed them my singing.

We move along the crowd and I swear to God, not one person realises that we are just skipping the queue. Everybody single person here is delusional, they all think they're going to be the next big thing and obviously they aren't. 'Cause I am. Even though Mandy has kept on telling people that I'm 'special', I can't stop falling for her in a big way. She is class. Although I'm feeling pretty shit about being talked down to by everybody. Even though I feel shit, I still ask her if I should act a bit more special, just to make it more believable, but she said I'm retarded enough and laughs. I still want her so bad. I then realise I haven't checked my phone in ages which is so not like me. Like I said, this girl has me smitten like a kitten.

In just over two hours we have made our way to near the front of the queue. There's about 30 people in front of us when Mandy tells me this will do, we're close enough. Next thing an important-looking woman with a megaphone comes out of the building and makes her way from the front of the queue. She gives us all a number on a sticker and an armband. She reaches us and doesn't say a word, just tells us to hold out our right arms, and don't take the armband off or we will be refused admission. I'm number 3046 and Mandy is 3047. The megaphone woman then does the same to about 10 people behind us, then makes her way back to the start of the queue and shouts into the megaphone:

'OKAY, COULD EVERYBODY WEARING GREEN ARMBANDS
MAKE THEIR WAY TO THE MAIN DOORS OF THE ARENA
WHERE YOU WILL GET FURTHER DIRECTION. STICK THE
ALLOCATED NUMBERS ON TO YOUR CHEST AND MAKE
SURE THEY'RE VISIBLE. LET'S GET THIS MOVING QUICKLY
AND SAFELY, WE HAVE A LONG DAY AHEAD OF US!'

I turn to Mandy:

'We're in! I can't believe we're getting in!'

'Don't ever doubt me, Mickey. Now, swap numbers, I don't want to be
an odd number, it's bad luck.'

Shit, now I'm the unlucky number.

All of a sudden we're running into the arena and directed into a room
with a sign saying 'holding area'. The place is huge and there is already
about 50 people there. Next thing the woman with the megaphone
comes forward and starts shouting again:

'OKAY, CAN YOU ALL LISTEN CAREFULLY? YOU WILL BE
HERE FOR THE NEXT FEW HOURS AND THE CAMERAS WILL
BE ROLLING. YOU WILL BE AUDITIONED IN THE
AFTERNOON SO MAKE YOURSELVES COMFORTABLE. YOU
CAN NOT LEAVE THE WAITING AREA AND IF YOU DO YOU
WILL NOT GET BACK IN. WE WILL BE FILMING
THROUGHOUT, SO YOU WILL BE EXPECTED TO FOLLOW
ANY DIRECTION FROM ME OR ANY OF THE CREW AT ALL
TIMES. ANYBODY WHO DOESN'T COMPLY WILL BE

EJECTED FROM THE ARENA. YOU HAVE ALL BEEN GIVEN A NUMBER AND WILL BE CALLED TO THE AUDITION ROOMS IN TIME. THANK YOU.'

Mandy makes a 'wanker' sign to me and says:

'She thinks we're a bunch of fooking animals!'

She then takes me by the hand and leads me to a corner where there's a free sofa. Then she pulls out her phone and takes a selfie of the two of us. I pull my phone out and give it a check.

I have three missed calls from my ma, she's probably realised I hid the dog's eye drops before I left. I also have a load of messages: one from Marty saying that him and the lads were chatting last night in the Bentley and we need to sort things out. He also said he scored with three Playboy bunnies who were in town last night. Lying fucker. He also wished me good luck. I can't help but laugh, though, and realise how much I miss the lads. Mandy hears me laughing and says:

'Wot's so funny, retard boy?'

She's lying on the sofa with her feet in the air. Pure sexy.

'Ah, it's just one of the lads texting me to wish me good luck. I think I should give them a shout.'

She then looks me straight in the eye and moves towards me with really sexy movement. Like a model on the catwalk. She takes my hands and pulls me towards her. I can see right down her top and she takes my hand and puts in on her arse. She then kisses me on the lips for a good 20 seconds. She doesn't give a fuck who can see us. I'm hoping everybody can.

'How many of your so-called friends are here with you now, Mickey?'

'Well, none. But that's 'cause …'

She puts her finger on my lips to stop me talking.

I'm lost in her eyes, even though that sounds gay.

'None of them are here 'cause they fooking don't care, man. You got to get used to the fact that people will be jealous of you now that you've been on the X-Factor. Remember, Mickey, people aren't always what they seem!'

I get a sudden flash in my head and I remember George telling me to beware of wolves dressed up as sheep. This must be what he's talking about 'cause I've seen wackos here dressed as sheep, cows and even men dressed as women. That must be what he meant. Smart kid, you got to give him that.

The other messages are from my stalker, Laura Dillon. I open the first one and it says 'Good luck my hero'. I don't even bother reading the rest 'cause the last thing I need at the moment is a psycho woman in my life.

Other groups of 50 people have been let into the holding area, and it's getting packed in here. Kinda reminds me of the Fleadh, only without the beer and Irish music. Loads of people who recognise me from the queue are coming up to me and patting me on the head and talking to me like a child. Mandy is just sat in the corner, laughing. At least I can make her laugh.

Then the girl with the Megaphone comes out roaring again:

'CAN I HAVE YOUR ATTENTION, PLEASE? THE CAMERAS HAVE BEEN SET UP AND WE WILL BE DOING SOME SHOTS. ONCE YOU GET THE CALL FROM ME I NEED YOU ALL TO

DANCE AND GO CRAZY. THIS COULD TAKE A FEW SHOTS, SO KEEP THE ENERGY GOING!'

A few shots?? Every few minutes we would be told to face a different way and 'go crazy' , this lasted for almost two hours! In between takes we were all instructed to face a large screen on the wall at the back of the room. Next thing Simon Cowell comes on the screen with his white T-shirt, amazing tan and posh accent:

'Good evening Manchester, I'm so sorry that my judges and I couldn't be there in person, but my amazing production team will look after your auditions at this early stage. Thank you all for coming today, and I hope to see many of you in a few weeks' time. Thank you.' Then he winks.

We are all cheering, then I realise that Simon isn't actually here! Again, the penny tok a while to drop. Luckily enough, I seem to be with people on the same wavelength as me 'cause I can hear pennies dropping all over the place, and people getting explained to that Simon isn't here. Then Mandy finally decides to leave her phone and come over to me:

'Did every fookin' twat here think that Simon Cowell and the other judges were going to spend all fookin' day listening to thousands of people trying to sing? Fook that. The producers narrow down the numbers, then you're called back in a few weeks if you're lucky. The rest go back to their sorry little fookin' lives.'

And with that good news she goes back to her phone. I try to kiss her on the cheek as she goes back to the sofa, but she gives me the middle finger. I want her so bad!

We wait in the holding area for another three hours. There is some filming going on, but mostly I just practise my singing. I really don't want to talk to anybody else 'cause most of them think I'm 'special'. Then the mega-mouth woman comes back and tells us they will be seeing numbers 3001 -3099 in the main audition room. I'm counting on my hands to see if we're in that number range when I notice Mandy standing beside me, just staring at me:

'Please tell me you're not counting to see if we're part of this group?'

'No, I'm, er ... just doing my finger exercises. It's kinda something I do before I sing. Like a ritual?'

'Come on to fook, retard. Let's show them what we got!'

We go in through these huge doors and the security people check our numbers. We go into a massive room, it's like the actual arena part of the arena. We're told to sit down until our numbers are called and we'll be directed to a booth. There must be a hundred booths around the place, and we can hear the people who are in them singing. It's just like a big mix of noise! I don't even be sitting long when all of a sudden Mandy's number is called and then mine straight after. I wish her good luck but she says she doesn't give enough of a fuck about this. I can see in her face that she's nervous, though. It's the first time I've seen her look vulnerable, if that's even a word? We arrange to meet back at where we were sitting in the holding room afterwards.

This is it. Fuck!

Everything was a blur. I was told to go into a booth where three people were sat. I don't even remember what they look like. They took my details and my number then told me to sing. They just seemed like robots. I could hear other people singing around me in neighbouring booths and I could even hear people crying. It was so noisy. I took a deep breath and sang! Before I knew it, I was out of there and back in the holding area. I didn't know whether to laugh or cry. Mandy ran to me and hugged me, she was shaking and she told me she got through and that she's so happy. Then she caught herself on and said she didn't give a fuck. Then she asked me how I got on. Then I started crying and shouted:

'I GOT FUCKING THROUGH, TOO!!'

CHAPTER 7.

'Why in the name of sweet Jesus have you brought a stranger into our house, Mickey?'

My ma is being a drama queen as per fucking usual. Things are getting tense.

'She's not a stranger. I think she might be my girlfriend?'

'You were only away two bloody days! You don't even know anything about her!'

'I know plenty about her!'

'What's her surname then?'

'She doesn't really use her surname, she just goes by her first name.'

'She doesn't USE her surname? Do you think I came up the Foyle in a bubble?'

'She doesn't use it! Jesus, big deal! She's like Rhianna in that way.'

'Eh? Her surname is Rhianna?'

'Naw ,her surname isn't Rhianna, I'm just saying that she doesn't use her surname, like the way Rhianna doesn't.'

'Who the fuck is Rhianna, then?'

I swear to God, sometimes I wish I was adopted. I'm only in the door five minutes and my ma has dragged me into the kitchen to question me about Mandy. Not even a well done on the X-Factor auditions. Mandy stayed with me at the hotel in Manchester last night. (We had sex, twice, just saying.) Then she decided she was coming home with me today. My ma is just being a dick. Mandy is in the living room with my da, who hasn't been able to stop looking at her tits, the dirty fucker. I've a feeling that's why my ma has gone OTT on the whole thing, she's just jealous there's a better rack in the house than hers.

'Jesus, Mickey. Right, I'll make up the spare room, then. You could have gave us a bit of warning and not just arrive at the front door with her!'

'I didn't think it would be any bother. And Mandy is staying in my room, by the way, so just so you know.'

'Oh no she isn't, young fella! There will be none of that craic under my roof, I can tell ye! It's the spare room or she finds somewhere else to stay. End of.'

She's definitely jealous.

Mickey Doc

I don't bother to argue, there's no point when she's like that. I need to get back to the living room anyway, to save Mandy from my da. I get in there and she's flirting her arse off with him. She's showing him how she can wrap her leg around the back of her head and he's just sitting there with his mouth wide open.

'I hope my da isn't wrecking your head!'

'No, your dad is cool, man.'

She gives my da a playful wink and that silly fucker winks back. Unfortunately for him ,he doesn't know my ma is standing at the door watching him:

'John, could I have a word with you in the kitchen, please?'

My da nearly jumps out of his skin when he hears her. I give him the middle finger as he walks out. He's like a school kid going to the headmaster's office.

'Sorry about my ma and da, they're a pair of saps!'

'That reminds me, I'd better text my ma and tell her where I am. I don't even know why I bother, it's not like they give a fuck anyway.'

My ma and da come back into the living room, they've obviously decided they're going to be nice. My ma has a big fake smile plastered across her face:

'So, tell us all about the X-Factor!'

Mandy doesn't even look at them, she just keeps texting on her phone.

'It was amazing, there was thousands of people there all trying to get on the show, but loads didn't. Me and Mandy have to go back next week to sing in front of the actual X-Factor judges!'

My ma tries to include Mandy in the conversation, but I can tell it's killing her to be nice to her:

'And you got through too, Mandy, that's great!'

She doesn't take her eyes off her phone:

'Yeah, it's alright.'

'And what do your parents make of you getting through?'

'They don't really care. I hardly know my dad, he ran off when I was two. My mum remarried a fookin' stiff called Richard, and they are too caught up in each other to really give a fook.'

'And do you live with them?'

'Yeah, well I did, kind of.'

'And do they know you're here?'

'Just texting them now.'

My ma looks at my da and rolls her eyes.

Mickey Doc

Then she turns to me:

'So when do you have to go back over?'

'Back over on Thursday night 'cause we have to be there early Friday morning.'

'And what about your work? How are you going to get more time off?'

'I'm going to quit tomorrow.'

'You're what?'

'I'm going to quit tomorrow.'

My ma blesses herself in that way mas do when they get bad news.

'Are you serious? Are you fucking serious?! What happens if you don't get through? Don't be thinking you'll be living here sponging off your da and me!'

My da decides to pipe up too, obviously acting the big man:

'You know that jobs are few and far between in this town, Mickey, you can't be just quitting 'cause you're on the X-Factor, you need something to fall back on!'

'Do you two have no belief in me at all?'

I'm starting to shout now:

'I don't need you two stiffs holding me back any longer. I have dreams ye know!'

Then my da tries to be the voice of reason:

'Listen son, I had dreams when I was your age and I ended up back here, and it was tough trying to get work. I don't want to see you doing the same.'

'I've made up my mind, I'm calling into work tomorrow and that's the end of it.'

'I swear to God, you have me and your father's hearts broke!'

My ma is always a last-word freak!

Suddenly, Mandy peels herself away from her phone and stands up:

'Right, no offence but I'm getting bored now. Mickey, you said we would see the city.'

She has a look about her like she doesn't give one flying fuck. Which I'm pretty sure she doesn't.

'Aye, I need to get away from these two anyway, this was supposed to be a CELEBRATION! Da, could you drop us into town?'

'I'll drop you in, but I'm not happy about your decision, Mickey. It's your life to fuck up, though.'

Mickey Doc

My ma gets up and storms out:

'Your life to fuck it up?? Amazing parenting skills, John Doherty,
AMAZING!'

Told you, she's a last-word freak.

I hadn't noticed before, but that mutt of a dog is sitting in between the
two chairs, staring out at me with an evil look. As I'm leaving the
room, I give it the middle finger then make a throat-cutting sign with
my finger. Mandy asks:

'Why are you doing that to the dog?'

''cause it's a prick.'

She shrugs her shoulders and says 'yeah … It looks like a prick.'

My da drops us into town and he starts to give us the credit we deserve
about our X-Factor achievements, which is nice to hear. He says that
my ma will be grand in the morning, she just doesn't like unexpected
guests blah. Blah, blah.

It's 10 o'clock on a Tuesday night, and I reckon The Metro is the place
to take Mandy. It's one of the more classy places in town. Problem is

I'm pretty skint, so let's hope she likes to pay her way. Come to think of it, she has hardly dipped her hand in her pocket since I met her, I've been paying for everything and I'm close to broke. We get to the front door and the bouncer is on that doesn't like me. I try to take Mandy's hand, just to show off that she's mine, but she pushes my hand away and tells me to 'fuck off with that holding hand shite'. The dick of a bouncer seen this and he has a big fucking smirk on his face when we get to the door:

'Here he is, Derry's answer to Elton John. Haven't seen you around in a while, I heard you were on the X-factor?'

He is the typical bouncer. Shaved head, big muscles, and he seems to be always chewing gum and scratching his balls. Marty told me before that the fella is riddled with that many diseases that he has to chew gum to stop himself from swallowing his tongue. I don't know if there's any scientific proof behind that, but then again, it was Marty that told me so it could be just made up. I'm still afraid to stand near him, though. Not because I'm scared of him, I just don't want to catch anything he has. Stevie calls him 'The Crustacean'. I don't know what it means, but the lads think it's hilarious. He can't take his eyes off Mandy, he keeps looking her up and down while chewing his gum in that cocky way that bouncers do. He doesn't even try to hide it:

Mickey Doc

'There's no way you're here with him tonight, love?'

Fuck, this could go either way!

'What?'

'I said that…'

She interrupts, she's good at that:

'I heard what you said, I'm just wondering what happened to somebody like you. My money is you were dropped on your head as a kid, put in the special class at school and then touched up by your uncle who was supposed to be babysitting you when your mum was out walking the streets.'

The other bouncers and people at the door burst out laughing. Crab boy is fucking fuming and looks a bit uncomfortable:

'You've got some tongue on ye, girl'

'I can do things with my tongue that would make your eyes water. But I'd rather dip it in sulphuric acid than put it anywhere near you, you ugly, steroid-laced retard. I've seen better-looking things at the zoo attached to the back end of a gorilla. Actually, that's what your face reminds me on, a gorillas arse!'

The other bouncers are egging her on now, they obviously don't want to get on the wrong side of her. Wouldn't blame them. Crab boy is fuming, he tells us to move along 'cause we're holding up the place. His face is bright red. We put our coats in the cloakroom and Mandy asks me where the toilet is. She tells me to get the drinks in while she goes to the toilet. She wants a double vodka and red bull. Fuck! I wait till she's gone before I start counting out what money I have left. I should have enough to do me if we drink slowly. I'm at the bar waiting to get served when I hear some familiar voices behind me and I know right away it's the lads. Marty is saying how he once kung-fu-kicked a bank robber in Shipquay Street, but just walked on and let the police do the rest. He says it was the sweetest kung-fu kick he has landed since he knocked out the boxer John Duddy in Aberakebabra. I burst out laughing and as I turn around the lads are standing right behind me. We all just stare at each other for what feels like ages, then Stevie gives me a hug, then Marty does the same, then Decky steps forward but hesitates...

I look him in the eyes before giving him a big bear hug. Everybody cheers and I feel like a huge weight has been lifted from my shoulders in that instant. Not in a gay way, though. Then Decky says:

'We only came out tonight to celebrate you getting through. I rang your house yesterday and your ma told me the news. We didn't think you'd be out ,to be honest. I'll get the round in!'

Mickey Doc

Everybody wants to hear about the X-Factor and I feel like a new man standing having the banter with the lads. Then I remember about Mandy:

'Hi, Decky, I met a girl at the X-Factor, her name's Mandy and she's here with me tonight, she's at the bog.'

'Nice one, man, what's she drinking?'

I bet he knows I'm broke as fuck, he's always been good like that. It's his third sense again.

'Vodka and red-bull – double.'

'I like her already, is she from Derry? Do we know her?'

'Naw, she's from Manchester! She's a fucking cracker, too!'

'No bother to you, man!'

He gives me a high five, then Marty and Stevie do the same.

Next thing I hear is a commotion going on behind us and I can hear girls screaming and glasses smashing. Before I even look around, I know in my heart that Mandy has something to do with it. She is dragging a girl by the hair while other people try to pull her off. They're not having much luck. I run over to try to get her away, but the bouncers are on the scene now. The crab bouncer hits me with his shoulder as I get near and sends me flying through a table full of drinks.

Girls are screaming like mad and shouting:

'That bitch tried to steal her purse in the toilets!'

'Yer wan started it that has a houl' on her hair, the psycho bitch! She tried to steal her purse!'

'Get her off her, get her off her!'

I'm then lifted off the ground by Stevie and Marty and I'm covered in drink. I think there's some glass in my hand and it's bleeding. I need to get her out of here quickly. She is being dragged towards the front door by the bouncers, and the lads are helping me get to the door to meet her. Mandy is like a woman possessed and I can see she still has clumps of hair in her hands. I get out the front to her and I don't know how she's going to react, she could hit me, too. The bouncers are telling me to get her the fuck home before they call the police. Mandy is having none of it:

'Fok you and the filth ye fookin' pricks! I was jumped on!'

The bouncers just keep repeating:

'Get her away from here, get her away from here now!'

Suddenly, Mandy sees me and comes running. I close my eyes 'cause I don't know what to expect. She grabs on to me and hugs me really tight, she's shaking like a leaf and whispers in my ear:

Mickey Doc

'Get me out of here, Mickey.'

I then take her away from the club to try to get a taxi. I look around and I can see that the bouncers are keeping the girls she was fighting with from getting out. Marty and Stevie are trying to calm things down and giving us time to get away. Just as we're about to go onto Shipquay Street, a car comes flying up beside us and slams on the brakes. The driver's window rolls down and it's Decky telling us to get in. We both jump in the back and it's a great relief to be safe.

'I take it you're both going to your house, Mickey?'

Mandy is cuddled into me, I've never seen her this affectionate.

'Aye, just to my house. Don't be saying to my ma what happened if you see her, will ye, Decky?'

'No bother. I'm Decky by the way.'

'I didn't do what they were accusing me of doing. I have no need to be stealing purses and I wouldn't do it even if I had to.'

I rub her head and she cuddles into me even tighter. Before, if I had rubbed her head, she would have told me I'm an asshole and to get my hands of her head. She seems to be liking it now. I ask Decky:

'Who owns the car, man?'

'It belongs to a friend of mine who was in the Metro, I asked him for the keys when I saw what was going on.'

Always one step ahead is Decky.

We pull up outside my house. Mandy's top is ripped and she looks a bit shaken up, so I tell them I'm going to nip inside to see if my ma and da are still up. I don't want them seeing us 'cause they'll only be dickheads and ask too many questions. Anyway, I don't think my ma likes her as it is.

I leave Mandy in the car with Decky for a moment while I quietly go into the house. My da is walking up the stairs in just his boxers and a football top. I think I gave him a fright:

He's talking quietly so my ma must already be asleep.

'Jesus, you nearly gave me a heart attack! What are you doing home so early?'

'We just left early, there wasn't much going on.'

'Where's your woman, Mandy?' He fixes his boxers and looks over my shoulder when he says this.

'She's in the car with Decky, he dropped us home. She's asleep so I thought I'd make sure the spare room is ready for her before I wake her. Must be the jetlag that has her wrecked.'

Mickey Doc

'You can't get jetlag on a 20-minute flight, Mickey.'

'Really? Well, she must be just tired then!'

'Your ma has the spare room all made up for her. Anyway, I'm away on up here'

'Thanks. Da.'

I head back out to the car where Decky and Mandy are chatting away. She's leaning in between the 2 front seats listening to him tell the story of how I once got my head stuck inside the grab machine at the bowling alley. I had tried nine times to win a teddy bear for a girl I fancied that was there. I think we were only about 14 at the time. I had the claw thing positioned perfectly over the bear each time but the fucking thing just wouldn't grab it. Marty told me that he climbs inside those things all the time and takes whatever he wants. I figured if I could get my arm and my head into the collection slot at the bottom, then I could reach across and grab the bear. I managed to get my arm and head in, but then I became jammed. The lads were pulling my feet, trying to get me out, but I just wasn't budging. After a while, all the staff who work there had a go of trying to free me but they eventually called the fire brigade who had to cut me out. I'm glad they're getting on well.

Mandy laughs and calls me a 'fookin' idiot'.

'Thanks for taking us home tonight, man, I'll give you a shout tomorrow?'

'Cool, Mickey. Chat to you then. Nice to meet you, Mandy.'

'You too.'

I help her into the house as she seems a bit sore, but she wouldn't admit it.

I whisper to her:

'We have to keep quiet, my ma is asleep and I don't want to have to listen to her tonight.'

She whispers back:

'Okay.'

'Do you want some tea and toast before bed?'

'Yes, please.'

As soon as I turn on the kitchen light the fucking dog is standing at the door staring at me, and showing his teeth. It frightens the absolute shite out of me! I'm not in the mood to be fighting with this prick tonight, so I tell him to get out of the way and nobody will get hurt. He must know that I mean business because he walks back towards his bed in the corner. I like looking tough in front of Mandy.

'Do you believe me that what happened tonight wasn't my fault, Mickey?'

'Of course I do, Derry girls can be total bitches when they see they have some genuine competition around. Sure, look at the way my ma reacted.'

'I don't want to stay here anymore, why don't you come back to England with me tomorrow? We could stay in my friend's house then do the audition on Friday.'

She's looking at me with big sad eyes and it melts my heart:

'Aye, I'll go with you. I just need to call into Valuesaver tomorrow and tell them where to shove their job. I can't wait to see the face on my dick-face manager, Barry, when I tell him.'

I also need to go to the Credit Union and take out whatever money I have left.

'I'll pay for our flights back, Mickey. It's the least I can do.'

She must have read my mind!

'Unbelievable that somebody could accuse me of stealing their purse. I bet I have more money than them all put together.'

I begin to feel like me and Mandy could actually go somewhere together. Not just to Manchester, or do really well on the X-Factor, I mean we could be a great couple and I think she is really starting to warm to me. She's being really nice. We have our tea and toast, then we tip-toe to the spare room. We have a nice long kiss at the door. She then pulls me in, hugs me, and says something that hits me like a bus:

'Your mate, Decky, he tried to come on to me when you were in the house earlier.'

'WHAT??'

I actually shout it, then catch myself on:

'What? Decky is gay, Mandy! He came out before I headed to Manchester.'

'Are you calling me a liar?'

'No, of course I'm not, it must of just been a misunderstanding!'

'He had his hand on my leg!'

'He's just a friendly guy!'

'Look, you believe what you want to believe. I'm just saying I don't trust him.'

She then kisses me on the lips and tells me to get some sleep.

I head into my room. My head is spinning from all that went on tonight.
I'm still buzzing from making up with the lads, but I feel like shit about
what happened to Mandy. There's no way Decky would try that, even
if he wasn't gay. Would he? I don't know what to think anymore. Fuck
it, I have to stop worrying. I have the X-Factor again on Friday and I'm
going with a fucking cracker chick. What more could I want?

Just as I get into bed my phone beeps. It's a message from Stevie:

'Hey, man, it was great seeing you tonight. Maybe we could all meet
up tomorrow? Look, I don't know if you've seen them or anything, but
Decky has had his wallet and iPhone nicked. Just check it hasn't fallen
out of the car outside your house or something.'

Jesus fucking Christ. I know what they're thinking. But there's no way.
There's no way she would do that…

CHAPTER 8.

I couldn't sleep a wink last night. I have far too much going on in my head and I'm not used to it. There was a time that my thoughts used to get lonely on their own, now there's too much going on. My English teacher used to say that although I was at high school, my brain never made it out of the maternity ward. He'll be one of a long list of people beating their words when I win the X-Factor.

It's Wednesday morning and I need to get packing. The X-Factor people told me that I have to wear the same clothes and have my hair the same way as I did for the first audition, because they mix the recordings of the two days. They said they do this because they want to create the illusion that it was all filmed in the one day and that the main judges (Simon and co) were there all along. Mandy had to explain this to me four times on the plane and, to be honest, I still don't really get it, but I'll just do as they say. She said it was about continuity? I don't think that's even a word, but I didn't have the heart to tell her.

I didn't bother texting Stevie back about Decky's wallet going missing, because I know they're blaming her. What sort of a boyfriend would I be if I let that happen, even though I'm not really her boyfriend?

Mickey Doc

I just need to keep looking forwards.

Mandy is packed and ready to go. She told me to come and get her in the spare room when I've told my parents that we're leaving 'cause she says she's 'not in the mood to be listening to bullshit this morning'. My ma and da are both in the kitchen, so after I get packed I go down to tell them I'm going back to England early. I take a deep breath outside the door then go into the kitchen. My ma is making sausages and I'm wondering if I should wait until I've eaten them before I tell her. Then I see the dog in the corner with a smug look on its face, and I remember there's probably none for me anyway so I give the mutt a dirty look.

My ma turns around when she realises I'm there, she seems really cheery:

'Ah, there you are. Must have been the smell of sausages that got you up, was it love?'

'I prefer bacon ...'

That's a lie. I love sausages. But I'm still annoyed with her for being a fucking bitch.

I grab the newspaper from the table to check if there's anything about me and the X-Factor in it yet. I should really have rang them, given them the story, and pretend to be a 'friend'. That's what the really famous do. They'll definitely report it when I get through the next round. Then, as I'm scanning through 'who was up in court in Derry' section my da grabs the paper out of my hands:

'It's time for me to go drop a load son, and I can't do that without the paper to read.'

'Hi, I was reading that!'

'Tough shit!'

Then him and my ma start laughing and he slaps her on the arse. I can see the ripples of fat move through her leggings like one of those big waves … a tiramisu? He kisses her on the cheek, too, the dirty fucker. Then she waves a sausage at him, like seductively if that's the right word? Now I know why she's smiling today. That's when I lose my head:

'You can both fuck off! I'm packing in my job today then going to England with Mandy forever! You two can live happily ever after! And don't think you can come running to me when I'm famous, either! I HATE YOU, I HATE YOU, I HATE YOU!!'

My face is bright red like it's about to explode. I slam the kitchen door really hard then I open it again. My parents are standing open-mouthed. I point at the dog and shout:

Mickey Doc

'AND YOU CAN FUCK OFF, TOO!!'

Me and Mandy are sitting in Cappucino's café on Foyle Street after getting the bus into town. My ma had tried to talk me out of it, but I just ignored her. My da just went ahead and had his morning shit, I could hear him whistling away in the bathroom like he owned the place. We have our luggage with us and the plan is to have some breakfast, then go to Valuesaver to tell them I'm leaving, then hit the airport. It's 11am in the morning now, and our flight isn't till 3pm, so we have plenty of time. I ordered the all-day breakfast then called the waitress back to tell her I'll have extra bacon instead of sausages. I think I've been put off them for life. Mandy orders tea and toast. She seems restless:

'How long will it take you to do what you have to do in Value-what-ever-the-fook-you-call-it?'

'Five minutes should do me. I can't fucking wait. I've been dreaming of this day for years. I love having you here with me for it.'

'You're a dick.'

I think I seen a little bit of a smile though. Either that or a frown. It's hard to tell with her sometimes. She's got her phone out again, texting like mad, so I try to start some intelligent conversation:

'Do you know the difference between an Ulster fry and an Irish fry?'

'Nope.'

'An Ulster fry doesn't have any beans in it. Naw, houl' on a minute …
An Irish fry has? And there's something about bacon fat too, but I can't remember. But they are different. Stevie told me about it when we were in Bundoran.'

'What am I to take from this attempt at information?'

'Beans?'

She shakes her head then stares at the table for about ten seconds.

'Where the fucks Bundoran?'

'It's in Donegal. which is also in Ulster, but they serve Irish fries. That was just one of the times I got Stevie on a technicality. I'm not sure about the English fry though. We'll have to check when we're over.'

I'm thinking how this is probably her first time seeing my smart side when she suddenly bursts my bubble:

'Jesus, Mickey, you don't half talk crap.'

'That's what I do when I'm excited.'

'I noticed. IF I decide to sleep with you again, don't be talking shite while we're doing it this time!'

'I told you, when I get excited I can't shut up.'

'It's a bit off-putting when you're talking about your mother's dog when we're having sex. I thought it was kinda weird. You're into some mixed-up shit, man!'

'Was I? Fuck! I'm not into animals like that, ye know?'

'Whatever!' Then she holds up her finger and thumb in an L shape. Basically, she's calling me a loser. Which, of course, I'm not.

Then I get the district feeling that we're being watched. Before I turn around, I know who it is. I can even smell her perfume. It's Paco Rabanne, Lady Million. (It's not Paco Rabanne watching us by the way, what the fuck would she be doing in Cappucino's?) It's definitely my stalker, Laura Dillon. She's sitting at a table behind Mandy, and she's just staring at me. I look over Mandy's shoulder and catch her eye. She doesn't even flinch, she just stares at me and she still seems sad. This goes on for five minutes. Even though Mandy hasn't taken her eyes off her fucking phone all morning, she still catches on to what I'm doing:

'What the fuck are you looking at?'

'Er, nothing. Just keeping an eye for our breakfast! I'm fucking starving, I can't wait for my fry. Are you looking forward to your toast ...'

Shit, I talk a lot when I'm nervous, too. I just can't stop myself...

'... Are you going to have marmalade with your toast? Or maybe some jam? What the fuck is the difference anyway? I must ask the waitress when she comes down. Maybe it's like the Ulster fry and the Irish fry ...'

I can't help but glance over at Laura Dillon when I'm talking. She's still staring. Fuck, I don't want them two to meet, Laura could say anything and there's a possibility Mandy could kill her. I keep rambling on though:

'... You know they call it 'jelly' in America? How fucked up is that? They call the stuff you have in ice-cream 'jello'. I'm not sure I'd want to go there, I'd probably have jelly on my toast and jam in my ice-cream.'

I can feel sweat on my brow as Mandy glances over her shoulder:

'Who's that girl you keep looking at?'

'Nobody. I'm not looking at her. Who? What?'

'The girl sitting behind me who you keep looking at like an idiot, who is she?'

'Aw, her. Well, she's kinda my stalker.'

'Your stalker?'

'Aye, my stalker.'

'Your fucking stalker?'

'Well not in a bad way like, she just kinda follows me around and stuff. She says she watches out for me which is kinda nice really, when you think about it?'

'Did you sleep with her?'

'No! Of course not! She just kinda hangs around everywhere I go.'

'I'm going to go have a word with her.'

Mandy gets up, she has that same look on her face she had last night in the Metro, like psycho-angry! I get up to ask her to stop:

'Mandy, don't ... please!'

She leans over the table, right into my face, causing me to fall back on my arse onto the chair. She has that crazy look in her eye, and she's talking through gritted teeth:

'Listen, I'm just going to have a word with the girl, right? Now if you get off that fookin' seat then I'm going back home on my own. Got it?'

I just nod like a fool and put my head down. I can't bear to watch 'cause it's going to be a slaughter. Mandy walks over to the table, cool as fuck, kinda like a tiger stalking its prey. A sexy as fuck tiger at that. (Again, I'm not into animals, just to be clear.) She stands over Laura for a few moments, just looking down at her. Then she pulls up a chair and sits down across from her. There's no screaming or shouting or hair pulling, but Mandy seems to be the one doing all the talking, although I can't hear what's being said. After a few minutes, Laura gets up and walks out. She doesn't even look at me when she passes, but I can see a trickle of tears running down her cheek.

Mandy returns:

'How long was she stalking you?'

'A few years.'

'A few years, and I sorted it for you in a few minutes. How the fook did you ever do without me, Mickey?'

I force myself to smile:

'I really don't know.'

We arrive at Valuesaver and Mandy has a stuck-up head on her, like she's too good for the place or something?

'So THIS is where you work?'

'Well, aye, but in a few minutes it will be the place that I USED to work!'

'And you had to wear THAT uniform?'

'Aye, but I wore the collar UP? Totally changes the look of it.'

'I always wanted to go out with a man in uniform, but that isn't really what I had in mind.'

'When we're rich and famous I can buy any uniform you want me to wear, baby!'

She's definitely smiling this time:

'Don't call me baby, you dick.'

We've just walked into Valuesaver, and for the first time ever I start to doubt my decision. Fuck, it must be my ma and da putting these thoughts in my head! There's no way I can win the X-Factor if I think I'm going to lose before it gets properly started. Then I see a customer at Jenny's till (I better not let Mandy know I used to fancy Jenny, or she'll have her leaving in tears, too) which reminds me why I need to get out of this fucking place for good. She's about 60 years old and seems like a right moaning oul' fucker. She has one of those annoying shaky old people voices:

'Your spuds are while dear, love!'

'Are they? I'll pass that on to one of the managers.'

Jenny just keeps scanning the items through. She has that dead look in her eye that you get when you've worked in retail too long.

'It's not just the spuds are dear, either, everything's got while dear.'

'Have they, aye?'

'You know you can get two of those things of bleach up in B&M for less than wan of them in here?'

'Right?' Now that's £18.67 please.'

The woman shakes her head as she pays for her groceries.

'And another thing, I bought chicken in here last week and it was out of date.'

'Oh God, that's not good. You should have brought it back?'

'I have it here …'

Suddenly the woman reaches into her granny trolley and pulls out a massive raw chicken which has turned a funny shade of blue and stinks like fuck, then leaves it on the till and walks out. Jenny runs to the bathroom holding her hand over her mouth.

Thank fuck I'm not working, or I'd be the one cleaning it up. Mandy is just walking around, holding up items like they're trash then turning up her nose and throwing them back onto the shelf. You would nearly think I brought her into a fucking food bank.

I ask Mandy if she wants to come with me to hand in my resignation, but she says she'd rather 'check out the rest of this dump'. I would have liked to have shown her off to Barry though. Then I see him. He's standing in front of the frozen foods section with a clipboard in his hand, and I can feel my muscles tighten! I always get tense when I see him. Maybe that's how I got such a great physique? It's the over-sized suit and the stupid moustache on his rat face that gets me every time. One time I almost passed out in the canteen because I spent a lunch break sitting across from him. The first aider had to get me to breathe into a brown paper bag. From then on in, I had to go on a different lunch break from him.

I pull the resignation letter out of my back pocket and unfold it, then I walk up and just hand it to him. I don't even say hello or anything. He just looks at me, then looks at the letter. I notice I spilled some beans on it when I wrote it in the café. He unfolds it then reads it out loud.

126

His stupid glasses are on the edge of his nose. He starts reading it in the voice of a five-year-old:

'Dear Valuesaver, I want like to hand in my resignation ...'

Fuck, I should have got Mandy to check it first.

'... I have worked here for far far too long and I want to go now that I'm going to be a star. I would like to thank everybody for helping me along the way except Barry Templeton...'

He actually smiles at that part.

'... He has been nothing but a dick from day one.'

I'm just standing nodding and listening. Barry stops and looks at me:

'There's more ye know, keep reading!'

He continues reading:

'Ps you should definitely sack him because he is a dick.'

Then I look him straight in the eye and deliver my final line:

'Now, I'm walking out that door and I'm not coming back.'

I turn around and walk off, that had to have been one of the best resignations EVER! But then dick face says something. I don't give him the satisfaction of turning around to look at him:

'You do realise, MICHAEL, that you're contractually obliged to give us at least two weeks' notice? But since you are nothing but a useless, lazy distraction when you're here, I will accept the resignation as of now.'

I don't say anything or turn around, I just put up my middle finger and walk out the door, holding my finger up the whole way. Mandy is standing outside on her phone, she says the smell in there is revolting.

We arrive in Manchester airport at 3.30pm and I get a message. It's from my wee cousin – George, the priest boy:

'Good afternoon, Michael. I've heard you are on your way back to Manchester for your second audition. I would like to wish you the very best of luck from me and the rest of the parishioners. Just remember, Michael, the story of The Prodigal Son – Luke 15:11-32. You will always be welcomed back with open arms.'

That kid has some serious issues that even the great Jeremy Kyle himself couldn't sort out.

I just text back:

'You need to get laid.'

Then I remember he's only ten years old and I could be charged with grooming or some shit, so I text back:

'I meant to write – you need to get more laid back!'

It's just lucky I can think on my feet!

Mandy is on her phone to somebody, and I'm left just looking after our bags. I'd go look in the shops and maybe buy Mandy a gift but I really need to watch the wee bit of money that I have. I buy two pre-packed sandwiches in case we get hungry on the way to the house we're staying in. There are so many different types of people and different languages here. Like, apart from the main countries where they speak English, there must be like loads and loads of other ones? Countries I wouldn't even have heard of. Mandy seems to be flat out on the phone, every time she hangs up on one call she dials another. I decide to use this free time to educate myself, it's something that I want to do from now on. I don't want to be doing interviews and not being able to give educational answers. So I Google 'bow many countries are there in earth?'

The internet is pretty slow here, must be loads of people using it. Should I have asked how many countries are there IN earth or ON earth? Google, the smart fucker, asks me did I mean 'How many countries are there ON earth?' which means that is the right way of saying it. Turns out there are 195 countries ON earth! I thought there would be about 20 or 30! 195! Fucking hell! I open up a list of countries and there's no way the half of them are real! They have a country listed called 'Guam'. That's not even a word, that's just a noise. And a place called Chad! There's even a COUNTRY called Iceland, like the frozen food shop! This has to be made up. See, that's the thing about learning stuff on the internet, you never know what's real and what's a load of shite.

Finally, Mandy gets off her phone and comes over to me. She says that she has arranged that we stay with friends of hers and that they live a few miles away from the airport. She just lets me carry her bags as well as my own, and tells me to follow her to the bus stop. Then she says 'fuck it, we'll get a taxi'.

We're in the taxi for about 15 minutes and, of course, Mandy has her head stuck in her phone. That's something I'll have to talk to her about when we're a proper couple. Actually, that's a lie, I know I won't say anything to her 'cause she'll just tell me to fuck off. Then we arrive at an estate. I'm not talking a fancy country estate with wild deer running about, I'm talking a proper estate like in Shameless, with wild dogs and wild children running about. Jesus, and I thought Shantallow was bad! This place would make it look like somewhere the Queen would live.

(Actually, there isn't a hope the Queen would be allowed to live in Shantallow, but you get what I'm saying.)

We pull up outside a house that has all the curtains pulled and it's still light out. Mandy hops out of the taxi leaving me to pay AND carry our bags. She does a really big long stretch and I swear to God my jeans are getting tighter. There's no doubt about it, she is unbelievably gorgeous.

'What the fok are you staring about with your gob hanging open? You look retarded.'

Fuck, I didn't even realise I was staring. I just look about me, the front garden looks like it hasn't seen a lawnmower in a while, I'm kinda afraid that something might jump out of the grass, to be honest, like a fucking horse or something. Mandy looks around at me and she can obviously see that I'm a bit shocked:

'Look, don't you be a fookin' dick in here and embarrass me in front of my friends, right? Not everybody gets to live with their mum and dad and get waited on hand and foot. Alex and Karen are good friends of mine and have always been there for me.'

Right away I'm wondering if Alex is a girl or a boy, 'cause it's one of those names that can be used either way. I hope it's a girl and they're both hot! Jesus Christ, my mind is running away with me!

I don't even notice at this stage that the front door has opened and there's a man with a beard standing:

'Fuck, it's a bloke!'

Then the realisation hits me that I said that out loud. The bearded man speaks:

'Yeah, mate, I'm a bloke alright, the names Alex'

He puts out his hand to shake it as I'm going in for a fist pump. He just takes his hand away then hugs Mandy and I can hear him whisper to her:

'Is he alright?'

The house isn't half as bad as I thought it was going to be inside. Actually, it's pretty fucking sweet. They have one of those big leather sofa's that goes around in an L shape and a fucking massive flat screen TV hanging on the wall. Plus the place is REALLY clean. Then a girl comes running down the stairs. Her and Mandy hug and then do like a kind of cool handshake/slap kind of a thing. The girl looks really tough, she's wearing a vest and she has muscles like a man, really toned and she has a few tattoos. I still would though.

'So this must be the fookin' Mickey Kid, then?'

I put out my hand, making sure to shake this time and not fist pump:

'The one and only!'

She shakes my hand and I swear to God I almost let out a scream 'cause of how tight she squeezes.

'So, you guys just fookin' make yourself at home right, and stay for as long as you fookin' need right?'

Mandy tells me to follow her to the spare room with our bags. The spare room is pretty big and it has a big double bed which is the main thing. It's going to see some action tonight I'm fairly sure. There's a TV on top of the chest of drawers at the end of the room which Mandy switches on and then throws the remote on the bed.

'Do you want to get washed up or anything, Mickey?'

'Why? Do I smell?'

'No you don't fookin' smell. I'm just asking, do you want to get washed up or maybe hang up the clothes in the wardrobe there, and pack the rest into the chest of drawers.'

'Aye, if ye want like.'

She moves over to me and puts her arms around me, pressing her boobs against my body. Then she starts kissing me on the lips. I'm thinking YES! Mickey is getting some horizontal action! But then she pulls away:

Mickey Doc

'I need to go downstairs and chat to Karen and Alex for a while about some things. You just stay here and wait for me, the remote is on the bed. We'll finish off what we just started then.

I'm still standing in the same position I was when I was kissing her with my lips still pressed when she walks out the door.

I flick on Hollyoaks, then I decide I'm going to have to release some of this tension in my pants before she comes back up, if you know what I mean?

I'm going to spank my monkey is what I mean.

Again, I'm not into animals in that way!! My monkey is my penis.

CHAPTER 9.

Well, depending on what way you look at things, last night went class. I managed to rehearse for the X-Factor for most of the night before falling asleep and getting a good night's sleep, instead of staying up all night 'getting jiggy with Mandy'. I really think my vocals are at the top of their game right now and I definitely have a recording voice.

Mandy didn't come to bed at all. At about 9 o'clock last night I went down to check on her, but she was in the kitchen with Alex and Karen plus a few other people I haven't met. They were drinking and the room was full of funny-smelling smoke. Mandy told me to go back upstairs as she had more stuff to sort out, so I just went back to the room and practised until midnight. Luckily, I still had the sandwiches from the airport. I was that tired I even managed to sleep through their loud music. She should really be concentrating on her audition because it's on tomorrow! I'm already up and dressed when she makes it back to the room. She looks pretty rough, but obviously I'd still dive in there.

'I need to get a few hours' sleep. Fook, I feel rough, man!'

'Did you get things sorted out?'

'What?'

'Did you get whatever you had to get sorted with Alex and Karen?'

'Oh, yeah, right. Yeah, we got things sorted, just some crap is all.'

'Is there a shop nearby that I can go get something for breakfast? I'm starvin' marvin'!'

'There's bread on the counter in the kitchen and you'll see the toaster. Just don't be wakening anybody. A few friends of Karen and Alex's came over to sort some stuff out, too.'

I feel like telling her it's 11:30 in the morning, but I don't want to aggravate her.

'Grand job, that'd be cheaper anyways!'

She's just climbed into bed with her clothes still on and pulled the duvet over her head. Then she sits up again:

'Oh yeah, about that Mickey, come here a minute.'

I sit on the bed beside her, she snuggles into me. I think I could get drunk just sitting beside her:

'You know the way we're going to be here a while and you have like, no money?'

'Aye'

'And we have to travel to our audition tomorrow and eat and stuff.'

'Yep.'

'Well, there's this mate of Karen and Alex's who was around last night, and he works as a ... how would you put it … he works as an independent banker? In other words, he will lend you as much money as you need without having to go near the fookin' bank and fill out all those forms, and basically beg the pricks to give you money before they turn around and tell you to fook off.'

'Right?'

'So I was talking to him last night and he said because you know me then he would lend you whatever your need. I told him it won't be long before you're making big cash through the X-Factor and your singing career, so you would be able to pay him back pretty quickly.'

'You said that? I'm flattered!'

She pulls me in close to her and kisses me.

'Now, I'm going to get some sleep and when I get up we'll give Knuckles a shout and get the ball rolling.'

'Knuckles?'

'Don't let his nickname scare you, he's a big softie really. Goodnight. Oh, and bring me up a glass of water when you come back up, and try not to wake anybody. Including me.'

Within seconds she's fast asleep and snoring. I head down to the kitchen and make myself some toast, then spend the rest of the day in the room watching TV while Mandy sleeps. Eventually, she gets up and we go to McDonald's for dinner. She says that Knuckles is going to meet us there:

'I'm not too sure about taking money from a stranger.'

'He's not a fookin' kidnapper offering you candy to get into his van, Mickey, stop being such a fookin' plank!'

'I know, it's just I don't know him.'

'I know him, and it's his job to lend people money. He doesn't just do it out of kindness, man!'

'Still doesn't feel right, somehow.'

'Look, Mickey, here's the way it is: you're practically skint, right?'

'Right.'

'And you're going to need some money to tide you over, 'cause I can't be carrying the both of us, got me?'

'Aye'

'So my friend is going to give you the money until you get rich off the X-Factor. It's basically your money, you're just getting it a little bit in advance.'

'I suppose when you look at it like that ...'

'That's the only way to look at it. Now, stop worrying. I told you before I'm here to look out for you.'

The McDonald's in Manchester looks a lot like the McDonald's in Derry, only bigger. Mandy orders a salad, which is something I really don't get! What is the point of going to McDonald's if you're going to order a salad? It's like going to the cinema and reading a book. Salads and books are two things I have absolutely no time or patience for.

We are just finished eating when Mandy's phone beeps and she says that Knuckles is outside. She texts him back and the next thing this huge fucker comes through the door and over to our table. He's about 6ft 5ins and built like a monster. He could be a WWE wrestler, no bother. He has a shaved head and a few scars on his face, and his eyes look like he's constantly squinting. He is pretty scary looking. Mandy gets up and gives him a hug: she has to stretch to get her arms around him:

'Knuckles, this is my friend, Mickey, that I was telling you about.'

'Awight, Mickey, your d'fella that is gonna win the X-Factor then?'

'Aye that's me, how's it going?'

'It's going good, son, going good. So you need a few sheckles to keep you going?'

They look at each other and can see by my confused look, I don't have a clue what he's talking about.

'Sheckles, son, mullah, a bit of dosh to keep you going?'

'Aw aye, money! Aye.'

'He ain't too bright this one, eh, Mands? How much you lookin' for, son? How much you lookin' for?'

'Am, I'm not really sure …'

'Four? Five? Six? Ten? Whatever you need, Irish boy, I know you're good for it.'

Jesus Christ, I was thinking about £200, tops. I suppose a couple more hundred wouldn't do any harm.

'Would five be alright?'

'Of course, Mickey son, of course. Why not round it off to six. Don't you know odd numbers are unlucky?'

':then, six!'

I'm fucking shaking like a leaf.

'Six it is, no bother son, no bother. I'll have it dropped around to Al's house tonight. You just pay it back when you get it, alright?'

'That's while sound of you, Knuckles, cheers man.'

'No bother, Mickey son, no bother at all. Now, I have some business to take care of so I'm gonna have to shoot off. Nice seeing ya both, nice seeing ya.'

Then he just gets up and leaves.

Mandy is smiling like a cat that caught the cream:

'Now, that was easy wasn't it, Mickey?'

'Aye, definitely! I can't believe how easy that was. He seems sound.'

'Yeah, he's a big teddy bear really. We won't have to worry about money from here on in, we're on the pigs back now, man, me and you against the world.'

Suddenly, I get really bad cramps in my stomach. Not sure if it was the Big Mac or the thought of borrowing 600 quid off a stranger.

Mickey Doc

It's the morning of the audition, and I didn't sleep a wink last night. It wasn't because I was nervous or anything, I didn't even have time to think about the audition. What kept me up all night was not the thought of owing Knuckles 600 quid; it was the thought of owing Knuckles 6 GRAND!! Apparently, people like Knuckles don't deal in hundreds, they deal in thousands. So when I said I'd take six, he was talking thousands while I was talking hundreds. I told him there had been a misunderstanding, but he said that I entered a verbal agreement and the money had been supplied. He said a lot of work went into freeing up that cash and it can't be put back, so I have to take it. I was too scared to say no. Me and Mandy are getting ready to leave for the auditions, she seems really happy:

'Are you still worrying, Mickey?'

'It's a lot of money, Mandy!'

'It depends in what context you look at it, man. When you were earning shit money in that vile shop you were working in, then yes, it would be a lot of money. But soon, very soon, you're going to be making the kind of money that makes six grand seem like spare change. You got me?'

'Aye, I suppose when you look at it like that.'

'Now, how do I look?'

'You look fucking amazing!!'

Which she does, she's dressed the same as the first time I met her, and she looks class.

'How do I look?'

'You look like a superstar. We make a fucking gorgeous couple.'

'You mean we're a couple now?'

'Yeah, man, why not! I didn't want to rush into anything before, you know, in case we don't click. But then last night I thought to myself "fook it, I'm falling in love with this boy!"'

My heart almost jumps out of my chest! That is the best news I have ever heard!

'I think … actually, I know I'm falling in love with you, too, Mandy.'

'Well, let's not go telling people. It's better if we keep it to ourselves for a while. Those X-Factor marketing people would rather have you single, know what I mean? Now, come here and kiss me.'

We go to the bank on our way to the X-Factor to lodge the cash. My bank account has never seen so much money in it. Actually, I've never seen so much money! The taxi waits outside with Mandy in it as I

queue in the bank for 20 minutes, I'm absolutely shitting myself having

this kind of mullah on me. Finally, I get to the front of the queue and

lodge it, all the time thinking I'll just dip into it when I need it, it's only

for day-to-day expenses.

We get to the arena and make our way in through a different entrance

this time. There isn't as many people milling about 'cause this is the

room-auditions where you have to sing in a room in front of just the

four judges: Simon, Cheryl, Mel B and Louis Walsh. There's still a lot

of people, just nowhere near the amount that were here for the first

audition.

We are directed into the main holding area where we spent so many

hours the last day, and I recognise a few faces. Mostly the people who

thought I was special needs. Mandy is on her phone as usual, and I'm

trying to get the wrapper off a lollipop. It has been in my pocket all

morning and the wrapper has really stuck to it. Three people have

already patted me on the head. Maybe they think I'll bring them luck?

The producer woman with the megaphone comes out and welcomes us

all to the audition and tells us that Simon and the rest of the judges are

now in the building. This gets a big cheer from everybody, except

Mandy of course. She just rolls her eyes and makes a wanker sign with her hand. We're then told to listen out for our numbers to be called, and that it's running numerically, which I think means they're running in order? I'm number 38 so I think I have a wee while to get myself properly prepared. I'm going with the same song again, One Direction's What Makes You Beautiful. It's my own slowed-down version of it. I've been listening to it on my iPod all morning. I think of Mandy every time I hear the song now. It's strange 'cause I used to think about Cheryl Cole when I heard it, and now in a few hours I'm going to be in front of her! Mandy comes over and sits beside me. She has that 'I don't give a flying fuck' look on her face, the one she practically always has:

'There are so many fookin' pricks in this place, man. It's making me feel sick. There's a few of them I want to punch in the face.'

'Aye, some of them are a bit OTT!'

'That's why I'm not going into the audition, this place is fookin' lame, man.'

'Jesus, Mandy! Are you sure? People would kill for this opportunity!'

'I don't feel too good, so I just couldn't be fookin' arsed, man. I'll still be here to support you, though. I'm going to the loo, I think I'm going to throw up.'

Mandy has been gone for ages and the next thing I know, my number is being called. I go over to the producer woman with the megaphone, and she tells me they're going to do an interview before I go in. The next thing I know, I'm in front of a camera and some woman is hooking a microphone on to my chest and there are crew members fussing all over me. Luckily, Mandy comes back and waves over. Then she pushes her way over and leans in. I think she's going to kiss me so I close my eyes, but she just whispers in my ear:

'Don't be fookin' mentioning me in the interview.'

I just nod and she steps away. Jesus, there's Sarah Jane Crawford, she's fucking gorgeous! She'll be the one interviewing me. There's a woman putting make-up on my face. None of the crew even talk to me, they just keep fussing about doing their jobs while I try not to get caught looking at Sarah's body. They're just shouting random stuff:

'Okay, can I get a test shot please?'

'How are the lights coming along with camera four?'

'Camera four ready.'

'Okay, can I get some more foundation here, I'm getting a shine off his forehead.'

'Alright, Mickey, this is Sarah, we're just about ready to go so if you can just answer in your own voice and speak clearly.'

Sarah reaches in to shake my hand, it takes all my power not to look down her top.

'Okay, guys, everybody ready and we're good to go in 5-4-3-2-1...'

Then he points at Sarah and she's starts:

'Hey, and our next contestant is all the way from across the Irish Sea in Northern Ireland.... Tell me a little about yourself.'

'Well. My names Mickey Doc, I'm 25 years old and I'm from Derry in Northern Ireland.'

'Ooohh, Mickey Doc! Is that a nickname or is that your real name?'

'I suppose it's a nickname, but it's what I've been called since I was a wain.'

'Since you were a what?'

'A wain? A child, like?

'A child like what?'

'Naw, I mean I've been called Mickey Doc since I was a wain, or a child I mean.'

'Ooooooo-kay, now, let's hope our judges are able to understand that accent, Mickey! Now, tell us, who are your musical influences?'

'I'm a big fan of One Direction, and I'm going to be doing one of their songs today. I also love Little Mix, Katy Perry, Beyoncé, Matt Cardle and Rihanna.' '

'That's quite a mix you've got there. What do you do back in Derry, Mickey?'

'Well, I worked in a shop called Valuesaver up until a couple of days ago, but I quit because I was coming here to win.'

She looks a bit shocked:

'Whoa, now that's confidence right there, ladies and gentlemen!'

'They were dicks anyways... Shit, sorry!'

Luckily, she's still smiling:

'It's okay, we'll edit that out, but just mind your Ps and Qs. So, what's your biggest dream in life, Mickey?'

'I'm living my dream right now. I've dreamt about this since I was a wean – a kid, so now I'm going to go on and win and prove everybody wrong.'

'And is there anybody with you here today, Mickey?'

'Yes there is!'

'And who would that be?'

'Actually, no … there's nobody with me, I just thought there was earlier.'

Again, thinking on my feet.

'Okay. Well, good luck in your audition and let's hope you have the X-Factor!'

'CUT!'

That was one of the crew, he gave me a bit of a shock. Then he points to a woman with a clipboard and tells me to follow Jessica. Suddenly, I'm walking across a corridor then standing outside a huge set of doors. Jessica looks at her clipboard then holds her headphones, somebody must be talking to her:

'Okay, so if you just follow me through here and when I give you the thumbs-up, you walk around this screen here and the judges will be in front of you. You stand in the middle of the wooden floor. Okay, here goes … everybody ready? Check lighting, sound …. And we're good to go.'

She gives me the thumbs-up, and I take a deep breath as I walk around the screen and onto the middle of the wooden floor. I really thought I'd be more nervous when I saw the judges, but I don't feel too bad. These four people in front of me have the power to change my entire life. Then I think, naw, fuck it, I have the power to change MY entire life. They all look so unreal and look every bit the celebrity. Simon speaks first:

'Welcome, and your name is?'

'My name is Mickey Doc, I'm 25 and I'm from Derry in Northern Ireland.'

They all smile which is good. Mel B and Cheryl look at Louis Walsh. Simon continues:

'So what's you background?'

'Well, I lived at home with my ma and da but I left there to come over here to follow my dreams.'

Cheryl jumps in:

'You left Derry? You mean permanently, pet?'

'Aye, well this is what I want to do, so I jacked in my job and came over here.'

Simon raises his eyebrows like he's shocked, shakes his head and sits back in his chair.'

Cheryl keeps talking:

'And what did you work at?'

'I worked in a supermarket at home. I never liked it, I always knew there was something else for me.'

'And what's your musical background?'

'Well, I haven't really sung in front of anybody before. Well, except in front of my ma a few years ago.'

Simon rolls his eyes, then says in a cheeky sort of way:

'So you've never done any sort of public performances, but you decided you would give up your job to try to audition for the X-Factor?'

He has a condensating look on his face.

'Aye, pretty much.'

He rolls his eyes again:

'Okay, let's hear what you've got.'

I take a big breath and wait for the music to come on. I've heard this music a thousand times, and I know where every note should be. The music comes on. This is it. All of a sudden, I'm lost in the moment:

Mickey Doc

You're insecure

Don't know what for

You're turning heads when you walk through the door

Don't need make-up to cover up

Being the way that you are is enough

Everyone else in the room can see it

Everyone else but you

Baby, you light up my world like nobody else

The way that you flip your hair gets me overwhelmed

But when you smile at the ground, it ain't hard to tell

You don't know

You don't know you're beautiful

If only you saw what I can see

You'll understand why I want you so desperately

Right now I'm looking at you and I can't believe

You don't know

You don't know you're beautiful, oh oh

That's what makes you beautiful

So come on

You got it wrong

By Fintan Harvey

To prove I'm right, I put it in a song

I don't know why

You're being shy

And turn away when I look into your eyes

Baby, you light up my world like nobody else

The way that you flip your hair gets me overwhelmed

But when you smile at the ground, it ain't hard to tell

You don't know

You don't know you're beautiful

If only you saw what I can see

You'll understand why I want you so desperately

Right now I'm looking at you and I can't believe

You don't know

You don't know you're beautiful, oh oh

That's what makes you beautiful

Na na na na na na na na na

Na na na na na na

Na na na na na na na na na

Na na na na na na

Mickey Doc

Baby, you light up my world like nobody else

The way that you flip your hair gets me overwhelmed

But when you smile at the ground, it ain't hard to tell

You don't know

You don't know you're beautiful

If only you saw what I can see

You'll understand why I want you so desperately

Right now I'm looking at you and I can't believe

You don't know, oh oh

You don't know you're beautiful, oh oh

You don't know you're beautiful, oh oh

That's what makes you beautiful

Now I come out of my zone and realise again where I am and what I'm doing there. The judges are silent and I try to get my breath back. Simon is smiling. The other three are just staring at me. Mel B is the first to speak:

'Mickey Doc from Derry, where have you been hiding that voice? That was incredible!'

I can hardly speak, I'm that happy. I feel like I'm going to cry, but there's no fucking way I'm doing that on TV.

Cheryl speaks then:

'Pet, I thought is this guy crazy, having never performed before and you came out and did that and blew us all away. That was one of the most passionate performances we've had so far, and you almost made me cry. So sincerely, well done.'

Then it's Louis' turn, he's happy and almost shouting:

'Mickey, what an amazing performance. That is bound to make everybody back in Derry 100% proud of you. You have the look, and what we want here is somebody who has a recording voice and you definitely have that. Plus, you're from Ireland!

All the other judges laugh, then Simon speaks:

'I thought with your lack of experience you would be looking for your job back on Monday morning, then when you started, I thought- he's pretty good. Then you went on and totally made that song your own. Now I'm not saying it was perfect, there were a few notes there that could have been better, but all in all that was a wonderful audition.'

'Thank you, thank you all very much.'

Simon smiles and winks at me then says:

'Okay, now it's time to vote. Louis, yes or no?'

'Mickey, Mickey, Mickey. A one million per cent yes.'

'Okay, Mel ...'

'I must say yes.'

'Cheryl ...'

Cheryl smiles at me:

'Yes, yes, yes, yes, YES!'

Jesus, I spent most of the past ten years wanting to hear her shout that. I think I'm crying. Then it's Simon's turn. Yep, I'm definitely crying:

'I can see how much this means to you. You've given up a lot and I can tell you it was worth it. You're through to the next round. Well done.'

I almost run out of the audition room to find Mandy. When I get out through the corridor she comes running towards me and jumps on me. I'm on cloud 9!

'Mickey, you were fookin' amazing! I got to watch it on the screen over there! Jesus Christ, I thought you were going to be fookin' shite!'

I'm too happy to even care about what she said. I just stand there hugging her and crying on her shoulder.

CHAPTER 10.

Three weeks have passed since my successful audition. Manchester has been a rollercoaster, to say the least. I don't mean it's an ACTUAL rollercoaster, I just mean I've been all over the place and I got sick a good few times along the way. We're still staying with Mandy's friends, Karen and Alex, but we're planning to get a place of our own soon. We have been doing a lot of partying! Her friends seem to have parties every night, plus me and Mandy have had nights out in the city a few times too. I don't think it's the partying that's been making me sick, though, 'cause back in Derry I was known as a bit of a party boy in the local scene. A bit of a playa. I think it's the added worry that us famous people have to deal with, even though I'm not famous yet, because the audition won't be on the TV till the end of August and it's now the first week of June. The next stage of the X-Factor is up next week – the Bootcamp round. But I'll even have done that before the X-Factor starts on the TV. It's all a bit confusing, to be honest.

I'm sitting on my own in McDonald's eating a sausage and egg McMuffin, and monitoring (if that's the right word?) a very important part of my musical development, which is: can I now pull off wearing sunglasses everywhere I go , even indoors? The good thing about having the sunglasses on is that I can look around and see what people's reactions are without them knowing that I'm looking at them. Spies should definitely wear sunglasses. There's a family sitting a few tables away from me and the kids seem to have noticed the sunglasses, they keep staring over at me. When I went up to order, the girl that was serving definitely fancied me, and I'd say the sunglasses really set her waters flowing. She was looking at me like 'holy shit, we don't get many people like this in here. I wish he would rescue me from working in McDonald's and take me away somewhere nice'. I give her a look as if to say 'I'd love to darling, but this man is already spoken for'. I hope she understands and doesn't take it too badly. A man came in wearing a motorcycle helmet and left it on while he ordered and got his stuff. Motorcycle helmets indoors are definitely NOT cool. The poor girl behind who was serving put her arms in the air when he came up to her, she thought she was being held up, that's the sort of place this is. I had to do a double-take when I looked across and could have sworn I seen Laura Dillon standing there. Must be all this pressure getting to me. Not many other people have really looked at the sunglasses. Maybe they're just playing it cool 'cause they say it's rude to stare. Nobody told that to the kids, though, that are sitting across from me and still staring. One is about seven and the other is about five. They both have hardened snot streaking across their faces and their ma and da are both wearing tracksuits, but they don't look like the sort of people who would go running, if you know what I mean? They're both fat. I'm looking in their direction, but I'm in a daze thinking about why fat lazy people wear tracksuits and never do any exercise, when all of a sudden I'm snapped out of it by a loud women's voice. She sounds foreign:

'Hey, why you stare at my kids?'

It's the ma of the two kids!

'Shit, sorry, I was just daydreaming!'

'You like look at little boys. you sick fuck?'

'Jesus, naw!'

'You pervert, eh? You take off glasses pervert!'

'I swear to God. I didn't know I was staring! I was just daydreaming about fat people in tracksuits!'

Oh fuck, I didn't mean it like that …

'Who you calling fat, pervert?'

Can I just say, none of them have stopped eating. The man still hasn't looked up from his tray.

'I wasn't calling anybody fat and I'm not a pervert!'

Other people are starting to look around now, to see what's going on which makes the woman get louder.

'Hey, watch your children, pervert in sunglasses like small boys!'

I look around, sort of talking to everybody:

'I'm not a fucking pervert! I was just daydreaming then this fat woman started shouting at me!'

Fuck, I shouldn't have included the 'fat' bit. Some other dickhead from another table pipes up:

'You some sort of fuckin' kiddy fiddler, mate?'

'Jesus, naw! Fuck this, can a man not even daydream in this place!'

'Call the police, pervert like small boys!'

Holy fuck, time to get out of here quick!

'Pervert like small boys, fucking pervert!'

I'm throwing the last of my sausage McMuffin into my mouth as I'm running out the door and shouting:

'Can't we even daydream anymore, this meant to be a McDonald's! A FUCKING MC DONALD'S!'

She's now shouting out the door:

'PERVERT LIKE SMALL BOYS!'

I just put my head down and walk as fast as I can. I think I'll leave the sunglasses off for a while.

I head back to the house, Mandy is watching a Davina McCall fitness DVD and doing exercises … while wearing jeans! What kind of a fucked-up place is this? She still looks fucking class though. I stare in through the living room door for a few minutes. She's touching her toes, then raising her arms to the ceiling, then touching her toes again, over and over. I get sort of hypnotised by the sight of her arse going up and down, up and down, up and down when the next thing I know I fall through the living room door and land on the floor. Mandy screams:

'Jesus fookin'Christ, mate, you nearly gave me a fookin' heart attack!'

'Sorry, I must have tripped over the rug in the hall.'

I go back to the door and pretend to fix whatever tripped me, knowing full well there was fuck-all there.

She hits pause on the DVD just as Davina has one leg in the air.

'So, where did you go for something to eat? Let me guess … McDonald's? That stuff will fookin' kill ya, man.'

'Don't I know it, I won't be going back there for a while.'

'Right, I'm going to get showered then I need to head out for a while, I might not be back tonight.'

'Okay, sure, text me and let me know.'

'Do you think I'm some sort of child? I ain't your fookin' property, Mickey.'

'Naw, I know that, it's just that I worry about you when you're out and you don't text.'

'Jesus, do I come across as some sort of a little princess who can't survive in the big bad world?'

'Naw ye don't, but I still worry.'

'Well you know where worrying will get you!'

She lifts her bottle of Lucozade, takes a swig out of it then throws it to me and walks out the door:

'Here, have the rest of that, Princess.'

I just manage to catch it, then I throw myself down on the sofa all in one move, cool as fuck like, and put my feet up and stretch out. It's then I realise the top of the bottle isn't on properly, and the Lucozade spills all over the front of my good jeans. I'm trying to wipe it up with a tissue I have in my pocket when all of a sudden Alex and Karen come in. Alex is the first to speak:

'Jesus Christ, Mickey, have a bit of respect, mate!'

'Sorry, I just spilled a bit on myself, It's alright, I didn't get any on the sofa.'

Karen is looking at me like I just killed a bunny rabbit, then she looks at the TV which is paused on a sweaty Davina McCall with her leg in the air and her fantastic arse in full view.

I'm still wiping away, quite fast, at the Lucozade on my, like, crotch area?

'That stuff is sticky as fuck too, imagine what it does to your inside, eh?'

'You sick fuck!'

I'm still rubbing away when the penny drops… they think I was having a wank to Davina McCall! Sometimes, I'm thicker than a … something that's really thick.

'It isn't how it looks, I swear, I was just cleaning up some Lucozade that I spilled! Mandy gave it to me before she went upstairs!

They don't seem to believe me. Alex says:

'Hey, mate, we're not here to judge, just keep that sort of shit to your bedroom.'

Then they both walk out. I swear to God, this day can't get any worse. I get a text message and when I whip out my phone, even that's sticky. It's from George the priest-boy, he texts me at least once a day now, and I'm very close to telling him to fuck off, only my ma would kill me:

'You promised me Lord,

that if I followed you,

you would walk with me always.

But I have noticed that during the most trying periods of my life

there has only been one set of footprints in the sand.

Why, when I needed you most, have you not been there for me?"

The Lord replied,

"The years when you have seen only one set of footprints,

my child, is when I carried you."

I swear to God, the priests back home must be feeding him altar wine for the craic. If God had any sense, he wouldn't let that wee fucker into Heaven 'cause he'd be a cert to empty the place within a week. I check my Facebook to see what the lads are at. It's my only way of seeing what they're up to these days. Seems that Stevie and Marty were out last night and they're both dying, but planning to 'hit d'town' again tonight. Decky has a big cup game coming up on Saturday, so he's not up to much. He's some professional is Decky. I go to have a wee nosey

at Laura Dillon's Facebook page, but I can't get into it for some reason.

Fuck, maybe she's blocked me after Mandy spoke to her in the café in

Derry. Just as I think this day can't get any worse, Mandy comes in

with a favour to ask and I know by the way she's looking at me it's

going to be HUGE. I might be dumb as fuck, but even I can see this is a

biggie.

'Right, Mickey… remember my mate Knuckles who kindly lent you

the six grand?'

'Of course I do, even I wouldn't forget something like that in a hurry.

What about him? Fuck, he doesn't want it back now does he? 'Cause

I've … we've been dipping into it a bit!'

'No, no, no! '

Thank fuck for that!

'It's just that he needs a bit of help and he asked me to ask you if you

could give him a hand?'

'Me? How the hell could I give him a hand? One of his hands are

bigger than my head!'

'Well, you really won't have to do anything, you'll just have to keep watch while he goes and gets something that belongs to him. You'll be like an observer.'

'An observer?'

'Yeah, man, somebody has something that belongs to him and the guy isn't there but Knuckles really needs this thing back right away, so he's gonna take it. Unfortunately, the pigs wouldn't see it that way if they came along. This is why he needs an observer and he needs somebody he can trust. He said he knew from when he first met you that you were an A1 bloke and totally trustworthy. He likes you, man'

'Really?'

'Yeah, man, he likes you.'

'And the person who has his thing is okay with him taking it back?'

'Well that's the thing, the person is out of the country at the moment and Knuckles has been trying to contact him, but he just can't get him. So he's just going to go take back what's his. Easy-peasy.'

'Ah, well that sounds fair enough! When does he need a hand?'

'He'll pick you up at half ten tonight.'

'Okay. What should I wear?'

'This...'

I suddenly get a bad feeling when my girlfriend hands me a balaclava and black gloves.

A few hours later, I'm sitting in the living room with the balaclava and gloves on, while watching Made in Chelsea. Mandy comes in and is about to tell me it's almost time to go when she stops mid-sentence and looks at me funny:

'Why are you wearing them now?'

''Cause I'm trying to get used to having them on. It's roasting in these things!'

'That's 'cause you're indoors,, in the heat. You'll be glad of them when you're out. Now make sure you're ready to go as soon as they pull up.'

'I will. I'm ready already. Houl' on ... what do you mean "they"? Who else is going?'

'A few of Knuckles's mates offered to go with him, too. They're good like that.'

Next thing a Land Rover pulls up outside and Mandy tells me to hurry up, then as I'm going out the door she tells me to take the balaclava and gloves off, and not to put them on again until Knuckles tells me. I put them into my pockets and walk over to the Land Rover. There's two

people in the front and I have the back to myself. Knuckles is in the

passenger seat and the driver is as tough-looking as he is. I'm already

shitting myself. Nobody is speaking as we drive out of the estate. I'm

looking through Facebook on my phone as we're driving along. I really

feel like putting up a picture of me with the balaclava on, and write

under it 'Going to work lol!', but if Mandy sees it she'll probably go

mad so I just leave it. We're in the Land Rover for about 45 minutes,

then we stop in an industrial estate that has , like, I suppose 'big shed'

type buildings. The driver flashes his lights and a white van appears out

of nowhere and pulls up beside us. Knuckles and the driver jump out.

I'm having trouble unbuckling my seatbelt when Knuckles tells me to

stay where I am and wait for his orders. Good job 'cause I think I've

fucked up the seatbelt holder so I can't get out anyway. Knuckles and

our driver talk to the men for about a minute then the driver gets into

the back of the van. Knuckles comes back to me and hands me a

walkie-talkie:

'This is a walkie-talkie, Mickey. It's not a toy, it's not to be played with

or messed around with. It's set at channel 16 and it stays at channel 16.

Your job is, if you see anybody coming anyway near this area then you

press this button and say 'There's a mouse in the barn, repeat, there's a mouse in the barn'. If you don't get a reply within 15 seconds then you say it again. You get that?'

'Got it.'

Knuckles hands me the walkie-talkie then comes close to my face:

'You fuck this up, boy, and you'll be in some deep, deep trouble. Right?'

'Right. Do I put on the balaclava and gloves now?'

'Make sure you leave the gloves on but just keep the balaclava handy, you might not need it. And don't touch anything!'

'Grand.'

He taps me twice on the face and says:

'Good boy, Mickey. Good boy.'

Knuckles jumps out of the Land Rover and into the van. Then the van drives around to the back of the warehouse leaving me out front keeping watch. I'm not actually as scared as I thought I would be because technically I'm only sitting in a jeep with a walkie-talkie and I really don't think that's a crime. I wonder how many of the other contestants who will be at the X-Factor Bootcamp will be doing the same as me at this exact moment. The lads would never believe me if I told them about this. I'm waiting for about 20 minutes, but it seems like hours 'cause there hasn't been a sinner in sight. I decide to turn on the radio, I'll keep it low. Music helps me concentrate anyway. I try again to take the seatbelt off, but the fucking thing is twisted so I take the gloves off to get it untangled 'cause I can't reach the radio from the back seat. After about five minutes I manage to get the thing off and I climb into the passenger seat. The keys are still in the ignition so I get the radio turned on, but I can't find any music I like. It's all either crap music or people talking. Why the hell would anybody want to listen to people talking on the radio? You can hear people talking anywhere, the radio should be your way of getting away from people talking. I eject the CD and out pops 'Disney Movie Favourites – Part One'. This evening is getting worse. After another 20 minutes, I see the van appear again from the back of the warehouse and it parks beside me. Thank God, I was getting really bored. Knuckles jumps out of the van and hurries to the window:

'Out of the car, quickly!'

He's sweating like mad. I decide it's not a good time to tell him it's not a car, it's a jeep.

'Get into the back of the van, Mickey.'

I jump out and close the door. The side door of the van is open so I jump in and Knuckles gets in behind me, then the van speeds off and nearly makes me fall over. I sit down on a box. Knuckles is breathing very heavily:

'Did you see anyfing, Mickey?'

'Not since you left.'

'Good boy, Mickey, good boy! Me and the boys here have plenty more jobs coming up that you're going to help us with.'

'What kinda jobs?'

'Are you going to pick up the Land Rover later?'

'You what?'

'The Land Rover. Is somebody going to pick it up later?'

'We'll not be going near that fookin' thing again. The only people that'll be picking that up will be the forensics people.'

He can see by the blank look on my face that I'm not following:

'The jeep was stolen about 20 minutes before we picked you up, we're leaving it there.'

He then looks at my hands and loses his temper:

'Mickey, where the fook are your gloves?'

'Em … in the Land Rover?'

'Did you touch anything in the jeep?'

'Well, I tried to get a radio station then I put on a Disney CD till you came back.'

'And you didn't have your gloves on?'

I'm shitting myself right now:

'It's hard to do anything with them on!'

'Ah for fook sake! I told you not to fookin' touch anything!'

'Does the filth have your prints?'

Again, he recognises the blank expression:

This time he shouts:

'DOES THE POLICE HAVE A COPY OF YOUR FINGERPRINTS ANYWHERE?'

'No! I've never given my prints before!'

'Right, you're going back to Ireland tomorrow morning until the heat dies down.'

'Seriously? I have an audition next week!'

'I said you're going back to Ireland tomorrow! You fly back for your audition next week in the morning and you go home again that night! I need you out of the way. If the filth comes sniffing around and they get your prints then you're up shit creek, Mickey. I said you're up shit

creek! If you get caught then you're on your own. Got it?'

This is no time to be arguing with him, because he looks like he wants

to tear my head off. I'm pretty sure he could easily do it, too. They drop

me at the McDonald's which means I have a ten-minute walk back to

the house. I hate walking through this place during the day, but at night

you're really taking your life into your own hands. As soon as I get out,

I see a group of teenagers standing in front of me. I'll be lucky to get to

my bed tonight alive! One of the teens comes over to me, he looks a bit

like Marty, kinda scrawny with a shaved head, but you know to look at

him he's tough. He seems to be the leader:

'What's the story, kid?'

Kid? I'm at least eight years older than him, but I don't say anything.

I'm actually too scared to speak, but I manage to say:

'I don't want to fight.'

'Ain't nobody going to fight with you around here, kid, when you're

part of Knuckles's crew.'

Jesus Christ, I'm part of a crew now.

'Thanks.'

'You need anything taken care of then you come to us, alright kid? Knuckles knows us well.'

I'm physically shaking:

'That's grand, I'll remember that.'

Then I just put my head down and head home. This all doesn't seem real. What the hell am I going to tell my ma and da when me and Mandy land back tomorrow? Fuck, what's Mandy going to say when she finds out we have to go back to Derry? I'm walking back to the house and the whole time I'm expecting a police helicopter to come overhead and shine a spotlight on me, and a SWAT team to surround me. Luckily, I make it back to the house safe and sound, but there's nobody home. Then I remember Mandy is out for the night so I whip out my phone and text her:

'Somefing happnd 2nite - Knuckles said I have 2 go bk home 2moro 4 while. We have 2 leave 2moro morning. Will I pack 4U?'

She doesn't reply, so I go upstairs and start packing for the both of us. Every few minutes I have a look through the curtains to see if there are any cops about. Still clear. Then as I start to think about things, I realise there's no reason why they would come here if they don't have my fingerprints. This calms me down a lot, so I go downstairs after I've packed and make some cornflakes. My phone beeps and it's Mandy:

'Knuckles just told me what you did. You're such a stupid prick! I can't go with you, too much to do here, text me when you get home.'

My heart sinks! This will be the first time I've been away from her for any length of time since we met. Apart from the times she stays out all night without me, but that's different.

I text her back:

'I'll miss you!'

She texts back right away:

'Suck it up princess: I'll see you at your audition. Now go get some sleep. Xx'

Two kisses. That's good. I text her back:

'xxxxxxxxxxxxx'

But she doesn't reply. I can't believe I'll be back in Derry tomorrow! At least I'll be away from the filth, and I'll have a few quid in the bank to play with.

CHAPTER 11.

Derry hasn't changed much since I was away. The school kids are still gathered around the bus station, acting like dicks like they always do. The crazy old woman who feeds the pigeons is still throwing her bread up in the air and screaming as the pigeons go mental around her. The Guildhall still rings its bells every hour or so, Foyle Street still stinks and it's still raining. I'm feeling a bit sentimental about the old place. In fairness, though, I've only been away three and a half weeks, but it's still kinda nice to be back home. I just wish Mandy was here with me, but she says she's got way too many commitments in Manchester to be running back with me every time I fuck up. I wonder how many times she's expecting me to fuck up? It also feels good not having to look behind me everywhere I go in case the police are following me. I was like a nervous wreck going through the airport this morning. At one stage, I was getting checked in and I almost confessed everything to the girl who was working there. She asked me my name so I thought she was on to me and this was the first part of the interrogation process. I've seen the movie 'In The Name of the Father' enough times to know that you should tell them what they want to know right away or things spiral out of control. My da watches that movie at least once a month, the sad fucker. He told me once when he was drunk that if he ever ended up in a cell with me, for a crime that he didn't commit, he'd batter me. I felt a whole lot better when I got to Derry, though, 'cause there wasn't many people on the plane and I'm pretty sure none of them were filth who had followed me over. I'm just going to tell my ma and da that I missed them and wanted to come home for a few days before the Bootcamp stage. I'll have four days in Derry then back to Manchester the night before the Bootcamp. I feel like an international jet-setter with the amount of air miles I'm doing. At least I'll get a chance to practise my vocals here, but I'll have to go out the town a few nights and show people that I've made it now, and I'm not afraid to splash the cash.

I jump into a taxi to take me back to the house. I'm in the back, usually I'd jump in the front seat, but lately I've started sitting in the back. It makes me feel like I'm being chauffeured around. The taxi driver obviously wants to talk, but I just want to stare out the window like somebody would in a music video, kinda all thoughtfully like?

'So where are you from, young fella?'

'Eh- I'm from Derry, the house you're dropping me to?'

'Are ye? You must have been away a while, I can hear a bit of an English accent there.'

Mickey Doc

Fuck, I was afraid of this happening. My ma and da had to stop me from watching One Tree Hill when I was 15 because I developed an American accent. The last straw was when my da brought me to watch a football match and I told him I'd rather sit on my fanny and drink soda, because football is shit and basketball is like 'oh my God, so much better'. I don't even like basketball, I just got caught up in the whole American dream thing. If … I mean 'when' I make it to the Judge's House on the X-Factor, I really hope I get to go to America and hopefully it's with Simon. I can just picture the two of us driving around Downtown Los Angeles in his sports car with the hood down.

'Well I've been in England a while, I'm competing in a music show over there.'

'Really? Which one?'

He's struggling to look around to see if he recognises me.

'I can't say which one, I'm not allowed to talk about it till after it airs.'

'You're probably one of the shit ones are you? Is that why you don't want to tell me?'

'No! Simon Cowell said I was incredible and Louis Walsh said I have a recording voice! That's hardly shit now, is it?'

'So you're on the X-Factor, then?'

Fuck!

'I can't tell you which one, I just gave you those names to throw you!'

The rest of the way home he just keeps looking at me in the rear view mirror while shaking his head and laughing. He thinks it's a joke, but he'll be laughing on the other side of his face when he sees me ripping the show a new one. We pull up outside my house and my da's car is there and my Aunty Margaret's. Let's hope George the priest-boy isn't with her. I throw the taxi driver a tenner and tell him to keep the change. I was trying to put it in his shirt pocket like they do in the movies, but he just looked at me weirdly when I bypassed his hand and tried to reach his pocket. Just as I'm about to close the door he shouts after me, I turn around and pull a pen and paper from my trouser pocket. He's obviously looking for an autograph:

'You better not be shite.'

Then he just drives off, leaving me standing with the pen and paper in my hands.

I get into the house and my ma meets me at the door:

'There's our wee superstar!'

As she's saying it she's looking over my shoulder with a big head on her. She's just making sure that Mandy isn't with me. Then my da comes out of the kitchen:

'Well, how are ye getting on, son?'

'Grand, da. I'm climbing the ladder of success and I'm loving it.'

'Well, just make sure to ring your ma a bit more, she be's worried about you.'

'Shut up, John, let the young fella live his life! But a wee phone call every once in a while to make sure you're okay wouldn't go amiss, son.'

My da just shakes his head, lifts the newspaper and goes up the stairs:

'I'm away for a dump.'

That's all that fucker seems to do. I go into the kitchen and my Aunty Margaret gives me a big hug and kisses my forehead. She says she's so proud of me and that she always knew I'd be a superstar which is very nice of her to say, although she has been a fan from the start. She stinks of perfume, though, so I get out of the hug as quickly as I can. Then I get a fright when I hear a voice behind me, it makes me jump:

'Well hello there, Michael. How lovely it is to see you again.'

Where the fuck did he even come from!? He's standing there holding my ma's dog in his arms like a baby, and the wee fucker of a dog is just laying back like butter wouldn't melt. I stare the dog out of it for about 20 seconds before I answer. Just to show the bastard that the boss is back in town:

'Eh, hello, George. How's the whole like religion thing going these days?'

I never know what to say to him.

'The whole religion thing is going very well, Michael. Thank you for asking. How are you finding the sermons in England as opposed to here? And could you please look at me and not the dog when you're talking to me?'

I release the dog from the death stare and look at George.

'Am ... pretty much the same only the accents are different.'

He just gives me that look he gives when he knows I'm lying. Which is pretty much all the time when I'm around him.

My ma then starts going into one, telling me absolutely everything that has been happening in Derry since I've been away, with my Aunty Margaret joining in from time to time to back up the story:

'Did you hear about Majella McCafferty?'

'Nope, can't say I did.'

'Well, she's pregnant again. Fourth child from four different fathers!'

Then Aunty Margaret pops in:

'Aye, I heard her Aunty Mary telling somebody at the bingo last Friday. She says thank God her mother isn't alive to see it or she'd be spinning in her grave.'

'And did you hear about Johnny McLaughlin?'

'Johnny McLaughlin that lives in Springtown?'

'Naw, his uncle.'

'Don't know him.'

'Aye ye do. Started working at the fish counter in the butcher's a few months ago!'

'Nope, don't know him.'

'Red-haired fella. Looks a bit like a ginger David Cameron.'

'Who the fuck is David Cameron?'

She shakes her head, just 'cause she knows fucking EVERYBODY!

'Well, anyway, wait till I tell you what happened to him, he got caught doing the double. Turns out that he was claiming social allowance the whole time he was working in the butcher's!'

Aunty Margaret pops in again, nodding away at her head like the fucking dog from Churchill insurance:

'And it was his wife that touted on him 'cause she was fed up with him coming home stinking of fish every day.'

This shite goes on for a good half an hour before I tell them I need to make a phone call and fuck off to my room. Then I remember my da hadn't come back down the stairs since I came in, so I pop my head into his room. He's just lying on the bed listening to Radio Foyle:

'Your turn to listen to them for a while there, son, I had an hour of it before you came in.'

I go to my room and text Mandy. I haven't heard anything from her all day. Then I text Stevie to tell them I'm back, and hopefully they'll still want to go out for a drink with me. I want to show the lads I have a few quid about me now and I'm not even working. He texts back right away:

Glad 2 hear from u! Were goin out 2nite to celebrate!

I just text back:

Happy dayz, where and when?

He just texts back:

Bentley, 6-ish!

Mickey Doc

You see, after all that me and the lads have been through lately, they'll still come out to celebrate me coming home.

I arrive at the Bentley bar at 6:30, I always like to be fashionably late as well as fashionably great. I go to the bar where I spot Decky, Marty and Stevie in the corner. They don't even notice me, but they seem to be in good spirits. I head over to their table and Marty is the first to see me. He looks half-cut already as he jumps off his stool and comes out to shake my hand:

'Mickey Doc, my oul' mucker! Glad you could be here to help me celebrate! What do you want to drink, buddy? Champagne?'

'Champagne sounds good, I'll grab us a bottle.'

'No way, man, I'm getting the champagne in, we've already went through a bottle!'

'Last of the big spenders! Where did you get money all of a sudden?'

Then it hits me, he said 'glad you can be here to help ME celebrate'!

'Didn't you hear? I won 20 grand on the free state lotto yesterday!'

'Jesus Christ, 20 grand!?'

'Aye, won it in the bookie's, too!'

Fuck, he has more money than me!

Then the rest of the lads come over, it's like I've never been away. I'm still in shock, though, that Marty of all people has more money than me! And I'm supposed to be showing off how rich I am tonight! I need to get the champagne, just to show he's not the only one with cash to flash!

'I'm getting the champagne, lads, you boys sit down and I'll bring it over!'

'No fucking way, man, I won the money, I'll buy the drinks!'

'You're not the only one with money, Marty. I'll get the champagne.'

'Fair enough.'

Then he sits down again.

I go up to the bar and order a bottle. Then I think 'fuck it', I'm not going to be outdone by Marty so I buy four bottles of champagne, a bottle each. The barman stares at me like I've lost the plot. Obviously, they don't get many people like me in here, even though I used to drink in here all the time.

'Do you want the four bottles now?'

'Of course I want them now!'

'But do you not just want to drink one at a time?'

'No, I want the four of them now, Jesus Christ!'

'But that means I'll have to get four ice buckets.'

'So?? I want FOUR bottles of champagne, NOW!'

'You realise they're £60 a bottle?'

'Oh, so you only have the cheap stuff then? I suppose I'll take it!'

Jesus Christ!! 60 quid a bottle! After doing a quick bit of maths in my head, I realise that's nearly £200!

'That'll be £240 please.'

Fucking stupid maths.

The barman gives me the first bottle in an ice bucket and I take it to the table. He says he'll bring down the rest of them. The lads have obviously been chatting about me, because they shut up when I get there. Stevie is the first to speak:

'So, where did you get the money for champagne? Usually, you can't afford a pint!'

'Well, when you're about to become a superstar, money just seems to come to you.'

Then Marty pipes in:

'Mickey's a rent boy!'

Everybody starts laughing, including me. It just feels so good to be with the lads again. All the other shit that's been going on seems a million miles away. Then I remember that Mandy still hasn't text me back so I send her another message:

'Miss u babe! Xxx'

Then the barman comes to the table with the other 3 bottles of champagne. Stevie tells him it must be a mistake and is about to send them back when I stand up:

'There's a bottle for each of us, lads, from now on we live the good life!'

Then I stare at Marty:

'And some of us actually EARN our money!'

He just makes a 'wanker' sign with his hand then says:

'There's no way he's a rent boy anyway 'cause he wouldn't be able to afford a packet of crisps, never mind champagne!'

So then I buy all the crisps that are behind the bar which costs me another 100 quid.

This acting the big shot is costing me a fortune, but it's worth it to see the lads think that I've made it. We're all getting pretty hammered and having the craic. Even Decky is knocking them back. In fairness, though, he spent enough money on me over the years, it's about time I spent some on him. The stick is flying and before long the conversation turns back to where I got the money. People ALWAYS want to talk about money. Stevie brings it up:

'So, where does an unemployed Derry man living in England get the money to be buying four bottles of champagne?'

I make sure to remind him:

'And all the crisps behind the bar!'

'And all the crisps behind the bar. So go on, tell us.'

'Well, if you must know, I got a loan until I start earning from the X-Factor.'

They all look at each other then look back at me. Decky pipes in:

'What kind of a bank would give an unemployed person a loan? No offence.'

'None taken. It was Mandy that set it up for me. One of her friends kinda runs his own bank.'

The lads are all suddenly looking worried.

'You mean, you got money from a loan shark?'

'That name makes it sound dodgy. Knuckles is a sound fella. No filling out forms, no speaking down to me, no questions. He just gave me what I needed then got it for me that evening.'

They're all looking at me like I'm thick. I hate that look. Decky is suddenly Mr Serious Head again:

'You're saying you got the money from a loan shark called 'Knuckles'? You realise this guy is more than likely a gangster who'll squeeze you for more and more money, or get you to hold stuff for him, or be involved in his illegal activities. You've done some pretty dumb things before, man, but this is huge … '

The other 3 lads have their mouths open and just nod.

'… How much are you talking?'

'Just six grand.'

They all gasp, if that's even the right word? I had convinced myself that it was okay to get six grand from somebody. Now I'm starting to doubt myself:

'Maybe he'll be cool and just take the money back after I start earning from the X-Factor.'

They all look at Decky, then he speaks:

'Mickey, you know we all love you like a brother, and don't be taking this the wrong way, but … what happens if you don't make any money from the X-Factor?'

'Woah – woah – woah! You can call me stupid for taking money from a loan shark, then going on a robbery with him and his gang, but don't ever, EVER say that I'm not going to do well in the X-Factor!'

I'm all of a sudden standing up with rage now. The lads look stunned again. Marty says:

'What do you mean 'went on a robbery with him and his gang'?

'Yeah, man, you went on a robbery – with a gang?'

Fuck, I didn't mean to tell them about that. This calms me down and I sit again:

'Knuckles asked Mandy to tell me he needed a hand. I thought it was a wee bit mad at the time.'

'A wee bit mad? What the fuck, man?'

'Well I was only sitting in a jeep keeping a watch. I didn't really see anything. It's not as mad as it sounds.'

I can tell that they're still a bit shocked. Then Marty lightens the mood with one of his made-up stories, the lying fucker:

'I know somebody who can sort this out for you, ye know.'

I just roll my eyes:

'Don't tell me, your da is Superman!'

'No, seriously, a guy that used to live down the road from me in Galliagh, Big Sean. He's a massive player in the criminal world in England right now. One of the top men in Europe, too …'

This is coming from the same bloke who once told me that he met Angelina Jolie in Buncrana and went out for dinner with her, only to find out she was trying to get him into a threesome with her and Brad, so he done a runner on her. It's good to know that your friends imaginary friends are always there to help out.

'… If you want me to give him a shout for you, I will. I'm sure he could sort things out pretty easily. Plus, he still owes me a favour.'

As I said before, Marty is a total moon-man sometimes.

'Cheers, Marty. If I need him I'll give you a shout.'

The lads keep asking me questions about my time in England until I've had enough and decide to go home. That and the fact that I'm absolutely rubbered. I don't tell anybody that I'm leaving, because they'll just talk me into staying longer. I check my phone and there's still nothing from Mandy. I haven't heard from her since I left England.

Mickey Doc

I illiterally fall into my bed and text her with one eye shut and the other working overtime trying to concentrate:

'Missing u boby xxc'

Holy sweet mother of fuck! I've just woke up with the worst hangover in the world. I can't open my eyes yet, or lift my head, so I just feel around the top of my bed for my phone. I find it under the pillow, so I very slowly move it to the front of my face. Then, very slowly again, I open my eyes. Jesus, the brightness hurts, so I give myself a few seconds to adjust. My mouth is so dry I can hardly open it. My tongue is kinda stuck to the top of my mouth and every time I move, my head hurts. I look at my phone to check if Mandy has got back to me. Still nothing. All I have is a few texts from the lads, checking that I got home alright. The fact that Mandy hasn't got back to me is really freaking me out right now. I check her Facebook and her Twitter, but there has been nothing new since she last text me. I check my e-mail too, just in case. But there's nothing from her. I have 4112 new e-mails. I'd really need to start clearing them 'cause they're usually all shite. Nothing from Mandy, though. Then I see an e-mail from the X-Factor and it was from a few weeks ago. Shit, I hope this wasn't important. I quickly open it and read it:

Michael,

Just a quick mail to remind you that the Bootcamp stages will take place on Saturday August 24th at the SSE Arena, Wembley. A total of 114 acts have successfully reached the Bootcamp stage this year. You will be put into groups and take part in a sing-off where the judges cut half the acts, leaving 57 contestants to compete for the 6-seat challenge. We will expect you to be at the main office of the SSE Arena at 8am sharp Saturday August 24th, bringing with you the pass you had been given at the last stages along with ID and a copy of this mail.

We would also like to remind you that the first auditions of this year's X-Factor will begin airing on ITV the following week – Saturday 31st August at 8pm. Your audition will be on in the very first week of the new season.

If you have any other questions, then please do not hesitate to call me on 026 7854 6523.

Sincerely,

Robert Abbott

X-Factor Assistant Producer

Now, that just helped with the hangover. Three more days till the Bootcamp and ten more days till the auditions go out to millions of people across the world, and people finally get to see a new superstar in the making. I'll not be touching another drink until after the Bootcamp 'cause I really need to be giving it 100 per cent. I really need to practise for the next few days, then head to London on Friday night. I just hope that Mandy gets in contact very soon, because I'm getting pretty worried about her not texting. I start thinking about what the lads said about getting money from a loan shark and how dangerous it all is, but at the moment all I can think about is the X-Factor. For years, it has taken over my thoughts, and now I'm on the verge of fame. That's all I want. Fame and fortune. Nothing more, nothing less. I really want Mandy to be there with me at the Bootcamp, though. Then I remember that Mandy used my phone a few times to ring Knuckles, so I search through my call log and find the number. I clear my throat as the phone rings:

'Who is this?'

'Ah, Knuckles, it's me, Mickey Doc, I was just wondering if you've heard anything from Mandy. It's just that she hasn't been replying to my messages and I haven't heard from her. I just want to make sure she's okay.'

'She's here, mate, she's had her phone nicked. I'll put her on to you.'

Mandy comes on to the phone:

'Hey there! Some fookin' dickhead has nicked my fookin' phone, mate!'

'Ah, no way! Fuck that! What about the insurance?'

'Yeah, I'm getting a new one today, but that's not the fookin' point, I have a lot of sensitive stuff in that phone and it can't get into the wrong hands, know what I'm saying?'

'Maybe you can get the same sensitive stuff in your new phone?'

I don't have a clue what she means by 'sensitive stuff'.

'Jesus, sometimes I forget how fookin' thick you are, man! :Look, I'm just busy sorting something out here, but I'll text you when I get my new phone this afternoon. Hope you're not missing me too much!'

'I'm actually missing you loads and...'

Then I realise she has hung up on me.

CHAPTER 12.

Now this is living! I've just been picked up at the airport by an X-Factor car, and I'm being driven to Wembley for the Bootcamp audition. Now all I need to do is get the driver to pick up Mandy at the bus station and we're sorted:

'Okay, driver, I'm going to need you to take a diversion and pick up my girlfriend at Victoria bus station. She should be just arriving there now.'

'What?'

Seems like he's thicker than me:

'A diversion. It means to diverse the car to somewhere else. In this case being to pick up my girlfriend.'

I love getting the chance to look smart. Doesn't happen too often. He just looks at me in the mirror, dumb fucker. I start speaking slowly so he can understand:

'Diverse. The. Car. To. Victoria. Bus. Station. Please.'

He just keeps looking at me in the rear view mirror. Maybe he doesn't speak English:

'Do you speak Eng…'

He suddenly stops the car in the middle of a busy road and turns around. He looks pissed off:

'Listen, you jumped up little fuck … firstly, my name isn't 'driver', it's Ian. Secondly, I'm studying advanced chemical engineering and this is just a poxy little job to help pay the ever-mounting bills, so I won't tolerate getting talked down to by anybody. Especially someone who doesn't know what the word diversion means. Got it?'

'Erm… somebody pissed in their cornflakes!?'

He just looks at me for a minute, then shakes his head and drives off again. I ring Mandy to let her know. She has been pretty strange since she lost her phone. Like, stranger than normal. It's kinda like she has just given up. Either that or it's her time of the month:

'Hey'

'There's been a problem, honey. The car can't pick you up 'cause we have to be there right away for some big interview or something!'

'How will I get there then? Should I just go back to Manchester?'

See, she hasn't called me retarded or a dickhead once. Definitely must be her time of month.

'No, no. I'll pay for your taxi from the bus station to Wembley. Text me when you get here.'

Mickey Doc

'Okay, see you soon.'

'See you soon. Love you.'

Then she hangs up, I'm not sure if she didn't hear me saying I loved her, or if she just ignored it. I'm staring out the window, thinking about women's periods when all of a sudden the driver, I mean — Ian, starts talking to me in a nice way:

'Is that your girlfriend?'

'Aye, her name's Mandy.'

'Look, mate, I'm sorry I couldn't go pick her up. It's just that they have us running around so much we hardly have time to take a piss, never mind take diversions.'

'It's alright, she took it surprisingly well. Normally she would have called me a 'fookin' dickhead' at least five times in that space of time.'

Ian laughs, he seems pretty sound, actually. He starts telling me about his course and how hard it is to earn a few quid to pay for it and stuff. He tells me that he has a girlfriend, too, but she's studying in Edinburgh and he only gets to see her every few weeks. He also tells me that this is his third year doing work for the X-Factor, and from this stage onwards it's where things start getting real.

'Just remember, though, mate, these guys are ruthless and will drop you like a hot potato. Give it your all, but be prepared.'

'Cheers, Ian.'

He gets out of the car and opens the door for me, then shakes my hand and wishes me good luck.

This Wembley is some place. It's fucking huge! The producers called us all together into groups and explained what would be happening. Basically, there's 116 contestants here and we're going to be separated into groups. There's the boys group, girls group, bands group and the one I fall intok the over-25s. I argued for a while that I'm not technically over 25 'cause I'm actually just 25 and not over it. The producer reminded me that I'll be 26 in November so I'm in the over-25s category and that if I don't like It, I can go home. Fuck that, over-25s it is for me, then. Plus, he wore glasses. Never argue with somebody who wears glasses, they always win … or are dickheads.

After we're separated into our groups, we get a chance to sing, and then the numbers are cut down to 57 people. Then, tomorrow night, the judges do what's called the 'six-seat challenge' which means they do a final cut, leaving six contestants in each of the four groups. Then, the judges will be told which of the four categories they will be mentoring.

I'm sure it's all very confusing to people who never watched the show,

but to me it's just something that makes sense. Kinda like the way

some people can use 24hr time without having to count on their fingers:

I can't do that, but I do know the X-Factor. The producer tells us we

have an hour to get ourselves together then the work begins. We're all

put into a big room that has snacks and drinks laid out on big tables,

and sofa's against the walls. Next thing I see is Mandy coming through

the doors and she sees me straight away. She walks over to me and her

eyes look really red, like she's been crying:

'Hey, honey, are you alright?'

'I'm fookin' great, mate, never been better.'

I can tell that she's lying, she doesn't really have that wee spark she

normally has. I give her a big hug and tell her that I missed her. She

doesn't really hug me back but she was never much of a hugger

anyway:

'So what's happening now, Mickey? The dickhead at the door told me

I'll only be allowed to be here with you for another hour or so?'

'Aye, well, ye see that's when we start rehearsing songs and shit for the judges this evening. Will you be okay on your own for a while?'

'Of course I'll be fookin' okay, mate! I've got other ways of keeping myself entertained'

I wonder if she's talking about a dildo. I wondered that when we were apart for a while there, if she had a dildo to keep herself entertained. I hope it isn't bigger than me. I can hear that she's talking, but I'm not really listening anymore:

'So, are you nervous or excited about today?'

'Dildo.'

Fuck, I said that out loud...

'What?'

'Nothing.'

'You just said "dildo".'

'No, I didn't, you must have heard me wrong.'

'Nope, you definitely said "dildo".'

She's looking at me for like, 15 seconds, obviously waiting on an answer, or trying to figure me out. Luckily, her phone rings.

'You are one strange, strange boy, Mickey Doc. Watch my bag, I need to take this call. I could be gone for a while.'

Saved by the phone!

She throws her bag on the sofa that I'm standing beside. I'm about to tell her we only have an hour together, but before I know it, she's pushing her way past the other contestants with her phone to her ear.

I have a quick look around, not many people are chatting to each other, everyone is trying to get into the right frame of mind. There's loads of really hot girls, but obviously I'm not looking. I sit down on the sofa and a bloke comes over and sits beside me. He puts out his hand for me to shake it:

'Hello, I'm Richard.'

'How's it going Richard, I'm Mickey … Mickey Doc. Any craic?'

He looks at me like I have two heads. I know this is going to sound like the pot calling the kettle back, but he looks a bit thick. He's tall and thin and has blond hair that isn't really styled in any way, and his eyes look a bit lost:

'I wouldn't be in to that sort of thing, not at all. No way.'

'What?'

'Crack… wouldn't be my thing, I just like a few beers and maybe a whiskey at the end of the night. Drugs isn't my thing. No way.'

He leans in close to me:

'… I'm sure there's plenty of people here that's getting high on crack, but I'm not one of them. No hay, Jose!'

I burst out laughing. It feels good to laugh at somebody else's stupidness:

'I didn't mean THAT kinda craic! I just meant like 'any fun' or 'what's happening?''

'Oh, right, like the Irish say?'

'Aye, I'm Irish!'

'No, you're not.'

'Aye, I am!'

'Really?'

Shit, I don't know if this is one of those British/Irish things where I don't know which one I *actually* am.

'I'm from Derry, which is in like, Northern Ireland?'

'Are you? That's great, the Irish are good these days. It's the Muslims we need to worry about.'

I don't even know where the country- Muslim is, never mind what the Muslims are like.

He actually talks really funny. It's like he's constantly depressed and thinks it's the end of the world or something.

'Where are you from?'

'Oh, I'm from here in England. Norwich.'

'Is that far?'

'About three hours or so from London. Came up last night. I don't usually like coming up to London, because it's too busy, see. And the people are a bit, you know? They'd stab you for the laugh. I brought some cans of beer with, and drank them in the B&B. That's why I feel so sick today.'

'Maybe a wee aspirin or a painkiller will sort ye out?'

'I don't know, I'm not one for taking that sort of stuff. But today could be exception 'cause I'm feeling sick, and I also think I have a temperature …'

He puts his hand over his forehead. He actually looks like he's going to cry.

'… It was my own stupid fault, I felt like I was getting the flu, so I got drunk. Now I have a hangover on top of that. How am I supposed to sing like this?'

'My girlfriend's away taking a call, she usually has painkillers and stuff in her bag. She's like a walking chemist.'

I'll be doing a good deed and it'll also give me a chance to see if Mandy has a dildo in her bag. I lift the bag, set it on my knee and have a quick rummage through it. There's actually not much in, it but I do spot a packet of painkillers. I give them to Richard:

'There ye go, two of those and you'll be right as rain.'

'What do I do with them?'

'Just put two in your mouth then take a big drink of water and swallow them down. Don't chew them or anything.'

He lifts a bottle of water out of a plastic bag he has at his feet, places the tablets in his mouth, then washes them down with the water. Then he just sits there, staring forward, waiting for the tablets to work. I have one last look in the pockets to see if the dildo is hidden. Nope, definitely none there. I do find a thermometer, though:

'Those painkillers will take half an hour or so to kick in. Here's a thermometer to check your temperature.'

Mickey Doc

He just stares at it. I feel like an actual doctor right now.

'What do I do with that?'

'It's a digital thermometer, it'll tell you if you have a temperature and how bad you are. Stick it in your mouth … and don't chew that either! Just suck on it.'

At least I think you suck on it?

I'm trying to switch it on while it's in his mouth but the small screen isn't really doing anything:

'You have to leave it in a while, until it picks up the temperatures.'

Sounds right anyway. We don't talk anymore while he has the thermometer in his mouth, he's still just sitting there, staring forward while sucking on the thermometer as I take a look at the screen every few minutes. Next thing, Mandy comes back. Richard doesn't even look up at her and she barely looks at him, she just points at him with her thumb:

'Who the fuck's that?'

'That's Richard from Norwich, he's a contestant, too, but he thinks he has the flu on top of a hangover. I gave him a painkiller from your bag and I'm taking his temperature with your thermometer, I hope you don't mind, I'll buy you a new one tomorrow.'

She looks down at him with real disgust. He just puts out his hand to shake hers but she just snatches the thermometer from his mouth and shouts at him:

'FUCK OFF!!'

Richard just looks at Mandy then looks at me, he seriously looks like he's about to burst into tears now. He's waiting for an explanation from me, but I don't have one so I just shake my head. He looks back at Mandy who is getting angrier and angrier by the second, grabs his plastic bag and water:

'Sorry, if I...'

She just stares at me and says:

'That's not a thermometer, that's a fookin' pregnancy test...

'... a USED pregnancy test!'

It takes at least ten seconds for me to catch on to what she's talking about, then it takes Richard another five seconds on top of that. Next thing I know, he's throwing up all over himself and the floor. As I watch him blow vomit out of his nose, I'm still working things out in my head, like does this mean she's pregnant with my baby? Is Richard pregnant? I turn to Mandy who is still in shock:

'Is it ... did it ... are you? Are we?'

'Am I pregnant? No, I'm not fookin' pregnant! It was negative!'

She catches on that I still don't understand:

'Negative means I'm NOT pregnant you fookin' retard! Jesus Christ, Mickey, what the fook, man? I leave you to look after my bag for five minutes and you've done this.'

'So, you're not pregnant?'

'No!'

'And Richard isn't pregnant?'

She just stares at me like the way teachers used to stare at me at school when I said something stupid. Then she seems to, like, soften?

'No, look, I took the test before I got here, and it was negative ... not pregnant, then I just put it in my bag 'cause I had nowhere else to put it.'

Richard is still staring at his vomit and the pregnancy test that is lying amongst it. There's people with mops and wet-floors signs trying to get everything cleaned up quickly, and everybody is staring in our direction. Mandy lifts her bag:

'I need to get out of here, man.'

'Am I going to see you later?'

'I don't know. I just need to be on my own for a while. I'll text you later.'

Then she kisses me on the cheek and leaves.

We're all in our groups and we've been practising away like mad for ages. Anytime we haven't been practising, we've been doing interviews and I fucking love it! The competition is unreal in our category, but I know I have that extra something. I saw the faces of the other contestants when I sang, and I could see that they were shocked and impressed. I was really giving it everything. The judges all spent time with us throughout the day, and they all seem pretty sound. Cheryl is still an absolute babe. I saw her looking at me a few times and I could tell that she was thinking 'if I wasn't married, Mickey Doc, you'd be bringing the Cole back to Derry'. At first, I was a wee bit nervous around the judges, but they all seemed interested in our stories and where we came from, so now they're just a part of it … a very important part at that. They decide if I'm going on to win a one-million-pound record deal. Which I am, of course, I fucking need it. The song we have been given to sing is 'Against All Odds (Take a

Look at me Now). Luckily, my ma has been blasting out that song since I was a kid and I know every single part of it inside out.

There are loads of us all sitting backstage and waiting to go on, we're told we have 20 minutes left. Richard is one of them, but he hasn't really spoken to me since the pregnancy test incident. The poor fucker can't even look at me. There's a few that just aren't up to scratch and a few that I think will definitely get through. Everybody just seems so focused, although we have had a good laugh, too. There's Mike from Stoke, he works on a building site and has two young children, a son and a daughter. He's 34 years old, but you wouldn't think it, he just goes on like one of the lads. He says he really wants to win so he could give his children the type of upbringing he never had. Then there's Godfrey who is the complete opposite. He's 28 and from London, but he never had to work a day in his life and never will. His dad owns some big corporation and they're properly loaded, they have maids in their house and everything. He seems sound enough, but I don't think a lot of people like him, probably 'cause he has money. I can tell Mike the builder doesn't like him because he has a few quid about him, but that's the type of life he says he wants to give his children? I just keep my mouth shut, though. Then there's Minka from London. He's like a black gang member (his words) and he says he's only in it for the pussy and gold. It sort of makes me think of Knuckles and the money I got from him, and it has suddenly started to feel real now. I have to block that out, though, because if I start thinking on the fact I owe a gang member six grand then I'm fucked right away. And if I don't win this and pay him back then I'm definitely fucked. I push it out of my head again, then the time comes where we have to prepare to go out and sing for our lives. Illiterately. There is no audience for this part, the arena is empty only for the four judges. The audience will be there for the six-seat challenge tomorrow, after half of this crowd are sent home. I take a deep breath and just go for it.

That was really difficult. Each of us didn't get a lot of time to sing and the judges were just sitting there, making notes and looking at each other. I can't believe how well everybody sang, it was class. I know I was class, but let's hope the judges got enough time to hear it. The judges just thanked us and told us they'll make their decision shortly. The tension is really high backstage now, as we're waiting to be called again. Everybody must have the nails chewed off themselves. They're going to call us out again in groups and only two of those groups will be going home. Mike the builder sits beside me as we're waiting:

'I know if I'm in your group going out there then I'm through, mate.'

Mickey Doc

I'm literally shaking, but trying to act cool:

'I actually thought that about you, too.'

That's not just me bullshitting 'cause he said it to me. Even sitting at home every year watching it on the TV, I can always call who is going through. Mike puts his arm around my shoulder (not in a gay way) and we just sit there waiting to be called. I'd say Minka the gangster and Godfrey the rich dude will go through, too. Then the next thing a producer comes backstage and calls out the names of the first group to go out to hear if they're staying or not:

'Could the following contestants come with me please?'

'Minka'

Fuck, this could be a winning group.

'Paul'

Not so sure

'Gavin'

He's good, too

'Godfrey'

Me and Jack look at each other, we know this is one of the winning groups:

'And lastly…'

Fuck, my nerves are shot:

'Jack'

Jack gets up and whispers to me:

'We don't know if we're through for sure, but you'll definitely be in the next winning group.'

'Good luck, man.'

I high-five them all as they go past. Less than five minutes later they're running back into the room, shouting and celebrating. Then they stop as they realise some people here are going to get bad news. The producer is with them again and I'm called straight away. I can't even think anymore if I'm in a group that I think will get through or not. I'm the most nervous I've ever been in my entire life. We follow the producer down through some corridors and out on to the huge stage. The stage is mostly made up of a huge X that we walk on. The arena seats are empty only for the four seats at the front table. The judges' table. Everybody links their arms around each other. Simon is the only one to speak:

'Thank you all so much for taking part, the Bootcamp round was great, but it has given us a really big headache in terms of trying to pick who goes through to the six seat challenge, because the talent was immense today. Right …'

He pauses for what seems like fucking hours. He isn't smiling which isn't a good sign:

'… I hope you all enjoyed your time on the X-Factor, we have loved having you all here and I hope … I hope you will continue to impress in the weeks to come … You're going through.'

I almost faint with excitement. We all hug each other and jump around the place then run backstage again. All the other contestants are waiting for us to come back and hug and high five us. The people who have already got through are all on a buzz, then the other people who get called out and don't come back are just gone, we don't see them again. I do feel sorry for them a wee bit, but at the same time I'm just glad I'm on this side. The first thing I want to do is ring Mandy, then the lads, then my ma and da then post it on Facebook. I really can't do that, though]cause we've signed forms to say we can't talk about it on social media, and we're only allowed to tell family. I ring Mandy and she answers straight away:

'I GOT FUCKING THROUGH!!'

'Fookin' brilliant, Mickey! I fookin' knew you could do it, kid, I fookin' knew it!'

'Aw, Mandy I wish you were here with me now! Where are you?'

'I just spent my time going around London and I may have bought a few things with your card to make myself feel better. I hope you don't mind?'

'Darling, you can buy whatever you want! Fame and fortune is coming! Plus we're being put up in a flash hotel tonight!'

'Brilliant. Ring me when you're finished and I'll come meet you.'

'No bother, babes! Tonight we celebrate!'

'Well done again Mickey!'

Next thing I ring my ma and da. My ma answers:

'Hello?'

'Ma it's me, Mickey.'

I can hear her shouting:

'John, it's Mickey, it's our Mickey on the phone!' She seems really excited.

'How did ye get on, son?'

Mickey Doc

'I'm through to the next stage, ma! I got through! And your song helped me, too, Take a look at me Now!'

I hear her repeat it all back to my da.

'You've always been brilliant at that song, Mickey! I remember you used to stand up on the fireplace and sing that song to me!'

She's definitely crying now and she's making me cry a bit, too. She gives the phone to my da:

'Well done, son, you're doing us proud!'

'Thanks da!'

'We'll be over there to shout you on as soon as you want us to!'

'As soon as I get to the live finals, da!'

'And tell my ma not to be spreading it around, I'm under contract to keep it secret.'

'Hold on, I'll tell her when she gets off her mobile, she's just ringing your aunties to let them know!'

I'm too excited to even care.

CHAPTER 13.

It's 6am in the morning and I'm awake and feeling on top of the world.

Actually, that's stupid, everybody is on top of the world. If you were

below the world you would be dead. Or live in a really deep cave

somewhere? Do those places exist? I must remember to Google that

later. Mandy is still below the duvet, though, (see what I did there, I'm

really funny when I'm excited). I'd like to say she is worn out by all the

sex stuff we got up to last night, but she said she was tired and just

needed to sleep. It definitely must be her time of the month because

most of the night I could hear her texting away on her phone. She

wakes up in that sexy sort of way that women do, her hair is

everywhere, she has drool down the side of her face and her voice

sounds all raspy. Actually, that's not sexy ... I'm just horny as fuck:

'Good morning, Sexy!'

'What fookin' time is it, man?'

'Just after 6am ... in the morning.'

'What the fook are you doing up at this time?'

'Ah ... maybe because I'm on the X-Factor today and my life is amazing?? Sleeping in bed is just wasting time that you could be living!'

Jesus, I could become like a motivating speaking person at this rate.

'Aw, fook, man, don't be turning into one of those twats!'

'One of what twats?'

'One of those twats who gets up early in the morning and spends the whole day talking about how "life is for living" and "every second counts" and all that bullshit. Next of all you'll be a vegetarian, and start doing yoga. Life can be a cunt, man. The sooner you accept it, the better.'

Obviously still her time of the month. I wonder how long it lasts? I hope it's not a full month. That's another thing for Google to answer later.

'I'm just excited! I can't wait to get back there, and do what I do best!'

'Be a dickhead?'

'No, be a ...'

'Twat?'

'No, a ...'

'Retard?'

'No …'

'A retarded dickhead twat?'

'NO! BE A SUPERSTAR!'

I think that's the first time I've ever raised my voice to her. I'll make it

up to her later.

'Well there's no need to make so much noise at this time of the

morning, for fuck's sake. I'm going back to sleep. I'll talk to you later.'

'If you can come across to the stadium for about 5-ish, then I can see

you before the actual show starts. I have your pass sitting on the table

there.'

She puts the pillow over her face:

'You told me this last night.'

'Breakfast is served till ten-thirty.'

'You told me that last night, too!'

'The key-card for the room is in the light switch!'

She still has the pillow over her head.

'I fucking know, now fuck off!'

'Right, well I'm away down to get breakfast.'

'Don't be wakening me when you get back to the room. Actually, get ready in the bathroom.'

'I'll try not to wake you!'

'Just get ready in the fucking bathroom!'

Ok. I love you…'

She doesn't answer, she just pulls the duvet over her head and grunts. She's definitely not a morning person. In fact, I'm not sure what time of the day person she is. I make my way down for breakfast, but I don't really feel hungry. A few of the other contestants are already there. Mike the builder and Godfrey the rich bloke are sitting with a group from the other categories. I grab some scrambled eggs and a few bits of toast and head down to them:

'How's it going there, everyone?'

Mike and Godfrey both high five me and introduce me to the other people at the table. There's Paula from Bristol, who immediately hugs me and says:

'Alright me babbers! I heard you, you got a voice! Wicked! You from Ireland inchew?'

I just nod and smile.

Then there's Lola who's a real loud-mouth:

'Than' boy is white! Damn! A from Jamdown man … Jamaica! Rope 'een white boy!'

I don't have a clue what she's saying, but she pulls the seat out from beside her and points for me to sit down. I think she might be from Jamaica because she sounds a bit like Bob Marley. I only know that because my da listens to him.

Breda, Maggie and Sharon who are part of the over-25s are also there. They're a bit older than the rest of us, they're in their late 30s, and I think Sharon is actually 40. They are really nice and mix with everybody, even though they're older. They're like the mammies of the group, only much better looking than mine. Paul and Gavin from the over-25s are there, too, they're dead on but they like to keep themselves to themselves.

Then there's another two girls at the end of the table, Linda and Jen. They're about 18 or 19 years old, but seem very shy. Absolute crackers, though, the two of them. There are so many accents here that my head is starting to spin. I throw the scrambled egg and toast into me then head off to get ready. Even though I don't have a notion what anybody is saying, they seem pretty sound. As I'm getting up to go, another lad comes in the door wearing a big long pink dressing gown and one of those big feathery scarves:

'Hi everybody! Oh. My. God. Did you see the food they have laid out? It's like oh-my-God soooo many calories … but too delish to pass!'

He sees me getting up to leave:

'And what would your name be, young man?'

He says it in a really camp way. That's not me being bad, that's just the way he talks. I shake his hand:

'I'm Mickey Doc, nice to meet you.'

'And it's nice to meet you, too! I'm Phil … and what a manly handshake you have there. I'm sure those hands could hold you tight all night … am I right?'

'Most people tell me I've got small hands.'

'Well it ain't always about the size, Mickey, it's what you can do with them that counts.'

I can't even build Lego, but I don't say anything.

Then, before I know it, he's off air-kissing everybody at the table, and shouting things like 'Fabulous darling' and 'How are you my beauty?' At least I can understand him. I make my way back to the room, looking at my hands the whole way there. I think I have nice hands, they look even better when I have a ring or two on them, though. I open the door to the room really quietly, grab my clothes and bring them to the bathroom. Then, I take my time getting ready. I do 10 push-ups on the bathroom floor. After the shower, I do ten more push-ups and then get dressed. Then it's time for the hair. This always takes me a good 45 minutes to get right and styled to perfection. I then do some poses in front of the mirror and look at myself from every angle and in every way of standing. After a few tweaks to the hair and clothes, I'm ready for the challenge … the six seat challenge.

I managed to get dressed and leave the room without wakening Mandy. Before I go, I grab a pen and some paper and leave her a wee note:

I love you to the moon and back, you are my whole world. Now, my public awaits.

I can be really romantic when I want to be. Plus, I feel bad for raising my voice to her earlier. I meet with the rest of the contestants in the lobby where we're waiting to be taken to the arena. Everybody isn't as relaxed as they were at breakfast, most people have earphones in and some are standing on their own doing vocal exercises. Even Phil, the guy that was wearing the pink dressing gown at breakfast, looks a little bit nervous. He's still dressed madly, though. He's wearing a yellow belly top that reveals his stomach and chest with a pink tie. One of the producers, Tim, or clipboard Tim as I call him, gets us all together and gives a talk. It kinda reminds me on when we used to go on field trips when we were at school:

'Hey guys, right, are we all good? Okay, can I have quiet at the back please, this is very important. Firstly, there will be limousines picking us up at the front door in about five minutes time ...'

Everybody goes 'oooohh' and there's high fives all around.

'... It's very important that nobody wanders off and misses their lift, so I'm going to put you all in pairs so it's up to you to make sure your partner is with you. Also, when we get to the arena, you will receive a schedule for the day. This will mostly consist of times that you'll spend with vocal coaches, interviews, photo shoots and of course the six seat challenge itself. We will also have a rehearsal, telling you where you should be onstage tonight, and where to enter/exit. Plus, guys and girls: remember that the film crew will be filming all day so we need to see plenty of entertainment. Now, if everybody could find themselves a partner and buddy up then the limos should be here any minute.'

Mike the builder just happens to be standing beside me, so I turn to him to 'buddy up':

'Will we be buddies?'

'Well, Mick, I was kind of hoping one of those pretty young girls would be my companion for the day but …'

I nod and turn away to find somebody else.

'… I'm only fucking joking, mate, of course you can be my buddy.'

'Aw right, cool!'

'Do you take everything literally?'

I'm not even too sure what that word means, I know there's two versions of it, so I just nod.

Next thing, clipboard Tim is telling us to go out the front as the limos have arrived. Everybody is cheering and the craic is good, then we see the limos and everybody goes nuts. They're top of the range and fucking huge! The filming crew are loving it and trying to find the right angles. Me, Mike and ten others get into the first limo. I have my sunglasses on and we're all loving it. There are people gathered outside of the hotel, ordinary people who aren't on the show. Tim the producer and a few others are telling them not to be taking photos, but in fairness they're just staring in amazement. The windows are blacked out which doesn't help you much when you're wearing sunglasses inside. Just as we're pulling out, I suddenly jump off my seat and whip-off my shades. I can't get a good look at the person I seen, so I turn around to look out the back window but I can't see her now. I sit back down again, a wee bit in shock. Mike turns to me:

'Are you alright, Mickey mate, you look like you've seen a ghost!?'

A few of the others ask if I'm okay, too.

'I'm grand, I just thought I seen someone I know.'

'Well, mate, you won't see much with shades on in a blacked-out limo. Probably a fucking shadow!'

I only caught a glimpse, but even through the blacked-out windows and the shades, she looked me straight in the eye and she looked worried. There's no way it could be Laura Dillon … I think the pressure might be getting to me a wee bit.

We make it to the arena and it's all go from the start. The voice coach for our group is a man called Jeremy. He's about 50 or so, but he's cool and really knows his stuff about singing. At 11 o'clock we get a break and I check my phone. I have loads of messages and two missed calls from Mandy. I check the messages first. There are messages from my ma wishing me all the best and my aunties pretty much saying the same thing, which is nice to hear. They've all lit holy candles for me, too. I hope they work! Then there's messages from the lads saying they're proud of me, and that they can't wait to hear the craic. Sometimes I miss them, but it's nice doing stuff on my own for a change, it makes me less independent, if that's the right word? I ring Mandy back, but she doesn't answer. Then a few minutes later she rings me back:

'What was that note all about this morning, you dick?'

'Aw, aye, it was just a wee love note. Did you like it?'

'I think I should read it back to you?'

'Aye, but I remember what I wrote. Those words were from the heart.'

'How sweet ... you wrote '"I love you to moon back. You're my whore world, now my pubic awaits". What the fuck is that all about?'

I'm bad enough at writing at the best of times never mind writing in the dark!

'I meant I love you to THE moon AND back, you're my WHOLE world, now my PUBLIC awaits! I was writing in the dark, plus I was trying to do joined-up writing which I NEVER do.'

'You're a fucking idiot. I'll see you later, I'm off to get a spa treatment in the hotel.'

'Nice for some, I've just been practising with a vocal coach and now we're going to …'

Then I realise she has already hung up.

We're sitting around chatting about how the morning went, when I get another message on my phone. I think it's going to be Mandy saying her phone went dead or something, but I get a shock when I see the name… it's from Knuckles:

Hope X-Factor is going well. Just a reminder that your repayments will be starting soon. I'm not running a fucking charity.

Jesus Christ, that was the last thing I needed today. I'll chat to Mandy about it later, maybe he's just having a bad day. I don't even know how much of the six grand is left, I'd say I've blew half of it already. If I can make it through to the live finals, I'll get £200 a week which should stop me from dipping into the loan. My ma has already text me saying that if I need a few quid then she'll send it over, but there's no way I can ask her. Fuck it, I just need to blank it all out of my head and get on with the show. As the Queen once said, the show must go on.

Just before I go back to rehearsals, I get another message that I wish I hadn't opened. It's from my cousin, George the priest-boy:

When you pass through the waters, I will be with you: and through the rivers, they will not overflow you. When you walk through the fire, you will not be scorched, nor will the flame burn you. Isaiah 43:2.

He has to be on drugs of some kind. And why's he signing it 'Isaiah 43:2'? He must have been given his new cult name by the priests.

As I said before, we're doing a lot of work. And proper stuff, too, not like the crap I had to put up with in Valuesaver. The judges have spent some time with us today, too which is cool. After all the rehearsing, interviews and photo shoots, it's finally time to stop for dinner, then it's show time. They have caterers brought in who have loads of amazing posh foods. I don't have a clue what most of the food is, but I just dig in anyway. I love how everybody gets on so well, and we all support and help each other. Phil, the camp fella, is sitting beside me at dinner and he has everybody in stitches laughing. Even people who I was a bit afraid of like Minka the gangsta are pretty sound. And, I can understand them much better now. They say if you want to learn a foreign language, then you're best to go and live in that country. I'm living proof of that. We also found out who our mentors will be. They called our group (over-25s) into a big room and the mentor given to our category will come through the door. The judge hasn't a clue who they got either. I really don't care who it is to be honest. Then the door opens and it's Louis Walsh!

I'm sitting backstage with my fellow contestants, people who I now call friends. It's the turn of our category, the over-25s, to fight it out for six seats and a chance to go to the Judge's House round. As I look around the room, it's really difficult to say who will be going through. Everybody has come on so much, which is great, but also really worrying for me. Mandy is in her seat which is just off to the side of the stage. I didn't talk to her about the message from Knuckles because I didn't want to bring it up. The 14 of us who are left all get into a big circle with our arms around each other's shoulders.

Clipboard Tim then shouts:

'Okay, guys and girls, this is it. Everybody follow the prompts you have been given and remember where to move to when you have finished your song. Good luck everybody. We're ready to go in t - minus 2 minutes. '

Pretty much, we'll all be called out, one at a time and sing the song that we've been preparing all day. My song is Mirrors by Justin Timberlake.

I think I have everything down to a T. My hair is sitting perfect, my clothes are perfect and the song is perfect. After you sing your song, the judges will tell you if you're going home or if you get one of the 6 chairs. I'm seventh in line to perform which means all the seats could already be gone by the time I get there. Louis is the one who decides who goes through for us 'cause he's our mentor.

The first person to go out to sing is Mike the builder. Although he's a few years older than me, we have got on great. He's like a big brother to me, but I wouldn't tell him that, it sounds gay. I hope he gets through and I hope I get to see him again. His wife and two young kids are in the audience which makes it really hard for him. We all wish him good luck, and then Tim tells him to 'go-go-go'. We watch his performance on a TV and he totally smashes it! He sung Hey Ho by The Lumineers and the judges absolutely loved it. Mike gets the first seat, only five more left. Next up is Paul, he is one of the lads who kept himself to himself, but he's still sound as fuck. We all high five him and wish him luck, but it doesn't do any good. Louis tells him that he was good, but just not good enough. I can't help but feel a wee bit relieved, but when I see him coming past us as he leaves he looks broken. I don't want that to be me, so I get myself into a zone in my head and lock myself in. Everything else happens really quickly. Minka is up next and he gets a seat, then Maggie who also gets a seat. Sharon, the other one of the mammies of the group also gets a seat. Gavin is up next and he gets sent home. Simon said he was disappointed in his performance and he's let himself down. Fuck, that doesn't help me much being up next.

I'm standing beside clipboard Tim, waiting to be told to go on. There are only two seats left and I fucking want it more than anything in the world. My body is shaking, but it's not so much nerves, just pure energy going through my veins. Tim starts counting down:

'Ten'

This is it.

'Nine'

Concentrate Mickey.

'Eight'

This is everything you've always wanted.

'Seven'

Control your breathing.

'Six'

Sing from the heart.

'Five'

You're a star.

'Four'

Breathe.

'Three'

Come on!

'Two'

This is it.

'One'

Showtime!

'Go-go-go!'

I walk out from backstage and make my way down through the corridors and out on to the stage! The atmosphere is unbelievable, the crowd are going fucking nuts! I walk along the massive X on the stage and to the middle where I'll sing from. The lights and the noise could really make you lose it, but I keep my head focused. I'm standing there with a microphone in my hand. The crowd starts to quiet down and then it's just me standing in front of the four judges. Backstage they were smiling and good craic, but now they have serious heads on them. Louis is the first to speak:

'Mickey Doc, why do you think that you deserve one of the remaining two seats?'

'Because...'

I'm silent for about ten seconds, I know what I want to say, but there's just so much emotion built up in me I can't get the words out. I hadn't planned on speaking. A hush comes over the crowd.

'... this ... this is everything I've ever dreamed of. This to me is life ... this is it. Every breath I have taken in my life has led up to this moment right here and every breath I have left in me will finish the job. This is it, this is my destiny.'

I don't even know where those words came from, but the audience goes mental. They're all nodding at each other and I can see that my words touched them. Then Simon speaks:

'Okay, Mickey Doc, let's hear it, good luck.'

The crowd goes silent again and I start singing. Every note and every sound is delivered from a place inside me. I'm back in my bedroom in Derry, singing away and there's absolutely nobody else there. The song ends and the next thing I'm snapped back to reality and I'm standing in a room in front of thousands of people and four judges. The rest of my life will be decided in the next few minutes. The audience loved it and I can tell that the judges did, too. Cheryl speaks then:

'Mickey, Mickey, Mickey Doc. My word, you really gave that everything. You had me hooked from before the song when you made that little speech. It actually gave me goose bumps and I can see how much this means to you, man. That performance was one of the best of the series so far. If it were up to me, you'd have a seat.'

'Thank hi, cheers Cheryl.'

Then it's Louis's turn:

'Mickey, that was a brilliant performance. I've watched you backstage and everybody loves you, including myself. You definitely have a recording voice and nobody can question how much you want it. But …'

But? What the fuck?

'… I only have two seats left and this has been, by far, the best group I've had to mentor. The question I have to ask myself is can you go all the way? Have you got what it takes to win this show? I believe that answer is yes … Well done, Mickey Doc, take your seat.'

Mickey Doc

I feel like I'm going to explode with happiness at this moment! I thank Louis and thank the judges then I blow a kiss to Mandy. I'm shaking like a leaf and I'm trying my best not to cry. Somehow, I make my way over to Mike, Minka, Maggie and Sharon. They're all standing up applauding and I go to high five them. Then I realise that high fives aren't enough, so I hug all of them and nearly squeeze the life out of them. I watch the other acts perform and I can feel exactly what they're feeling when they're out there and I feel so bad for the others who didn't make it. The last seat went to Godfrey who was the last person I thought we'd see crying. This is the group I'll be going to the Judge's House with. This is my band of brothers ... and mammies.

CHAPTER 14.

Five days after the X-Factor six seat challenge and I'm back in Derry. The night after the show there was a party thrown for us in the hotel, and we all got absolutely pissed. Mandy said she wasn't feeling well so she wouldn't have a drink and went to bed early. She seemed pretty shocked when I told her about the message that Knuckles had sent me about the money. She said it was nothing to do with her, and then she went to bed. When I woke up the next morning (clean dying, of course), I asked her about it again and she told me I was 'a total dick', packed her things and left. It all happened so quickly. The last I heard from her was two days ago when she text me to say she 'needs time to sort her head out'.

My head has been well and truly melted about the whole thing, because, and I know this sounds totally gay, but I really do think I love her. It must be real love, too, because we haven't had sex in over a month and I still feel the same way. She always seemed to have a sore head or was feeling too tired, but that never put me off her. In fact, I think it made me want her more which is weird. The only thing keeping me going is knowing that my TV debut will be made tomorrow evening, when the first X-Factor episode will be shown. I just wish

Mandy was with me for it. My ma has invited everybody around to the house to watch it and I've invited the lads. That leaves me just one more day until I'm properly famous, and I can't fucking wait!

Ever since I've got back, there has been something that has been worrying me and it seems to be getting worse. It's not just the fact that I owe six grand to a loan shark, or that my girlfriend isn't talking to me, it's something closer to home. Everybody is well aware of the on-going feud that I've been having with my ma's dog. It's been going on since she first brought it into our house, many years ago. My ma used to treat it like another child, even though she had me. It was as if I wasn't good enough anymore so she got something else to look after. It used to try to be my friend at the start, but I was having none of it. Then as the years went on, it started to hate me as much as I hate it. This week, though, things have taken another twist: I've started to notice other dogs gathering outside the house and they bark at me when I go outside the gate. Every day there seems to be more, and I honestly think the fucker has gathered up his mates because I'm back in town.

It's 11am in the morning and I want to head into town to get a new top for my TV debut on Saturday night, but I can't leave the house because of the gang of dogs outside. My ma had spent the morning making sandwiches for tomorrow night and now she's gone to get decorations.

My da is in bed because he was working last night and only got home at 9 o'clock. I was about to leave the house about half an hour ago, but then I noticed the amount of dogs. There must be about 20 of them and they're all just pacing about outside our gate and looking angry. As soon as I stepped out, they started barking and growling so I went back inside to come up with a plan. My ma's mutt was standing at the kitchen door going mad too, so I fucked him out into the back garden and shouted after him:

'You're barking mad for thinking you could take me on. You've just declared war on the wrong guy, FUCKER!'

I just wish somebody had of been there when I came out with that cracker line!

I think I'll put it on Facebook.

My first plan seemed pretty solid. I got a tray of sandwiches that my ma made for tomorrow night and started throwing them up the street so the dogs would run after them, and I could make my getaway. Turns out even the dogs on the street wouldn't touch her food, they just sniffed at it, turned their noses up then ran back to the gate as I was about to slip out. So I ran back into the house and came up with plan B: make loads of noise and waken my da, then ask him to drop me into town. His car is parked in the driveway so it means the dogs couldn't get at me. If I had rung a taxi, then I'd still have to get past the gang. I can't believe I'm being held hostage in my own house by a gang of fucking dogs!

My da is really hard to waken up! I started off by banging doors – that didn't work. Then, I got the metal tray that the sandwiches were on and dropped it on the tiled floor in the hall – still snoring. Then I started running up and down the stairs really fast until I ran out of breath, but that didn't do it. In the end up I had to run in and start shaking him:

'Da, da, waken up, it's okay, it's just a bad dream you're having!'

He opens his eyes, but he doesn't have a clue what's going on:

'What the fu... what? What's wrong, why did you wake me?'

'You were having a nightmare, you were calling out 'help-help!' so I came running up to see what was wrong!'

'Was I?'

'You were, aye.'

'Jesus, I don't remember what I was dreaming about!'

'It must have been a scary one, I honestly thought something really bad was happening so I came straight away!'

He rubs his hands over his face really hard to wake himself up. He looks absolutely wrecked! I suppose, though, the poor fucker has only been in bed a few hours.

'What time is it?'

'It's nearly 12 o'clock.'

'Fuck that, I'm going back to sleep!'

'You can't go back to sleep straight after a nightmare, everybody knows that! Here, I brought you up a coffee to settle your nerves.'

He takes the hot mug of coffee and stares at it, still half-sleeping. Then his brain starts working again:

'How did you have time to make me a cup of coffee when you thought I was in trouble and came straight up?'

'Now, now… don't be asking questions, just get that into you and you'll be grand. Your body is probably still in shock after the nightmare.'

He's still staring at the cup:

'But …'

'No buts, just get it into you.'

I tip the bottom of the mug and move it towards his mouth and he drinks it. He'll be up out of bed in no time. I stay with him until he drinks the rest of it, then I head down to the living room and wait for him to get up. Five minutes later he's coming down the stairs, whistling.

'Where's your ma at?'

'She went up to the shops to get decorations, then she's heading over to my Aunty Margret's'

'Decorations for what?'

'Ah, for my X-Factor TV debut?'

Jesus, if I wasn't looking for a lift I'd be giving him a lot of cheek for that!

'Aye, sure I know it's your TV thing, but I didn't think there'd be decorations. Is there such a thing as X-Factor decorations?'

Even with me needing a lift, I'm still coming close to calling him a dick and storming out. Only thing holding me back is the four-legged wank gang that have the front gate surrounded.

'I think she's just getting standard decorations. Are you by any chance heading into town today?'

'Well, I hadn't planned to. Why?'

'It's just, I need to head into town and get a few things and it's … um … raining outside. I don't want to be getting a flu and me going to the Judge's House in a couple of weeks. But, if you don't want to then I can go and get soaked and possibly ruin the rest of my life.'

I can be an absolute dick to him, but I know how to get round him too.

'Aye, well I'll scoot you into town then, let me just throw on me.'

Works every time. He goes upstairs to get changed and while he's away, I go out to the back window and give the mutt the middle finger. Two minutes later he's back down again.

'Are ye ready?'

'Aye, I've been ready for over an hour!'

He grabs his keys and we head out the door. I'm walking like Johnny Big Balls, smiling over at the dogs and giving them the middle finger. They start barking and jumping on the gates like mentalists, which makes me get a bit carried away, and before I know it I have my top off and I'm swinging it around my head while hopping on one foot singing:

'Who let the dogs out, WHO –WHO-WHO-WHO!?'

Mickey Doc

I don't know how long I was doing this, but when I turned around again my da was just standing there with his mouth open. After about 30 seconds, he said:

'Are you alright Mickey? You're not into drugs, are you?'

'Jesus! Naw! Fuck that. It's just them dogs have been gathering outside the house and they've been annoying me. Can I ask you a question?'

He still looks worried:

'Aye, of course you can.'

'Can dogs talk to each other, like, to arrange something?'

'Well, they can certainly communicate with each other. Why?'

'No reason.'

We pull out of the driveway and the dogs are sniffing at the car and pushing into each other:

'She's on heat, ye see. She's bringing dogs in from everywhere!'

He says it with a smile on his face? I don't have a clue what 'on heat' means either. I definitely must Google it later. Then my da sees the sandwiches on the road. Seems like there was more on the tray than I thought:

'What in the hell is that …'

'…That's them fucking dogs causing a mess. That's it, I'm ringing the authorities!'

Fucking score! My ma's sandwiches might just do the trick! I give them the middle finger again as we drive off.

My da drops me off in town and I go around the shops looking for a new top, possibly even some new shoes, jeans and sunglasses. The worst thing about shopping in Derry is that if you get a nice top, the chances are somebody else is going to have it, and the last thing I want at my X-Factor party is some dickhead with the same top as me. So I head up to Austins department store, they have designer stuff that definitely nobody else will have. When I worked in Valuesaver, I couldn't even afford to look in the window of this place, never mind shop there. After about 45 minutes of trying stuff on and looking around, I finally decide on a totally class shirt that nobody else will have because it costs £150. I also pick up a pair of sunglasses at £50, too, then I start to get hungry. As I'm heading out the door of Austins, I whip out my phone and see that I have five new text messages. My heart misses a beat because suddenly I'm standing still, hoping that at least one of them is from Mandy and she has her head sorted. My hand is shaking and I feel myself starting to feel sick in my stomach. The first three messages are from Mike, Minka and Godfrey from the X-factor, basically seeing how I was and asking if I'm excited about Saturday night. It's great that we all text each other often. It's like we're part of something that nobody else can be a part of or knows what it's like to be a part of it. We've kept in touch loads, but they're not who I was hoping it would be. The next one is from Decky saying that him, Marty and Stevie are heading into town for lunch and if I fancy it. I text him back and we arrange to meet in half an hour in Fitzroys. It'll be my treat. Marty can fuck off if he thinks he's paying. The last message is a major fucking let-down. It's from my ma. It says:

Mickey, I'm not accusing you, but why is the full tray of salad sandwiches that I made thrown around the front street?

Salad sandwiches? That's why the dogs didn't eat them! I remember hearing one time that dogs are cannibals, so they only eat meat. Fuck!

Me and the lads are sitting in Fitzroys, stuffing our faces. I've been telling them all about my X-Factor adventures and they are loving it. They just can't get enough of my stories and they seem to be really looking forward to tomorrow night. Marty and Stevie start taking the piss a bit, but it's only banter:

'So, you're going to Louis Walsh's house then? Louis is going to get a bit of Mickey?'

'Fuck off, ye dicks!'

'Wouldn't be the first time!'

Then Decky jumps in and asks a sensible question:

'So when do you go to Louis's house then?'

'We go there in three weeks' time for three days. 13th of September, I have to be in London and then we go to the house the next day. I'm hoping it's somewhere really warm and glamorous!'

'Nice one, man, remember to take loads of photos!'

'Aye, I will alright. I need to ask you guys something serious now. I think I may need some back-up and I may need your help.'

The lads all look at each other like they seen it coming, but didn't want to say anything?

Then Marty says:

'Man, we were talking about this earlier, Decky and Stevie reckon you should go to the police. I don't think that's your best option. Remember the gangster bloke I told you about that used to live down the street from me? Well, I got in contact with him and he says he'll see what he could do, but he'd need to hear from you first.'

'Jesus, naw, I'm not talking about THAT problem! I'm kinda hoping when I get enough money together I can just pay off Knuckles and learn from my lessons …'

Not that this imaginary gangster could help me anyway.

'… No, this is a gang closer to home that is waiting outside my front door.'

They all look at each other in shock. Decky is the first to speak:

'Jesus Christ, Mickey, what sorta bother have you got yourself into now, hi?'

'Well, you know my ma's dog …'

They all just nod and look confused.

'… and you know the way I've always hated the fucker?'

'Aye, you were always putting it in the Buy and Sell, at least twice a week if I remember?'

'Yes, well, it looks like the fucker is fighting back. He's got all his mates to gather outside my house waiting on me, and I don't know what to do. I tried throwing sandwiches but that didn't work.'

Again, they're all looking at each other in … I think the word is disbelief?

'My da said something about them being on heat? Anybody know what that means? Does it mean they're angry? They definitely look angry.'

They all look at each other for a few seconds, trying to work things out in their heads. Decky is the first to speak:

'Mickey, firstly, the dogs aren't gathered up to give you a hiding. Secondly, your ma's dog is a she dog. And thirdly, she's on heat which means she's ready to reproduce. The dogs outside your house can smell it. They're not angry, they're horny.'

'Are you sure?'

'Mickey, you're our mate and all, but you're thicker than the River Foyle!'

Next of all, the lads are burst out laughing, like really bent over laughing with tears coming out of their eyes. People in the restaurant are turning around to see what's happening. The sight of them laughing gets me going too, and we all just sit there for the next ten minutes laughing so much we can't speak. Sometimes I surprise myself by how stupid I really am, but the laughing makes me feel better.

The big night is finally here, and we're all gathered around the TV in my house. My ma has the place looking well, fair play to her. All my aunties and uncles are here and a few of my cousins, including George the priest-boy. Doesn't he have mass or something to be at? The lads are also here and we're necking back the beers. The craic is good and everybody is wishing me luck and telling me how excited they are. I also got a text from Mandy today saying:

We'll be watching tonight, can't wait.

It wasn't much, but it just felt so good to hear from her and it put me in even better form. Marty asks me if Laura Dillon is coming over, but I can't tell him that she hasn't been stalking me anymore since Mandy pretty much threatened her.

Next thing I know, it's about to start. Everybody is saying 'sshhhh' at the same time which makes it really loud and everybody seems to be telling everybody else to sshhh, even though they're sshhh-ing too. Then a big cheer goes up when we see the opening credits of a large X zooming through space like a meteor and the familiar X-Factor tune in the background.. It's going really fast and it's heading for earth. It has a big flame behind it as it makes its way down to earth and into London, and the hairs are standing on the back of my neck! Then they start showing the queues that were outside the first auditions. I get flashbacks when I see the queue I was in, in Manchester. That was where I first met Mandy and she pretended to be a reporter and made me out to be a bit touched. I wish she was here with me, but I just text her:

Thats were we furst met.

I see a few people I recognise, including the bloke who was dressed up as a cow and Mandy threatened. I have a huge smile on my face. They introduce all the judges and everybody cheers. Everyone is having good craic and shouting stuff like:

'What's Cowell like in real life, Mickey?'

'Aye, Simon is sound.'

'Ooohh so it's Simon to his mates is it?'

'What's that Cheryl Cole one like. Is she a cracker in real life, too?'

'Aye, she is, da. She's married now, though, and called Cheryl Fernandez Versini!'

Mickey Doc

'That wouldn't stop me!'

A big roar goes up and I look around to see my ma giving my da a dirty look. He's half-pissed so he doesn't care. I get a text back from Mandy:

I should have battered that fookin' dickhead when I had a chance!

The first contestant up is absolutely crap! He's one of those ones that the crowd start booing and the judges slate him.

Somebody, I think it might have been my uncle, shouts from the back:

'I hope you're fucking better than him, Mickey?'

Everybody laughs. As I said, there's a good atmosphere.

Then an ad comes on and everybody starts chatting again. George the priest-boy comes over to me:

'Looking forward to seeing you, Michael. The whole family is extremely proud of you.'

I don't know if it's the drink or the excitement, but I end up giving him a high-five and telling him his messages are always nice to get when I'm away, but I can never tell if he thinks I'm lying or not. The show comes back on and a big cheer goes up again. The next thing we hear is Dermot O'Leary's voice:

Next up we have a contestant who has given up a lot just to compete in this year's X-Factor.

Then it cuts to me talking and the whole room explodes into cheers:

Well my name's Mickey Doc and I'm 25 years old and from Derry in Northern Ireland...

A big cheer goes up again:

Well, I worked in a shop called Valuesaver up until a couple of days ago but I quit because I was coming here to win. I'm living my dream right now. I've dreamt about this since I was a wain- a kid, so now I'm going to go on and win and prove everybody wrong.

Then it flashes to me in front of the judges. Everyone in the room is chanting:

'MICKEY- MICKEY- MICKEY!'

Then people start ssshhing again when Simon goes to speak. I must say, I look class on the TV:

'Welcome, and your name is?'

Somebody shouts from the back, I think it might have been my da:

'That's Mickey Doc, ye prick ye, Cowell.'

Everybody sshhh's him.

Mickey Doc

'My name is Mickey Doc, I'm 25 and I'm from Derry in Northern Ireland.'

'So what's you background?'

'Well, I lived at home with my ma and da, but I left there to come over to follow my dreams.'

My da shouts again:

'Woooo you gave your oul' ma and da a mention!'

'Shut up, John, or you're going outside!'

My ma is getting seriously pissed with him.

Cheryl speaks next:

'You left Derry? You mean permanently?'

'Aye, well this is what I want to do so I jacked in my job and came over here.'

Cheryl keeps talking:

'And what did you work at?'

'I worked in a supermarket at home. I never liked it: I always knew there was something else for me.'

'And what's your musical background?'

'Well, I haven't really sung in front of anybody before. Well, except in front of my ma a few years ago.'

This is the bit where Simon rolls his eyes, all my family and friends boo him:

'So you've never done any sort of public performances, but you decided you would give up your job to try to win the X-Factor?'

'Aye, pretty much.'

'OK, let's hear what you got.'

All of a sudden everybody in the living room goes absolutely quiet. I'm nervous myself even though I know I done class. I have tears in my eyes while watching myself sing on TV. It's an amazing moment in my life. Everybody is cheering and hugging me when the song is finished, then the room goes silent again for the judges' reaction. I look around but I don't see my ma, she's not where she was before. Maybe she can't watch anymore.

The judges are giving me all the amazing compliments and every time they do, a huge roar goes up! People are chanting my name and I feel like a superstar. I can tell by my da's eyes that he's pretty pissed, but he's looking at me like I've never seen him look at me before – with pride. I move through the crowd of people. Decky, Marty and Stevie are all hugging me and dancing about. I'm loving every minute of it. My da gives me a big hug:

'I'm fucking proud of you, Mickey, that was class!'

'Thanks da, where's my ma?'

'I think she went out for some air. It was all getting too much for her.'

I head out to find her, there's a few people in the back garden who are smoking and they seem to be all around my ma and consoling her, if that's even a word? Decky, Stevie and Marty are behind me and I walk over to her. She's absolutely crying her eyes out which sets me off, too. I promised myself I wouldn't cry. Then she says something that totally knocks me off my feet:

'I came out for air and seen him lying in the corner, not moving, he's dead, Mickey. My precious little dog is dead!'

I'm stunned. I can't believe the little bastard, even in his last breaths he's stealing my lightning. She's crying her eyes out.

Marty, Stevie and Decky are all staring at me like I've done something wrong:

'That had fuck all to do with me!'

CHAPTER 15.

This is a text I woke up to this morning:

I seen you on the TV last night. I spent the whole time trying to decide which of your legs I'll use to smash your ugly face in with. 5 grand before the end of September, otherwise your interest doubles and you lose a leg.

Ugly face? Seriously? This coming from a bloke who has a face like a melted wheelie bin! I'm illiterally shaking with anger!

After I calmed down about the disgusting insult, I realised that Knuckles isn't the person I thought he was and I might be in danger. I was about to text Mandy, to see if she could help, but we're not really on speaking terms at the moment. I text her back twice last night, but she never replied. My heart feels like it has been kicked about, but I know she'll come back to me sooner or later. I can't tell anybody else about the threat because they're all real proud of me for once, and I definitely can't balls that up. I have a full month to come up with the money he wants, if I don't get it sorted in the meantime. I need to push this to the back of mind for the moment and focus on being Derry's latest superstar. Actually, Derry's only REAL superstar, in my opinion. How could anybody become a superstar with an ugly face? They couldn't, that's how, it just wouldn't happen. Full-stop. Ugly! What a dick!

The main reason I have to put the threat to the back of my mind is that I have two interviews lined up already. The Derry radio station, Radio Foyle and the Derry News, were both on the phone this morning. Obviously, the local radio and newspaper people are going to be the first to get in there when somebody local makes the step from zero to hero. Not that I was ever an actual zero, I was always a bit more than that, probably a seven or an eight – maybe even a nine.

I need to be at Radio Foyle for 11 o'clock, then, I'm meeting a reporter from the Derry News at one. I think fame even helps with hangovers 'cause I ended up rubbered last night and I feel grand today. My da is going to drop me to the radio station when he gets up, it's only 9 o'clock now, but I can't sleep 'cause of the excitement. My ma is sitting at the kitchen table drinking her coffee and staring into space. She looks like shit.

'So I have to make my own breakfast, then?'

'I can't believe she's gone.'

'Who?'

'Who? WHO? A member of our family dies last night and you ask 'who?'

I just ignore her when she's in that sort of a mood. Anything I do say will end up in her being a total dick. She just sits there like she's in an episode of Eastenders or something. Pure drama queen. I can't help myself: I start whistling 'How Much is that Doggy on the Window', but she doesn't even flinch. I end up just making cornflakes because it's handy, then I go upstairs to make myself ready for my public. My Facebook and Twitter has gone through the roof with the amount of people following me and sending friend requests. People from everywhere have sent messages, but I'm not going to reply to any: there's no way any properly famous people would get back to you when you send them a message, it just doesn't happen.

It's 10.30 now and my da is about to drop me to Radio Foyle. For years, I've been practising doing press interviews. I'd sit in front of the mirror for hours and interview myself. I'd say I could even become a talk show host with the amount of practice I've had. I'm waiting at the front door for my da. He's in the kitchen trying to say nice things to my ma, to make her feel better. Somebody get me a fucking bucket! I end up shouting:

'Hurry up!'

Mickey Doc

I can hear him giving it loads to her:

'Look, love, how about you and me go out for a nice meal tonight and a few drinks. Just the two of us, it'll help take your mind off things?'

'That sounds nice, John.'

'Okay, I'll see you when I get back, love.'

These two make me sick. This is the start of the biggest time of my life and they're acting like someone just died. I'm just standing there tapping my watch when he comes out of the kitchen.

He talks to me quietly when he closes the kitchen door:

'Try to be understanding with your mother, she's just lost her pet – and she was like a member of the family.'

'In case neither of you have noticed, you already HAVE a member of the family standing right here.'

'It's just a hard time for her.'

'Blah, blah, blah… Am I going to have to listen to this all the time now?'

He just shakes his head and grabs his keys. He knows I'm right. We walk out to the car and one of the neighbours shouts across the street:

'Seen you on the TV last night, Mickey. Never knew you had it in ye!'

'Thanks, Jack! Onwards and onwards!'

Jack is about 50 and a bit nuts. Actually, he's proper nuts! He has a shaved head and shitty-looking tattoos all over his arms. They look like a child did them. Probably done them himself.

'And don't be letting those English bastards take the piss out of ye, Mickey!'

Then he just kicks the fence and sends one of the boards spinning across the street. It's his own fence, too. As I said before, the bloke is fucking nuts. We just jump in the car really quickly and drive off. See, if you give Jack an audience, he'll wreck the fucking street, he's done it loads of times. I look back and he's taking his top off like he's going to fight somebody, but there's nobody there. One time the Jehovah's Witnesses came to his door and he got angry and ended up burning a car. It was his own car.

My da leaves me outside the radio station and I head in, sunglasses and all on. I can see people looking at me like they know me. I go to reception, and there's a really hot blonde there. I'm just standing, leaning on the reception, looking really cool. She's probably used to shite people coming in to get interviewed about things like winning £100 in the bingo, or some crap like that so I must be a breath of fresh hair. And my hair looks fresh as fuck.

Mickey Doc

'Hello, can I help you?'

I just lift the shades up so she can recognise the face. She just keeps on looking at me. After about a minute of me standing there like that:

'Can I help you sir?'

She must be thick. I point at my face and take the shades off altogether, she still doesn't get it!

'Mickey Doc.'

'Sorry?'

'I'm Mickey Doc, I'm here to be interviewed!'

'Oh, okay, let me just check the schedule ...'

Even if I wasn't involved with someone else, there's no way I'd go out with her after that, the bitch.

'... oh, okay, Mickey Doc, here you are. You were on the X-Factor last night? I didn't get to see it, but I have it recorded. I heard you were brilliant, congratulations.'

Actually, she's not too bad. I probably would go out with her now If I wasn't already involved with Mandy, of course.

'Thanks very much, I'm just trying to keep my feet on the ground.'

'That's good, now if you'd just like to wait over there and I'll give you a wee shout when we're ready to get you sorted. You're due on in about half an hour, but before that, one of the producers will go through things with you. Would you like some tea or coffee?'

'I'm more of a champagne kind of a guy now.'

She looks at me like she's trying to work out if I'm serious or not. Obviously, she's not used to somebody as rock and roll as me.

'We just have tea or coffee.'

'Tea then... two sugars.'

Half an hour later and I'm sitting across from the radio presenter. It's a good job he chose radio because there's no way he'd get on TV with a head like that. I try to push this thought out of my mind so that the interview won't suffer. It's a kinda technique I discovered.

'Well, listeners, we have a wee treat in store for you this morning... millions of people throughout the UK and Ireland tuned in last night to watch the ever-popular X-Factor talent show, and, if you saw it, you will have been blown away by a young Derry man who lit up the auditions with his version of a One Direction song. That young man is here with me in the studio right now, and his name is Mickey Doc. Mickey, how are you feeling this morning after the show aired last night?'

'Pure class. It's like all my dreams are coming true. I've dreamt about this moment since I was a wean.... '

'That's brilliant, and wha…'

'I mean I dreamt about being on the X-Factor since I was a wean, not this radio show. Let me just clear that up first.'

I don't want this joker thinking it's all about him.

'Okay… well, we knew what you meant anyway, Mickey. So, tell us, what was it like standing in front of some of the biggest names in the music industry and singing to them? That must have been frightening?'

'Aye, well it was a bit scary alright, but I was focused on what I had to do and I'm sure you'll agree it went class.'

'Yes, it went very well indeed. Simon seemed to have a bit of a face on him when you told them you hadn't sung in public before. I think everyone thought you were going to fail miserably, did you get a sense of that when you were on stage, or were you just focused on the job at hand?'

'I think Simon was just playing up to the camera. He could see that I was a talent straight away, that's what he does.'

'And did you get to talk to him afterwards?'

'Well, I've chatted to him a few times since, he's actually pretty sound.'

'And what about your parents, Mickey? They must have been nervous seeing you standing up there?'

'They weren't actually there for the audition, but they did watch it last night.'

'They must be really proud today, then?'

'Aye, you would think so. My ma's dog died last night during the show and she's been pretty unbearable since.'

'Oh, my God! Sorry to hear about your mother's dog, that can be a big loss to a family. How old?'

'58.'

'Is that dog years?'

'What do you mean?'

'Isn't one dog year the equivalent to seven of human years? That would have made your dog... 8 and a half?'

'I don't have a clue what age the dog was. My ma is 58.'

'Your mother is 58?? Let's hope your mum isn't one of these women who don't like their age being discussed? Especially not on live radio!'

'She's definitely one of them. She tells people she's 52, but I could bring you in her passport to prove it?'

He laughs again, but it's like a nervous laugh?

'No, there's no need for you to bring in your mums passport. So, Mickey, do you think you can go far on the X-Factor?'

'I'm going to win the whole thing. I've been planning this since I could walk and there's nothing that's going to stop me.'

'Have you always been this confident, Mickey?'

'Not really, not in most things. I did always believe that I could sing though, and I know I have the looks to go with it.'

'And I believe that you gave up your job to pursue your dream? That's a very brave move that most people wouldn't make in such hard times, but I suppose that shows your confidence in your ability?'

'Aye, I worked in Valuesaver and to be honest I always felt that there was something bigger out there for me. I used to be bored out of my head every day, and all that kept me going was my dreams and my dream is to be a superstar. I want paparazzi following me everywhere I go. I want people to ask for my autograph when I walk down the street. I want to wear sunglasses all the time. I want more money than I know how to spend. I want to be like my heroes, Little Mix, and have people look at me and say: 'There's the fella that changed the music scene forever.' I want to be famous. I want to be a millionaire. I want to win the X-Factor.'

'You want all that?'

'Yep, but most of all I'll keep my feet firmly on the ground.'

'Well, Mickey, I admire your confidence. We'd like to wish you all the best with the rest of your exciting journey, and maybe you'll call into us again for a chat?'

'Is that it?'

'Ha, ha, ha, yes that's it, Mickey. Unfortunately, we have time schedules to stick to on the radio, but thank you again. Keep an eye out for that name in the future folks, Mickey Doc. Next on the show we have the news followed by an in-depth look into the decline in bingo halls around the country and how that is affecting rural life. Stay tuned folks...'

Then all of a sudden I'm being hurried out of the studio and back into the waiting area. It all happened so fast, I thought I was going to be in there for about an hour or so. The producer comes over to talk to me, but I just take out my phone and check my messages as I'm walking out the door. Fuck them, they get a local star on and they just want to talk for a few minutes. No thanks, dickhead! 120 new Facebook friend requests since I've been in there and I have a load of new text messages. The first one is from Marty:

Got d new wheels today, Marty's Mobile Shop is in business! Meeting the lads for pints this afternoon to celebrate if u fancy it?

Stevie and Decky send pretty much the same thing. The next one is from my da:

Proud of you, son, and all that, but stay out of the house for a while, your ma is throwing a wobbler!

I went and totally nailed the Derry News interview after I left the radio station. I definitely would have nailed the newspaper woman, too, absolute cracker and she was definitely flirting with me in a big way. She seemed really into me 'cause she kept asking loads of questions and gave wee smiles every time I answered. When she asked if I was

seeing anybody, I had to tell her that I was and I apologised if I may

have been leading her on. She seemed to take it pretty well, though.

She had a photographer with her, too, and I'd say he felt like a bit of a

third wheel with all the sexual chemistry going back and forth between

us. He seemed pretty sound, though, to be fair:

'Maybe we could head up the Derry Walls to get a few snaps, Mickey?'

'Aye, sounds good to me. Are you coming, too, Rochelle?'

I think that was her name anyway, I wasn't really listening when she

told me. She's putting her notebook into her bag:

'No, I need to get back to the office for another job, but thanks for your

time today, Mickey, and all the best on the X-Factor.'

She puts out her hand to shake mine, but I reach in and kiss her twice

on each cheek. Everybody does it that way when they're famous. She's

starting to blush a bit so I decide to put on a few moves:

'Rochelle, you are the type of girl I would totally go for. Why don't

you give me your number and if things don't work out with the girl I'm

in love with at the minute, then I'll give you a call and maybe I could

take you out for dinner or something?'

She looks over at the photographer bloke, I think she might be shy because he's standing there looking on. He's obviously never seen somebody with the confidence that I have because he looks pretty shocked.

'That's… that's… a great offer, Mickey, but how about you just concentrate on the girl that you're in love with right now?'

Yep, the photographer bloke has definitely made it awkward for her, I can tell.

'Aye, I will, but I'm just saying "if"… Add me on Facebook sure.'

'Em… okay… am… I have to get back to the office now, thanks again.'

Then I think 'fuck it, might as well':

'Actually, here's my number anyway, just in case.'

Then I whisper to her:

'And don't mind him, he's just jealous he ain't got the moves like Mickey.'

Then I give her a playful wink. Chicks love that craic.

All of a sudden, she turns to the photographer bloke and says something that almost knocks me off my feet:

'I'll see you later, darling. Ring me after you pick Aoife up from school and make sure she has her PE bag with her, she's always leaving it behind.'

Then he says:

'What time will you be back, remember we're going around to my mum's tonight, she's cooking for the whole family.'

'Of course! I'll be back about 6:30 and I'll pick up a bottle of red on the way.'

He followed that up with landing a big kiss on her lips.

As you could probably guess, the next hour up the Derry Walls was the most awkward hour of my life – and I've been in some awkward situations. We barely spoke the whole time, it was just him telling me where to stand and where to look as he took loads of photos with me in different poses. We went the whole way around the walls and he had a smug look on his face the whole time, the wanker! Loads of people stopped to see what was going on trying to figure out who I was, but it's only tourists that walk around the walls so nobody recognised me. One old woman from Scotland thought I was Daniel O'Donnel and asked for my autograph which made the photographer-wanker laugh out loud. After that, I just told him I've had enough and went to the Bentley to meet the lads.

It seems like life is moving on for all of us: Marty has his own business (his words, not mine. I think it's just a big tuck shop but I'm not going to tell him that 'cause he's a mate), Stevie just got a big promotion at his da's business and Decky is going out with somebody (a bloke, because he's gay). And I don't mean that in a bad way like, he is actually gay). We're all already pretty drunk and the craic is good:

'Right, this really calls for champagne!'

That was Stevie. I let him know that I won't be buying:

'You can fuck off if you think I'm buying four bottles this time!'

Everybody laughs. Then Marty has to get in a dig at me:

'I think you're in enough debt as it is!'

Everybody laughs again which makes me pull out my wallet:

'Fuck you, Marty, I'm going to buy eight bottles, ye prick!'

Then they all start telling me to put my money away and get down off the stool. I can't let it go but:

'Do you sell champagne in your tuck-shop, Marty?'

'Tuck-shop? Little acorns my friend, little acorns.'

'Who the fuck is going to buy acorns? '

Then they all start laughing again. Sometimes I don't know if they're laughing with me or at me. I could be a comedy genius and I don't even know it. Then Decky jumps in:

'Never mind the champagne, why don't we just drink beer like we always do and leave it at that? I thought I heard somebody on the radio today saying that he wants to keep his feet firmly on the ground?'

I think that was directed at me, but before I could figure it out, everybody starts laughing again which makes me laugh. I love having a laugh with my mates because it stops me thinking about all the other stuff that's going on: Knuckles, the loan, Mandy and all that. The lads never seem to mention Mandy and I can tell that it's because they don't like her, but that's just because they don't know her like I do. We end up doing shots at the bar and the last thing I remember is Stevie telling me something about Laura Dillon. He said that his cousin hangs around with her, but Laura has moved away from Derry to clear her head and to stop thinking about me. That knocks me back, because underneath her mad stalking ways she was actually really nice and supportive to me. I think the whole Mandy threatening her thing hurt her too. I'd love to talk to her again, to tell her I appreciate what she done for me, but I know that Mandy would go fucking nuts if she thought I got back in contact again. After that, everything is a blank. I don't even remember getting home, which is always a sign of a good night.

I wake up the next morning with the worst hangover ever! It's as if the hangover from the day before and last night got together and made a super-hangover. I check my phone and I have a message from Mandy. Then a sudden fear comes over me, it's not like a real memory, but I know somehow that I text her last night. I look at my phone for a few minutes, trying to remember, before I open her message. The most recent message she sent to me was:

Ok, I'm glad you understand, see you soon. **03:11**

As usual, I understand fuck-all, so I read back through our texts in the order they were sent:

I'll do that then. I love U Mandy. **02:59**

Fuck.

No mickey - things are complicated and I have things to sort out here.

Stay there for a while. You go to the Judge's House on the 13th?

Come over a day or 2 before and we'll talk.   **02:58**

What the…?

Im gona come over 2moro 2u. We can b family   02:46

Jesus, I must have been pished!

3 months. I don't know what to do.   02:44

3 months since what?

FCUK FUCK How long?   02:37

??

I'm pregnant.   02:36

Tell me!   02:34

There's something I need to tell you.   02:34

I miss U. U can keep doin.   02:27

*Things are different, I can't keep doing what I'm doing to you
Mickey.   02:26*

Hey. I miss U. Do U miss me?   02:18

CHAPTER 16.

I'm sitting at the airport looking at a family that's sitting across from me. It's a mammy, a daddy and a wee boy that's about five or six years old. He's running around with a sword and he's pretending to fight people with it. The mammy and daddy are both on their phones and not even looking at him. I can see that the wee boy is trying to get their attention, but they're too busy with their Facebook or whatever else they're looking at. I'm watching him for ages, and the only time the ma or da have looked up from their phones is when the wee lad fell over while trying to kick a fly. My first reaction was to jump out of my seat to help, that must be the parent instinct kicking in, but as soon as I did, the da lifted him up and told him to stop being so clumsy. I was already on my feet, so I had to pretend I was getting up to stretch. As I sit back down, I notice that there's a woman sitting beside me. She's about 70, so I'm way out of her league. I can sense that she's been looking at me a while, so I say 'hello'. I hope I don't give her the wrong idea. She says hello back then asks me:

'Do you have any children yourself?'

'Erm... no, not really. Actually, no, I don't. What about you?'

She answers, but she doesn't really seem to be talking to me, she's kinda talking to herself?'

'A boy and a girl, Jamie and Suzie.'

'Cool, what age are they?'

'They're twins and they're 35.'

'Twins? Are they identical?'

She looks at me and smiles:

'No, they're not identical. They live in Australia, that's where I'm going now. I haven't seen them in just over four years. Well, I've seen them on Skype and in photos, but ... but it's just not the same is it?'

'Naw, I suppose it's not.'

She's looking into the distance again:

'They both have their own lives now, they've even given me grandchildren. Last time I went to visit, Jamie's child was only a few weeks old. Aw, he was gorgeous, and still is of course. I remember holding him in my arms and looking into his little eyes, you would swear he'd knew I'd come all that way to hold him because he stopped crying as soon as I nursed him. And now Suzie has had a little girl, four weeks old she is, and I'm going to meet her for the first time.'

I can tell she's crying without even looking, I don't want to look at her 'cause I know I'll cry, too. It has me thinking about the baby that Mandy is carrying … my baby. I hope my ma isn't going to be like that, having to see her grandchild in photographs.

The wee lad is using the sword now to try to cut the legs of his da's chair, probably wants him to fall off so he'd notice him. That's the sort of thing I'd have done. I probably still would if I'm honest.

'Well, sure, in a few hours you'll get to meet her and see them all again.'

'23 hours.'

'What?'

'23 hours, that's how long it takes to fly to Australia.'

I'm looking at her face to see if she's trying to take the piss out of me.

'You're taking the piss out of me? 23 hours? You could go round the world in 23 hours … I think?'

She just laughs and looks at me in, like, a nice way. She's lovely.

'No, son, 23 hours with a stopover in Dubai.'

Dubai must be like the Monaghan stop on the Derry to Dublin bus. I'm going to say nothing, though. I've learned over the years to keep my mouth shut when I don't know stuff. I spend a lot of time with my mouth shut.

'Now, I must bid you farewell young man, and go to catch my flight.'

She stands up and puts out her hand for me to shake it.

'And good luck in the X-Factor, son.'

I'm shaking her hand, probably much longer than I should, and just looking at her. I think she might be … like a ghost or an angel? A ghost angel? I can't talk. Luckily, she speaks:

'Even an old foogy like me can watch the X-Factor, Mickey. You were brilliant.'

'Thank you! Do you want my autograph?'

'Thank you, but I'm a bit old for autograph hunting. Just keep your feet on the ground, Mickey. Do nice things for others and good things will happen for you.'

'I'm trying to keep my feet on the ground, it's one of my main prirorit.. prirorit… pri… it's one of my main things to do in future. Good luck in Australia and with your family!'

She's turning to go, when I realise I'm still shaking her hand and there's tears in my eyes. I'm an emotional wreck these days! She smiles at me and walks off with all her luggage. I turn around to see if anybody else has heard the conversation about me being a star, but, the kid's ma and da STILL have their heads stuck in their phones. The kid is looking up at me now, I then do something I probably shouldn't do, I give the kid the middle finger. Now, before you all start judging me and stuff, the kid doesn't know what it means, I'm just teaching it to him to annoy his parents, it's nothing personal towards the kid, I have no beef with him. Within a few minutes he has it nailed. At first he was using the wrong finger, then for some reason his thumb? But, he got it right in the end. I pull out a bag of Starbursts that my ma gave me to stop my ears from popping and give him one, just to say well done. Then, a few minutes later, this totally shocks me, out of the blue he starts shouting ''FUCKERS'' at the top of his lungs whilst giving the middle finger! I didn't even know the kid could talk! All of a sudden, his parents take their heads out of their phones and jump out of their seats to stop the kid. He's really causing a scene at this stage, acting like some wild animal or something. I take a fly look around to see if anybody seen me teaching the kid to give the finger. I may be to blame for that, but there's no way I'm taking the blame for the cursing bit. The da actually has to cover his mouth to shut him up and the ma is holding down his hands to stop him giving the finger and he's putting up some fight for all the size of him. Luckily, it's time to get on the flight so I quickly get my shit together and go. As I'm leaving, I can see the kid looking at me and pointing (with his middle finger of course), I think the little fucker is trying to grass me up!

Before I know it, I'm through the check-in and into my seat on the plane. I check my phone, still nothing from Mandy, I haven't heard a thing from her since the night she messaged me to tell me she was pregnant. I've tried ringing her every day, but her phone is switched off. I sent loads of messages, but still nothing. It's eating me up inside. I just want to talk to her 'cause I haven't talked to anyone about it. It's now Monday morning and I'm due in London on Wednesday for the X-Factor meet-up and media obligations. I'm going to Manchester first to see if I can find her, even though Knuckles is probably going to kill me if he sees me there after the whole robbery thing, and me owing him six grand. All of a sudden, a message comes through and my heart skips a beat. Unfortunately, it's not Mandy, though, it's my da:

Hi son, hope you've got the flight ok. I don't want to worry you son but Laura Dillon's mother and father just called to the house. Apparently Laura hasn't been seen or heard tell of in a few weeks. They're really worried about her as she was in a bad way when she left. If you've heard from her then give us a shout. Ring me when you get there.

As if I'd know anything about Laura! There's no way she'd speak to me again after Mandy gave her a mouthful in the café! Maybe she just needs a bit of space away from people? I could be doing with a bit of that myself. Fuck, I hope she hasn't … No, there's no way she' d… Fuck, I shouldn't think like that!

To distract my mind, I send the gang a message:

On way over guys and girls, lock up your daughters!

When I say 'gang', I don't mean 'the lads' as in Decky, Marty and Stevie, I mean the gang that I'm on the X-Factor with- Mike, Godfrey, Minka, Sharon and Maggie. We've been really close lately, constantly sending each other messages and chatting on the phone. It makes it seem more real and less scary that I'm going through it with them, because we're all in the same boat and finding things out as we go along. As much as I love the lads (not in a gay way, obviously), they just have no way of understanding what I'm going through on my road to success. Then I remember that Mike and Sharon both have daughters!

Fuck! Sharon and Mike, I dnt mean yr actual daughters!

It doesn't take long for them to reply. Godfrey is the first:

One is looking forward to seeing you again my Irish friend. I'd get a bottle of my most expensive wine ready for your arrival, but we all know that would be wasted on your ass. Safe Journey! P.s, I'm locking up my Tibetan Mastiff's... just in case. :)

He's such a snob, but not in a bad way. He's a really funny and good person too! I don't even know what the fuck a Tibetan Mastiff is, he could have just made it up to confuse me. Actually, it could be one of the servants he has working in his house, I remember him saying once that they come from some far away country. Then it's Maggie that replies:

Lol I know what you meant sunshine! We'd need to lock up every girl in England on your arrival you little heartbreaker. See you soon darling. My nerves are killing me! Xx

Sharon is a lovely woman, and I mean that as like in a friend/big sister sort of way. I can't wait to get back to them all, and away from all the other crap that is going on in my life right now. I try Mandy's phone again before take-off. Still nothing. I don't even bother leaving a message this time. Then the pilot makes an announcement that the flight has been delayed due to a hold-up in boarding. I've already been in my seat about half an hour! I have a check through social media, it's going through the roof, illiterally thousands of people are following me and sending me messages. The X-Factor producers sent an e-mail, too, basically just telling us that from now on things are going to be hectic and will never be the same again blah, blah, blah. After the Judge's House, the people who get through will be living together in the X-Factor house and I'm going to do everything I can to make sure I'm there!

I'm sitting waiting on the plane to hurry up and also trying to stop myself from thinking too much, which usually isn't hard because thinking isn't exactly one of my strong points. Then, there's a bit of commotion at the entrance to the plane and someone else is getting on. Now, I've been a dickhead many's the time and I'm the first to admit that, but I've never left a plane full of people waiting on me for nearly an hour. I'm sitting near the door, so I'm practising my dirty looks to throw at the person, when suddenly I recognise the woman, then, I recognise the man, then the little kid that the man is carrying. The kid is soaked in sweat but he's not giving the middle finger anymore or shouting the word 'fuckers' at the top of his lungs. He obviously wore himself out and he's only been allowed to board the plane now. His da is carrying him and the wee lad is just laying with his head on his shoulder, probably asleep and totally exhausted. They're walking up the aisle, the three of them looking like they've just came off some battlefield, when all of a sudden I see that the kid is actually awake and they're heading in my direction. I look around for somewhere to hide, 'cause I know what parents are like, they need somebody else to blame and the kid is sure to grass me up, he already proved how much of a tout he is in the airport. I stick my head into my backpack, which I have on my lap, mostly because, well, there isn't many other places to hide when you're sitting on a plane. I start whistling, just so the man sitting beside me doesn't think I've completely lost my marbles. I hear the family getting closer, then, all of a sudden they stop and I know well that they're sitting in the seats directly in front of me. I'm wondering if I can keep my head inside my backpack for the entire journey, then my phone beeps and I jump all of a sudden. I peek my head out of the bag, just enough to see that the family have sat down looking forwards. I check my phone and it's Mike:

Hey buddy, not long to go now, just spending my last few days with the family before the real work starts. Enjoy your few days with your bird before Wednesday! You might be the one that needs locked up Mickey! :) Take care mate.

The plane takes off, and now I can relax, the devil-child will probably be asleep soon and the flight is only about half an hour long. I remember that I got a text from Decky last night, but I forgot to text back, he was out with the lads and he basically just wished me all the

best from everyone and good luck. I must remember to text him back

when I get to Manchester. I'm about to put my earphones in when I

hear the woman in front of me (the kid's ma) talking to the woman

that's sitting beside her:

'I don't know what came over him, one minute we were sitting

watching him playing with his sword ...'

Lying fucker, they were too busy on their phones to notice the kid!

'... then, without warning, he was shouting a rude word and giving the

fingers ...'

Finger, actually ... not FINGERS!

'... I knew when I looked at his wee eyes that he'd somehow gotten

hold of a sweet of some sort ...'

Uh-oh...

'... He's allergic to sugar, you see, it spikes his glucose levels which

sends him into hyperactivity.'

Without warning, it seems to happen in slow motion, I can see the top

of the kid's head in front of me as it rises up behind the seat. I try to

stick my head back into my bag, but it's too late, he makes eye contact with me. I stick my head in the bag anyway and hope that he doesn't recognise me, but then he starts shouting:

'SWEETS SWEETS SWEETS SWEETS' at the top of his voice!

I take out another sweet just to shut his mouth, and when I look up again he's giving me the middle finger and jumping up and down like he's found the key to Santa's house! Just as I'm about to give him the sweet, the mother turns around and catches me in the act:

'No! Do not give my son sweets, he's allergic!'

'Oh, I'm sorry, I didn't know, I thought he just looked like he'd like a sweet!'

The mother then turns to the child who is getting a bit mental at this stage:

'Max, what did I tell you about accepting sweets from people, especially strangers. We don't do that, do we!? And get that finger down!'

The kid isn't listening, though, he experienced the sugar rush and he wants more!

'Man give me sweets mummy the last time!'

'No I didn't!'

Mickey Doc

I still have the half a pack of Starburst in my hand, and the kid has his eyes glued to them. Then the mum pulls out a Starburst wrapper from her pocket:

'We found this in his hand when he took the attack …'

Fucking drama queen, it was hardly what you'd call an attack!

'… Did you give my son a sweet in the airport?'

'I did no such thing … how dare you!'

I gave that everything, by the way, had the back of my hand on my forehead and all, proper Oscar winning stuuf!

'He did mummy, he give me sweet! Nice man give sweets!'

The little fucker still hasn't taken his eyes off the starburst so I decide to get them out of harm's way by eating the whole lot in one go. There are ten left in the bag and I quickly get them out of their wrappers and into my mouth. The kid is sitting with his mouth open, there's drool running down his cheeks. He can't believe what just happened, neither can the ma or da, they're just staring at me while I have my face stuffed. Next thing, the kid absolutely loses it and goes wild again! The da is trying to control him while the ma is shouting at me:

'You sick fuck, you just ate a full packet of sweets just to annoy my child!'

I can't win! I'm fucked if I give him sweets, and I'm fucked if I don't! I can't even argue because my mouth is full! Plus they're the tropical ones so they're bitter as fuck! One of the stewardesses comes up to see what's going on and the ma blames the whole thing on me! The stewardess then asks me if I'd kindly move to another seat to help defuse the situation. I try to argue, but all I can do is just nod and get up. This would be highly embarrassing for anybody, but for a superstar like me it's even worse. The stewardess tells me there's a seat right up the front and she'll show me to it. As I'm passing the fucked-up family, the kid looks up at me so I give him the middle finger and I fucking mean it this time. This causes the ma to absolutely lose it now, and the da is using all his power to hold her and the kid back from me. Everybody on the plane is looking at me while tutting and shaking their heads. The stewardess shows me to my seat and even she gives me a disappointed look, the bitch. I spend the last 15 minutes of the flight sitting on my own and wondering if my own child is going to turn out a little touting prick like that.

As you can guess, I was first off the plane. Luckily, I had my earphones in to block out the noise from that mental kid who was still screaming his lungs off when we landed. I'm standing outside the airport debating

with myself whether to get a taxi or a bus to Karen and Alex's house, to
see Mandy. The money I got from Knuckles is drying up quickly, but I
can't be travelling by bus these days, I've got an image to keep. I do the
sensible thing and get a taxi, I enquire about a limo but the taxi
company just does normal cars. Luckily, the taxi driver isn't one of
those types that wants to talk, he just sits there with a big head on him
while I sit in the back thinking about what I'm going to say to Mandy.

We pull up outside the house. I'm sweating even though it's cold
outside. My stomach is doing summer-shots and I can't think straight. I
give the driver a tip then ask him to leave. He tells me to 'fuck off
Paddy' then drives off. He obviously mistook me for someone else. I
walk up to the door and all I can think of is that Mandy is inside that
house, and my baby is inside her. It kinda reminds me on that film –
Inception, even though I didn't really get it. I knock on the door and as
soon as I take my hand away, the door opens:

'Mickey! What the fuck are you doing here, man?'

It's Karen, Mandy's mate that owns the house.

'I'm here to see Mandy, is she in?'

'No, she's not here, Mickey. She don't live here no more, man, she
moved out two weeks ago.'

Fuck!

'Do you know where she is?'

'Mickey, I'm sorry darling, but she don't want to see you right now, she's going through a bit of a bad patch, man.'

'But I need to see her! She's carrying my baby and I can't get the both of them out of my head! I need to know where she is, Karen. Please, please, I just need to talk to her.'

I can feel the tears starting to run down my cheeks. I can hear voices from inside and I can make out Mandy's voice.

'She's in there, isn't she?'

Karen looks at me for a few seconds then steps out of the doorway and pulls the door almost shut behind her. Then she starts whispering to me:

'Look, Mickey, you need to get your Irish ass out of here before there's any trouble. You're a nice kid, you ain't suited for life around these parts. Please, Mickey, I like you, man, I don't wanna see you get hurt.'

'But I'm already hurt!'

Suddenly, the voices become raised and they're coming from upstairs. It's definitely Mandy 'cause I would know that voice anywhere. She's arguing with a man. Then out of nowhere there's a huge smashing sound and more shouting, then, someone comes stomping down the stairs and bursts open the front door. It's Knuckles. I get a fright when I see him, but he just grabs me by the throat. I've never seen anybody look as angry in my life:

'I fackin' told you to stay the fack away from here didn't I, Mickey … DIDN'T I?'

He's screaming in my face now, and I think I'm going to die! He's like a man possessed.

'I fackin' told you, you fackin' little Irish cunt, I fackin' told you stay the fack away from here! DIDN'T I? DIDN'T I?'

I can't speak 'cause he's crushing my throat. Then he just holds me there, looking into my eyes like a psycho. He looks like he's trying to figure out what way he's gonna kill me.

'I fackin' told her this was a bad plan, I fackin' told her from the start, but she wouldn't fackin' listen!'

Then he drops me and I fall to the ground, grasping for breath. Before he leaves, he kicks me in the stomach and shouts in my face:

'Next time I see you, I want you to put £1,000 in my hand. Then, after that, you can start paying me back the eight grand you owe me. You got that, you fackin' Irish prick!?'

I just nod, there's no way I'm going to tell him it's only six grand I owe him.

Knuckles storms out of the garden, kicking and breaking the gate on the way out, then gets into his car and speeds off. Karen helps me to my feet and brings me into the kitchen. She's half-carrying me and I fall onto one of the chairs. I didn't see the kick to the stomach coming, so I didn't have time to clench my six-pack, that's why it hurt so much. I'm just sitting there trying to get my breath back while Karen fills the kettle:

'You want a cup of tea, Mickey?'

I just shake my head.

'What about something a bit stronger, then?'

I shake my head again.

'Listen, he ain't so bad … he's just going through a bit of a rough patch, too, and unfortunately, he took it out on you … and my fucking gate.'

She looks out the window at the gate:

'I think the gate got the worst of it, Mickey.'

I start to laugh. It isn't even funny what she said and it hurts to laugh, but I can't help it, I just start laughing.

Mickey Doc

'You sit there, Mickey, I'll go see if Mandy is ready to speak to you.'

I must be sitting there for about ten minutes. I know this because when Karen left, the big hand was on five and when she came back it was on 15. I just sat there the whole time watching the clock. The kitchen door opens and in steps Mandy. She looks absolutely amazing. She's wearing a pair of skin-tight jeans, a low-cut black top and she has her hair done up all nice. She smells beautiful too. I stand up to hug her, but I still need to hold onto the chair for support.

She just stands at the door:

'What the fook did you come here for, you fookin' bellend?'

She then steps in and hugs me. I think I'm getting an erection. Either that or the pain is spreading down below.

'I just needed to talk to you, about the baby.'

She holds her belly, even though you wouldn't notice there's a baby in there yet.

'Well, what did you want to talk about then?'

'I wanted to tell you that I'm … well … I fucking love you, Mandy, and I want us to be a family. Me, you and the baby!'

She just stares at me with a kind of … like a blank stare, if that makes any sense? She doesn't have that fun look in her eye anymore.

'Okay, let's do it. You, me and the baby. Happy fookin' families!'

'Really?'

I can't tell if she's being sarcastic or not!

'Fookin' really! But, we need to get a few things straight … you don't tell anybody I'm your girlfriend, we don't sleep together. As far as anybody else is concerned there's nothing going on between us. Not until after this X-Factor business. Got it?'

'I got it, anything you want, Mandy. Anything!'

'Now, go get yourself washed up, you look like fookin' shit.'

I just can't believe she's agreed to be a family with me. This is the happiest day of my life! Then, I remember something:

'What did Knuckles mean when he said 'I told her this was a bad plan'?'

'He was just incredibly angry is all and you got the brunt of it. When he gets like that he just says things he doesn't even mean.'

Then she comes over and kisses me on the lips and says:

'It's just me, you and the baby now, babe. You better do us proud on the X-Factor.'

'I'm going to win it for us. You, me and the baby.'

Mickey Doc

I try to touch her belly, but she pulls away and leaves the kitchen.

CHAPTER 17.

This is exactly what I want to be doing. I've known all along that I wanted to be a mega successful singer, but actually doing it makes me know that for the first time in my life I have been right about something. I've spent the last two days in London doing promo work for the X-Factor with some of the best people in the world. It's like a big family. There's me, Minka, Mike, Godfrey, Maggie and Sharon: we're like the children. I'm the little brother and the rest are my older brothers and sisters. The production team are like our aunties and uncles and the judges are our parents. I've never had brothers and sisters before, it's like I've been reborn as the person that I always wanted to be. They told us when we got to London that the real hard work starts now, but this doesn't even feel like work. To me, work has always been trying to avoid doing things that I'm supposed to do, and get paid for it. This is me doing something that I love to do, although to be fair we're not really getting paid for it, but we do get loads of stuff for free, so that kinda makes up for it. I've got a whole new wardrobe (of clothes, not an actual wardrobe), which, along with stardom, puts me above the ordinary people on the street.

Mickey Doc

After two full days of promo stuff: interviews, photo shoots, stylists, videos and voice coaching, we're sitting in the canteen waiting to find out where we'll be going for the judge's house part of the show. We're all sitting around a table (me and my brothers and sisters) waiting for Louis to call us. We've heard rumours about where we're going, but we can't be sure. Godfrey is trying to make out that he doesn't really care, by doing a crossword while we all chat about our destination. The man is rich as fuck, and he goes on holidays all the time, so it's no big deal to him, but I can tell he's still excited. He reads out a clue from his crossword:

'7 across, the Oxford College that Margret Thatcher attended ... Starts with 'S'.... 11 letters?'

As if I'd have a fucking clue! All I know is she was the president? I try to get him in on the conversation:

'Isn't there anywhere you want to go, Godfrey?'

'Listen, Mickey ... I've been to almost everywhere in the world there is worth going to, and I can go again anytime I want, I'm easy as to where we end up.'

Then he just goes back to his crossword. I don't know why he feels he has to smarten himself when he's already rich and a star.

'Fair enough, I just want to get a tan. What about you, Minka?'

'You fink I need a tan, Mickey?'

Fuck! Minka's black!

'Naw, naw, naw! I just meant …'

He interrupts:

'I know what ya meant brother! You white boys fink ya get a tan, but all y'all turn out looking like a big boiling lobster …'

He's laughing:

'… Nah, man, I hope we going to L.A. –Los Angeles, baby, that's where it's at!'

Mike's playing a game on his phone and talking at the same time:

'I heard Louis has a place in Bermuda … now, that would be sweet!'

The two girls get excited by that, I don't have a fucking clue where it is, but it sounds nice. Sharon says in her high-pitched excited voice:

'Oh my God, imagine that! Golden beaches, crystal-clear water ... I always wanted to go to Bermuda! What you think, Maggie? Cocktails on the beach!?'

'Now that sounds like a little piece of heaven!'

Mickey Doc

All of a sudden, one of the production team comes over to our table, I think his name's Peter:

'Rightio gang, Louis is ready to see you. If you could all follow me …'

We all jump up right away, even Godfrey, who was acting like he didn't give a shit, almost falls off his chair, he got up that quick. We're all laughing about that and slagging him as we're walking down the corridor. Maggie and Sharon have both linked on to my arms and we're all just having a laugh, it's like something out of a music video. In my head we're walking in slow motion. Then, I think his name's Peter, brings us into a room where the cameras are all rolling and Louis is sitting on a table. I'm actually shaking with the excitement! Louis starts talking:

'Here we are! Now, I know you have all been dying to know where we're going, so I'm not going to leave you in suspense for too long. We're going somewhere that is very dear to my heart and it's one of the most beautiful places in the world …'

For fuck's sake Louis, spit it out!

'… When we get there, we'll be joined by a special guest mentor for the duration, I won't spoil that surprise by telling you who he or she is just yet … but what I will tell you is … the place you will be going, with me, is … my home county of Mayo in Ireland …'

Everybody takes an intake of breath, I think we're all waiting for him to tell us he's only pulling our legs, there's no way he'd bring us to Ireland for fuck's sake!

'… You will be my guests in the 13th century, five-star hotel in the village of Cong, Co. Mayo …'

He's serious. He's actually fucking serious!

'… Now, the competition is astounding this year folks, and two of you will be eliminated at the end of our trip, leaving four to go through to the live finals. So, I hope you're all as excited as I am, and I shall see you all tomorrow morning in the beautiful county of Mayo.'

Everybody cheers but it's obviously not the response that Louis was looking for. He whispers something to one of the production team, who then claps his hands, and tells us to listen up while he adjusts the headset on his head:

'Okay guys, we're going to shoot that scene again, only this time when Louis tells you where you're going, I want you to cheer like you mean it. I want you to hug each other, high-five each other, whatever it takes, but most of all I want you to look generally excited and happy.'

Louis doesn't even bother saying his line the second time, he just gets up and leaves. The production guy, I think his name's Martin, counts us down from five and we all have to cheer like we just received the most amazing news ever. It takes 12 goes at it before the production team are happy with our response. I still can't believe we're going to Ireland, I don't even know where Mayo is or why the hell anybody would name a place after something you put in a sandwich?

We arrive at an airport which is only up the road from where we're going, and I shit you not, the airport is called 'Knock'… which is in 'Mayo'… and our hotel is in 'Cong', which is also in 'Mayo'. Who the fuck comes up with the names of these places!? Apart from the fact we've been on the road since five in the morning AND we're not going to an exotic location, we're all super-excited about the next few days. Everybody keeps asking me questions about Ireland and I swear to God, they might as well be asking me the seven times tables … in other words, I don't have a fucking clue. We're in a limo to the hotel and the gang are asking me loads of things. I'm not sure if they're taking the piss, 'cause they know I'm thick as fuck, or if they actually want to know stuff:

'What's the population of Ireland, Mickey?'

That was Mike: he might actually be serious:

'Well, I can't be sure of the ACTUAL population at this moment as people are being born and dying every few minutes.'

I think I got away with it, I've learned how to get out of actually answering questions over the years. Mike is just nodding. Well, he's smiling too but that could be 'cause he's happy with the answer?

Then Sharon joins in:

'Would you consider yourself as Irish or a Brit, Mickey?'

'Again, it's hard to say. Like, if anybody asks me where I'm from, I'll say 'Ireland.' But on, like, official forms and stuff, they say I'm from the United Kingdom, which, I think is being like a Brit? So maybe I consider myself, like, half-Brit and half-Irish, so if you put the two together I'm technically, like, Brit-ish.'

I think I can hear sniggers. It's hard to tell in the limo with my sunglasses on 'cause I can't see their faces. Then Godfrey asks me a question. I feel like I'm on a fucking game show here:

'In our current economic climate, Mickey, with Ireland suffering badly at the hands of the EU and the subsequent debacle that was the Nice treaty: do you think Ireland will ever see the likes of the Celtic Tiger again?'

'Yes.'

I don't have a notion what he was saying: the smart fuck may have been using some Irish words to throw me? I think I done well at answering their questions, though, and I definitely think I may have got smarter since hanging around with this lot? I must Google if they have tigers in the south. Just at that moment the driver tells us we've arrived. He speaks in a proper Irish accent, took

'Howya there now, if ye look just up in front of ye, up there behind the trees, ye'll see the beautiful Ashford Castle.'

Everybody starts ooh-ing and aah-ing, but I can't see a fucking thing.

'I can't see anything!? Where are you looking?'

Then Mike knocks the smartness ideas out of my head:

'Can you not see it there, Mickey… through the darkness?'

'I can just see the darkness?'

'Maybe try it without the sunglasses?'

Everybody bursts out laughing, even the fucking driver. I whip off the shades and I swear to God it looks amazing! It's like something out of a fairy-tale! Everybody is still laughing and high-fiving and I can't help but join in. This is going to be a class few days, I'm with the best people in the world, doing the best job in the world, but, most importantly: this is the next step to me becoming a global superstar.

The cameras are still being set up as we pull up outside of the castle. We're told we can't get out until they're ready, so we all just sit there staring out the window with our mouths open. There's an actual old bridge, which is part of the castle that you have to cross on the way in, and it looks mega-old. The gardens are absolutely class, and that's coming from somebody who wouldn't know a dandelion from a weed. We're just staring for ages and pointing stuff out when one of the producers tells us to get out of the limo when he gives us the signal. He tells us the cameras are rolling so look like we're really blown away by it, but there'll be no acting involved here, everybody is, I'm going to use the word- mesmerized by the place? We jump out of the limo and look around at the surroundings. It looks even more amazing out of the car. We're standing at the bottom of the steps which leads up to the castle entrance doors, when suddenly the doors open and out walks Louis Walsh. We all go wild, jumping, hugging and high-fiving, just general madness. Then, Louis holds up his hands like he's about to speak. He looks like he owns the place and he's here to make a speech to his loyal subjects. For some reason, I'm picturing him wearing like a big white robe that just goes over one shoulder and a leaf headband ... I think it's called a yoga or a toga, or something?

'I am so excited to have you all here in my home county of Mayo in Ireland, we will have the most amazing few days here and I hope you all have fun. But guys, although we will have fun, this is where the hard work starts. I'm looking for four amazing acts to bring to the live finals and I really think I have the X-Factor 2014 winner in my team this year.'

We all cheer at that, but I know he's talking about me.

'So, let's have a look around the magnificent Ashford Castle and we'll get under way. If you'd like to follow me ...'

We spend the rest of the day getting shown about the castle and the huge grounds. I've never seen anything like it in my life. It has loads of gardens that look like they were painted and there's a huge big lake beside it. There's ancient walls and look-out posts from back in the time when they would have been attacked. The inside of the castle is like somewhere a king and queen would live, and I just wish Mandy was here with me to see it. She could be my queen and I would be the king of the castle. I send her a few photos and I tell her that I'll bring

her here when I become the X-Factor winner. She messages me back

right away:

'Oh my God that place is fookin' cool as fook man. When I seen the

picture our baby kicked!'

I text back:

'Me, you and baby will live here.'

We've been getting on great since after I visited her in Manchester.

Well, I didn't really see her much after she agreed to be a family, but

after I left for London she seems to have come around.

She texts me back:

'I had my 3 month scan today, I didn't want to worry you 'cause I

know you can be a dick. All is good ... but keep it to yourself.'

I just stare at the message, then my phone beeps and it's her again:

'And I got some money together and paid Knuckles some money back

for you, it's all good now.'

I'm sitting on my bed in my five-star luxury hotel suite and I can feel

the tears running down my cheeks. I feel that everything is starting to

come together now, and I know at this point that I'm the happiest man

in the world.

Mickey Doc

I just text back:

'I luv u.'

She sends me back a smiley face. In other words, she's smiling, which is good.

Me, Minka, Sharon, Maggie, Godfrey and Mike are all sitting in one of the hotel pubs having a drink and taking in all that has went on today. I feel like a new man, all the stress that has been building up inside me is starting to go away and I just want to shout it from the rooftops that I'm in love and I'm going to be a father. Mandy would fucking kill me if she found out I did, though. The people that work in the hotel are apparently sworn to secrecy about us being here because the Bootcamp stage still hasn't been shown on TV yet. It'll be on next week, so until then, nobody has a clue who made it through apart from us and our families and the people who work on the show. Minka says from next week, when it's shown, we are all gonna be mega famous. Then, like we're all thinking the same thing at the same time, we remember that two of the group will be sent home tomorrow and won't be with us for that. We all look at each other for a few seconds, then Mike raises his glass:

'No matter what happens tomorrow guys, I just hope that one of you lot are crowned the winner at the end. And after all is said and done, we'll be friends for life.'

We all 'cheers' each other. Maggie and Sharon are crying and I can tell the lads aren't far off it either. Then Godfrey stands up:

'I never thought I would ever be involved in something like this, but I'm glad I am, and I'm glad I'm experiencing it with you guys. Let's just enjoy our time here and not think about elimination. We are a team, we are a family. We win together, we lose together. No matter what happens from now on in, we've already achieved more than the tens of thousands of other people who applied. Let's be proud of that. Let's enjoy what we've already achieved.'

It's a beautiful moment, and I don't mean that in a gay way or anything. Sharon is the first to say she's off to bed, then Maggie, Godfrey and Minka follow, leaving only me and Mike left. It's just the two of us sitting at the table when Mike says:

'I'm not too sure I want to spend too long in my room, not with all the history behind this place.'

I honestly don't have a clue what he's talking about. History was never one of my strong points at school.

'Aye, History can be a bad thing alright.'

'I mean the history of the castle, mate, as in all the bad things that have happened here over the centuries and the ghosts that are said to walk the corridors and rooms at night.'

'There's no such thing as ghosts!'

I'm starting to shake, I fucking hate scary stuff.

'Ah, but there is, Mickey. This building has gone through many invasions, plagues and mass murders. This place is haunted alright. Didn't you get a strange feeling when you came in here? My family has always had a sixth sense when it comes to the supernatural, it has been passed down from generation to generation, and this place is most definitely haunted. There are tortured souls roaming about this building, unable to pass over to the other side.'

I am actually shitting myself now:

'I don't believe it, there's no way the X-Factor would bring its biggest stars to somewhere that has ghosts wandering around the place.'

He looks around him, in like a scared sort of way:

'Believe what you want, Mickey. All I'm saying is keep one eye open when you're asleep 'cause there's evil trapped inside these walls. Now, I'm off to bed too mate, I'll see you in the morning.'

I don't want to look around in case I see something I don't want to, so I just stare into my empty glass.

Mike has stood up and all, ready to go:

'Mickey, I said I'll see you in the morning, mate.'

'Aw, aye, I'll eh … see you then.'

Just as Mike is walking away, I realise I'm on my own:

'Hold on, Mike, can I walk up with you, man?'

'Of course you can mate: we'll be safer in numbers.'

The whole way up to our rooms, Mike is talking about ghosts and I'm actually shaking. We get to his room first:

'Right, Mickey, I'll see you in the morning.'

'Yep.'

'Are you alright?'

'Yep.'

'Are you scared, Mickey?'

'Nope,'

'You fucking are, mate, you're shitting yourself.'

'Tired.'

'Mate, I was only pulling your leg! Fuck's sake, man, just get yourself a good night's sleep. Honestly, I don't believe in ghosts, even if I did I wouldn't be afraid of them. You should be more afraid of the living than the dead.'

'Yep'

Mike goes into his room, then about a minute later his door opens again and I'm still standing outside his door:

'Aw, mate, I feel bad now. I was only having a bit of fun. Seriously, you have nothing to worry about.'

'Yep'

'Come on, I'll walk you to your room.'

Mike walks with me to my room, it's only about 20 steps away from his room, but I think I've gone into some sort of shock or something?

'Right, this is you now, Mick, take out your key card.'

I take the key card out of my pocket, but I can't get it into the door because my hands are shaking too much. Mike takes it off me and opens the door:

'Are you sure you're going to be alright, mate? I feel really bad now. I was just trying to play a joke on you, but I didn't think you'd fall for it. Go on inside now and keep the lights on if you're still afraid.'

'Yep'

'Sorry again, mate, look just get yourself a good sleep.'

Mike walks off and I step into my room. It looks so different now than when I came into it earlier. It looks bigger now with loads of shadows and dark places for ghosts to hide in. The curtains are shaking and I could have sworn I closed the window earlier. Everything in the room looks old and scary now. There's a painting on the wall of two children that I could of swore wasn't there before. They look about six and eight years old, but they're not smiling like kids usually do in photos. They're just standing there, staring at me, so I make a run for my bed and jump under the covers. It seems cold in here now, too. I remember hearing one time that if it's cold in a room then there are definitely ghosts in it. I check my phone and it's only 10:30 at night. I can feel those kids staring at me even though I'm under the duvets. What if they're not in the picture anymore and they're in my room, like on the floor? I decide I have to be brave and peek out from under the duvet. I stick my head out and the picture is gone! Oh Jesus, Mary and Joseph what the fuck is going on? Then I remember I was looking at the wrong wall, so I peek out again and thankfully the picture is still there, but the two fuckers in the picture are still staring. I decide there's only one person that can help me now, one person who knows about this sort of shit and can give me like a prayer or something. I'm just not sure if George the priest-boy will still be awake at this time. I hold my phone for a minute to stop myself from shaking, then I text my 10-year-old cousin who's practically a priest:

'RU stil awake? I need help?'

He texts back after a few minutes, but it feels like hours:

'Cousin Michael, so very glad to hear from you. I've been meaning to ring you regarding the lack of contact you've had with your family and friends this past few weeks. Now, I know you're quite busy with this little talent competition you're involved in, but I must reiterate how important family and friends are, especially in times of such upheaval. I won't even ask if you've been to mass since you've been there. Your family and friends feel as though they're being left out of this little adventure of yours.'

I wish I hadn't of text him now, but, it is an emergency. I text him back:

'Jst been busy. I'm in a castle and theres ghosts. Its really really old and cold. Can I say a prayer to get rid of them?'

He texts back:

'Have you been drinking? Are you taking some sort of drugs? I hope not, your mother would be very disappointed.'

What the fuck?

'no! at the x-factor, stayin in old hotel-castle. Place is hunted. Kids in painting staring at me. Cold to.'

He's really annoying me now, I come to him with a serious problem and he doesn't even realise it!

'Michael, do not be afraid. You are more than likely just letting your imagination run wild. Your hotel is not haunted and there are no ghosts in your room. I want you to say an 'Our Father' and two 'Hail Marys'. This will put you at ease and help you sleep. I also suggest that you ring your family and friends tomorrow, they all care for you. Goodnight and God bless you, Michael.'

I don't even bother texting him back. I Google the two prayers he told me about and I say them over and over until, finally, after a few hours, I fall asleep.

Luckily, when I got up the next morning, everything seemed a lot less scary. Maybe George's prayers worked? I don't think Mike told any of the rest of the gang, because when I went to breakfast, nobody mentioned it and Mike apologised again when he got me on my own. I told him I wasn't really scared, I was just playing along with the joke. I'm not sure if he really believed me or if he just pretended to, to make me feel better. Straight after we've eaten breakfast, one of the production people tells us that Louis is ready to see us and we'll meet our celebrity mentor. We are taken out into the garden where all the crew are flat out getting cameras, lighting and sound stuff set up. Within a few minutes, Louis comes out of a door behind us, again he's on top of steps, again like a ruler. The producer gives him the signal and he starts talking:

'Hi everyone! I hope you're all enjoying your time, but guys, I have to tell you, we are in for some hard work today to get you ready for your audition this evening. I think you're all really amazing and as I said before, I believe I have the winner in my team this year. Now, I have someone very special with me, someone who I'm sure you will all know, he has been a colossus of the music industry for a number of years now and he's here to help me today. Ladies and gentlemen, I give to you, Mr Ronan Keating!'

We all run over to Ronan and hug him. I've always been a big fan of his and it's great to have him here with us. He seems really sound, too, and says he's really excited because he's seen tapes of us and he thinks we're brilliant. This is a great boost for everyone and we can't wait to get going. The rest of the day is spent going over our songs with our voice coaches. My coach is called Yvie, and she knows everything there is to know about singing, probably even stuff there isn't to know either. She says she loves my voice and asks me what song I'll be singing. It's a song my mum used to always get me to sing for her, it's called 'Bridge Over Troubled Waters' and Yvie reckons it's an amazing song choice which will showcase my vocal talents. I've hardly seen the rest of the crew today, but anytime I did, everybody seemed a wee bit nervous, which was bound to happen. I don't really feel nervous 'cause I just know that I'm going to go all the way. I'm not even sure how I know, but I just know.

Finally, the time comes when we have to sing in front of Louis and Ronan. We will be singing in the garden, which I always think is pretty crap because the acoustics aren't good, and everybody will perform separately, although we will get to watch each other if we want. Then, Louis and Ronan will discuss who they think should stay and who should go, then they call us back and tell us, again, separately, who goes home and who stays.

I'm last to perform. I watched the rest of my friends give some class performances and suddenly I felt a little bit of nervousness. I try to remove the bit of doubt from my head, then I head to the garden where Louis and Ronan are waiting for me. Louis is the first to speak:

'Mickey Doc, the lad from Derry. How are you today, Mickey?'

Him and Ronan are smiling, which is always a good sign.

'Aye, great thanks, Louis. How's it going with you?'

'Things are going very well, thank you, Mickey. You've met Ronan already ...'

'Howaya Mick?'

'How's it going, Ronan?'

'... and it's time for you to give us your song, Mickey. What will you be singing for us, today?'

'Am ... I'll be singing an old song that my ma used to always get me to sing for her. It's called Bridge Over Troubled Water and it's by a bloke called Simon Garfunkel.'

The two of them start laughing, I didn't know what I said was even funny. Ronan clears it up for me:

' Mickey that's actually a song by Simon AND Garfunkel. They were a two-piece consisting of Paul Simon and Art Garfunkel.'

'There was two of them?'

'Yes, there was definitely two of them.'

'That's a good 'un. You learn something new every day!'

That seemed to put everybody at ease. Next thing the piano starts and I fall into my zone. I have the song down to a T and I blast it out from a place deep inside me. I have my eyes open for most of it, but I can't see the judges' faces, everything has changed and I'm no longer in the gardens of an old castle, I'm standing in my living room singing to my ma and making her proud of me. At the end of the song I snap back into real-life again. Louis and Ronan don't seem to be giving much away, they just smile and tell me they'll see me later.

The next few hours is just a blur. I'm hanging out with my crew, and we're trying to have the craic, but everybody is overcome by the nervousness of it all. Then we get the news, Louis is ready with his decisions. He has moved to another part of the castle grounds, an old remote garden area that has a huge wooden seat beneath a large tree. My heart is illiterally bursting out of my chest as I wait for everybody else to see him. Because I sang last, I'll be the last to find out the judges' decision. Minka is up first, then Maggie, then Sharon, then Mike, then Godfrey and then me. We all hug each other as people are called to see Louis. After seeing him, we have to walk around the long way back to the castle, so I won't know who else is through till I get back.

One by one, the gang get called and soon I'm the only one left. After about ten minutes of complete and utter torture, I get the call to say Louis is ready for me. I walk across the gardens and get shown to the seat where Louis is sitting waiting:

'Hello, Mickey, how are you feeling now?'

'I'm feeling great, Louis, just a long oul' wait there 'cause I'm last!'

'What does winning the X-Factor mean to you?'

'It means the world to me. It's illiterally everything I've ever dreamed of. This is what I was born to do and I'm going to go the whole way. No doubt.'

'Well, Mickey, you've impressed from the start. Your first audition was one of the best of the season. And your performance at Bootcamp was simply amazing. But ...'

What the fuck's the 'but' for?? There's no buts!

'... But, I wasn't sure if you could raise the level again at the Judge's House. This has probably been the most difficult decision I've had to make, simply because the talent this year is phenomenal and when that

happens, Mickey, somebody really brilliant will get left behind …'

No. No, no, no! It can't end like this!

'… You made that decision a little bit easier for me when you

performed today … because there's no way that a talent like yours can

fall through the gaps. Congratulations, Mickey Doc from Derry, you're

going to the live finals.'

CHAPTER 18.

To say that things have gone absolutely mental would be an understate, man. The Bootcamp episode was shown on TV at the weekend and my fame has exploded even more now. Everybody wants a piece of Mickey Doc. TV shows, newspapers, magazines: they all want to talk to me. Then, there's the fans! I can't even go out in public anymore without people wanting a piece of me. Messages and phone calls and e-mails and tweets and photographs and marriage proposals. Oh, and other types of proposals too, if you know what I mean?

Sex, by the way, in case you didn't know what I mean.

Old people, young people, smelly people, clean people, crazy people, binmen, shop workers, police officers, traffic wardens, teachers, nurses, doctors, farmers: they all stop me and ask me for a photo or an autograph, or sometimes they just want a chat. It's absolutely nuts – and I fucking love it!

I flew back to Derry the day after the Judge's House, mainly just to pick up some stuff, but then I left again that night and flew over to Manchester to see Mandy. My ma wasn't too happy about me leaving again so soon, she was planning a party and all, but I just don't wanna be in Derry anymore, it's not very 'pop starish'. I probably would have been better staying there, though, because when I got to Manchester, Mandy was heading out into town with friends from school, so I only seen her for half an hour or so. I thought she was going to invite me: obviously, it would look class for her if she had a star going out with her, but she said it was a girls-only night. She drank half a half-bottle of Vodka before she went out, too, even though I heard that woman who are pregnant shouldn't drink? There was no way I was for saying anything, though, she seemed annoyed enough with me being there without that. Maybe it's just her hormones that are making her like that? I'm pretty sure now she *doesn't* have a period when she's pregnant? I stayed the night in Alex and Karen's, Mandy didn't come home. She text me to say she's going back with one of her friends who got her drink spiked, which is understandable I suppose.

I'm now in a taxi heading to my new house and I can't fucking wait to get there. It's not really MY house, it's the X-Factor house for all the remaining finalists, but I'll be there till the end 'cause I'm gonna win. Oh, and it's not actually a house, it's more of a mansion! I just wish that Minka and Godfrey could be here, too, but they got sent home at the Judge's House. They both text me this morning wishing me good luck, which was a really nice thing to do, but I can't help feeling sorry for them. I can't wait to see Mike, Maggie and Sharon again. Even though we were only apart for two days, I missed them. It's 'cause

nobody else can understand what it's like to be in this position. I didn't

even meet up with the lads when I was back home 'cause they'll just be

talking about normal stuff and I'm past all that now. The finalists from

the other categories will be staying at the house and I'm looking

forward to seeing them again, too, even though I don't have the same

connection with them as I do my own group. But, I'm sure that will

change very quickly and we'll be a big happy family. The camera crew

and the production guys are all waiting outside the house for our

arrivals. The taxi man doesn't have a clue what's going on, he just

keeps looking at me in the mirror, even though we're both wearing

sunglasses. I'm way cooler, though, he must be about 50 … and he has

a bald patch and sounds like he should be in Eastenders, even though

he probably has zero talent:

'Are you famous or something, mate?'

I lift my sunglasses above my eyes:

'Eh, yeah? Of course I am?'

He does the same thing with his sunglasses:

'Eh, yeah, well you can't be too famous if I don't have a fackin' clue

who you are? Let me see your cod and plaice, mate…'

He turns around to look at me:

'… Don't know ya. Is that your Mickey?'

'What? I am Mickey, Mickey Doc. I knew you'd recognise me!'

'What?'

'I'm Mickey!'

'I said is that your *Mickey*? Your *Mickey Mouse*?'

'What?'

'Is that your Mickey Mouse? Your house?'

This guy must be on drugs or something, he's talking gibberish!

'Naw, it's not my house, it's the X-Factor house, but I'll be living there.'

'You on that show, then? You must be a bit Duke of Kent mate?'

'What?'

'Never mind. That's a macaroni mate.'

'I honestly don't know what you're talking about.'

He looks to be getting pissed off now:

'I said *that's a macaroni*! A pony! Are you a bit Jeff?'

I'll try to slow things down a bit:

325

Mickey Doc

'How. Much. For. Taxi?'

'25 quid. 25 quid is a pony, a fackin' macaroni.'

I quickly hand him the 25 quid:

'Erm … thanks!'

'Now, get the fack out of my jam-jar you little Scottish prick!'

I'm out of the car and all before I realise he called me Scottish, so I shout after him:

'I'M NOT FACKIN' SCOTTISH YOU BIG FACKIN' JUNKIE!'

Then I realise that all the production team and camera people are standing in the driveway staring at me.

The house, or should I say mansion, is fucking unbelievable! I didn't think anything could compare to the castle we stayed in, but this place is something else. The rooms are absolutely huge and there's even a swimming pool and a gym. Imagine how good my six-pack is going to look by the time I get to the final? I might even perform topless in the final if they let me? The kitchen is about the size of the whole bottom floor of my ma's house and that's no joke. It looks like something out of MTV cribs. Me and Mike are sharing a room, and Sharon and

Maggie are sharing the room next door to us, then the rest of the

finalists are in the other rooms. I'm in the room when Mike arrives:

'Well hey, here we are in the X-factor house, Mickey! Love it!'

We high-five each other, then decide a hug would be better.

'Aye, it's fucking unreal, man! Have you had a look around it yet?'

'Yeah, well I had a quick look around, I'll get a better look shortly!

There's a swimming pool out the back!'

'And a gym, too!'

'No way! I seen a table-tennis table and a basketball ring, too. Did you

see the size of the kitchen?'

'Aw, man, that kitchen is bigger than the whole downstairs of my ma's

house!'

He laughs:

'I live in an apartment, mate, with my missus and two kids and that

kitchen is bigger than our whole gaff!'

'Fucking hell!'

'Mad, isn't it?'

'Totally!'

Mike leaves his suitcases in the corner, then lays back on his bed:

Mickey Doc

'Have you seen any of the rest of them?'

'The other contestants like?'

'Yeah, is Sharon and Maggie here yet?'

'Don't think so, they're probably late as usual. I think I was first here because I didn't see anybody else.'

Just as I finish the sentence, we hear screaming from outside. We're in one of the rooms at the front of the house so we both run to the window to look out. It was excited screams by the way, not horrible screams. Everybody seems to be arriving at the same time and there's like a party atmosphere. Mike is just as excited as I am:

'There's the rest of them!'

I'm trying to make out who all's arrived:

'There's Belle from the girls group, fucking hell she's hot as fuck!'

'She's a little cracker, mate. There's Paula from Bristol, too. And there's the lads from Holda Beats. We'd better head downstairs.'

'Aye, come on, let's get this party started!'

We both run down the stairs like it's Christmas morning. Everybody is shouting and hugging and high-fiving each other. The first person I meet is Lola. She's part of the girls category and she's mad as fuck, but

I find it hard to know what she's saying half the time because she's Jamaican:

'Mickeey Doc! Waa gwan?'

I hug her 'cause I don't know how to answer what she just said:

'Lola, what's the craic! You were amazing in the other rounds! Your voice is class! How's things?'

'Mi nuh really hav much ti complain bout, mi life irie right now man!'

Sometimes I think she's an undercover pirate. I must remember to Google if that's a thing later.

Out of nowhere somebody grabs me around the waste from behind and kisses my cheek. I think it's one of the girls and I turn around to see Phil, the camp guy that was wearing the pink dressing gown and feathery scarf at the Bootcamp. He can see the shock in my face when I see it's him.

He's laughing away and he snorts when he laughs which makes me laugh too:

'Mickey Doc you thought it was one of those pretty girls trying to get a piece of you, didn't you darling?'

I just laugh again, he's such a nice and funny bloke:

Mickey Doc

'I knew it was you the whole time, Phil! Great to see you again! I seen your interview where you said I was one of the favourites, thanks for that!'

'Well, Mickey darling, you're definitely one of my favourites anyway.'

He taps me on the nose with his finger, then he just moves on to the next person he sees, it's like he owns the place and he's welcoming his guests.

Everybody is pouring into the front hall. It isn't really a front hall: it's like a huge big room on its own with a big winding staircase behind it. Maggie and Sharon are last to arrive (as usual). Me and Mike drop their luggage up to their room, I swear to God, I think they have a few actual flat-packed wardrobes in the bags. They weigh a tonne. The cameras are recording and there's people taking photographs all around the place, it feels a bit like we're in the Big Brother house … only we have *actual* talent. The rest of the day and night is spent just having the craic, telling stories and catching up on what's been going on with everybody. I thought it might be a wee bit weird having so many different people in the house, but I can safely say: it's the best feeling ever and things are only going to get better!

I'm woken up the next morning by my phone going mental. I look at my watch and it's only 6am in the morning! I answer the phone quickly before Mike gets woke up, too:

I clear my throat a bit so I don't sound like I was sleeping, even though I was?

'Hello!'

'Hello, Mickey, this is Peter Singleton from the X-Factor production team. Sorry for ringing you so early, but have you seen any of the morning papers yet?'

I could count on two hands and one foot how many papers I've read in my life, never mind this morning's:

'Naw, I haven't seen any papers yet this morning. Why? Am I in it?'

Then I get a feeling something is wrong:

'Well, yes. Yes, you are. But it's nothing to worry about. These sort of things happen every year where people sell stories about contestants to the gutter press. Don't worry, we have people who specialise in this sort of thing and there's a huge backroom team here behind you.'

'What does it say?'

'As usual with these things, it's a sensationalist story that has come from, what they like to call, 'a close friend' of yours and there's usually not a shadow of truth in these things.'

'Aye but what does it say about me? Is there a photo?'

'Well, the headline is a bit crude, but it's all that can be expected from such a smut paper. The top half of the page is the headline and it says 'Shit Factor', Then there's a picture of you, a picture of a cartoon turd with steam rising from it, and a story about how you went to a job interview in Derry at the start of the year and ended up … well… it says you ended up shitting yourself in the interview?'

Holy fuck! I just freeze. I can't even move or say anything.

'Hello, are you still there, Mickey…?'

'… Look, Mickey, we'll make this work for us. We just need to come and meet you and we'll figure this whole thing out. And remember, you're on the front page of a national newspaper, there's no such thing as bad publicity!'

'Front page?'

'Yes sir, front page of the Daily Star. Can I ask you a question, Mickey?'

'Yep'

'Is it true? Did you shit yourself at an interview and have to carry your soiled pants through the office on your way out?'

'I want to talk to my lawyer!'

I think I watch too much TV.

'Your lawyer is my lawyer also, we have a team of lawyers that work for us. I just need to know if it's actually true so we can work out what approach we take from here.'

'Yes, it's true'

I swear I can hear him snigger when I tell him it's true.

'Thank you for your honesty, Mickey. We'll sort this out, son, don't you worry.'

All I can think of is: which of my so-called friends sold the story to the newspaper?

****

It's only two days till the first live final, and most of my time seems to have been taken up by that stupid newspaper story. I actually had to change my phone number because so many people are ringing and texting me about it. My ma is annoyed because I ruined a good pair of trousers and the fact I told her at the time that she must have lost them in the wash. The only other people that knew about what happened at the interview were Decky and the lads. I haven't spoken to them in a while, because I just don't know what to say. I never thought any of my best mates would do something like that on me, but Mandy is convinced that they done it. She said that it was definitely Decky, that this is his way of getting back at me for falling out with him when I found out he was gay. It wasn't even because he was gay, it was because he was stealing my thunder and lightning, and now it seems he's trying to do it again. Everybody in the house is being really supportive about the whole thing, which is great, even the production team and the voice coaches are cool about it. Louis hasn't said anything to me yet, but he's coming towards me now and he looks like he wants to chat:

'Mickey, how are ya? Everything alright in the house?'

'Aye, it's grand, Louis. Better than that actually, it's amazing here, I love it!'

'And everybody seems to love you too, Mickey. You've made quite an impression on everybody here. Now, what I wanted to talk to you about is this story that appeared in the papers and all the talk about it. Every

TV show and stand-up comedian in the country seems to have mentioned it or tweeted about it. #shitfactor was the number one trending hashtag in the UK the past three days and even Loose Woman did a full segment on their show this morning about the topic. Mickey fever is sweeping the streets of Britain right now I can tell you.'

'Aye, but it's not the kind of publicity I wanted, is it? I want to be known for my singing, maybe even my good looks and nice hair, too, I don't want to be known for that interview.'

'I know you don't, but, look, listen to somebody that has experience in this sort of thing. I've been at the wrong end of a battering from newspapers all through my career. I've been to the highest courts in Dublin about them, too. And you know what I discovered, Mickey? There's no such thing as bad publicity. As long as your name's still being talked about, you're still in the public eye. Look around at some of the other people that are on the show … do you think they'll be remembered in a year's time? No, they won't. That's where you have the advantage over all of them. That, and you're a marvellous singer, Mickey.'

I'm actually starting to feel better already. We all know that there's nothing I like more than a good confidence boost. And no matter what people say about Louis, he knows how to look after people.

Mickey Doc

'Thanks very much, Louis, I'm feeling better already ...'

The bloke just looks so genuine, too, I can see actual tears in his eyes.

'... the thing that's annoying me most, though, is which of my mates sold the story to the paper?'

'How do you know it was one of your mates? Couldn't it have been somebody from the place you went for the interview?'

'Nope. I contacted the paper and they said they can't say who it was, but it was definitely one of my mates.'

'Look, Mickey, when you start climbing the ladder of success, you need to think very strongly about who you trust and who you don't trust. That includes your mates, fans, girlfriends ... everybody is trying to make a pound or two out of you. Mainly, though, trust nobody that's involved in the press. Don't let it get out either that you contacted the press, that's a big no-no on the X-Factor, but I'll let it slip, that's just between us.'

Louis stands up and gives me a hug:

'What I want you to do now, Mickey, is jump into this like a new man. I want you to work as hard as you can and let that great voice of yours make the papers, instead of silly stories. Agreed?'

'Agreed!'

I feel like I can take on the world again! Louis is such a nice guy and I'm so glad he's my mentor. From now on, I'm going to put all my focus on winning this show, then fuck everybody else. It'll just be me, Mandy, our baby and my celebrity friends. The people I can trust.

****

It's the day of the live finals. That was an absolutely crazy week in the X-Factor house! After all the craic about the newspaper story, I put my head down and worked as hard as I could. Now, everybody in there has a good head on them about getting stuff done, otherwise, they wouldn't be there, but at the same time they're just as fond of partying... and fuck, can they party! The lads from the boyband- Savage Punch and the girls from Passive X, spent most of their time getting pissed along with a few of the others. As you already know, I can party with the rest of them when I want to, but I decided that I'm going to put all my energy into the show, I'll have plenty of time for parties afterwards. Even having those kind of thoughts makes me feel mature and I think that being in the over-25s category has helped me. My phone isn't going half as much since I got myself a new number, there's only a few people I gave the new number to, which is why I was surprised to get a text from Marty of all people:

Alright man, got your new number from your ma! She said your working hard, bout fucking time! :) Only joking man, we're all proud of you. Decky got a new car last week. Got a new BMW so we're travelling in style these days! Stevie's Da has his business going again and Stevie is working for him now. He's turning into his da, flash as fuck! Hi I was chatting to the fella from down my road, Europes biggest crime boss, and he said if you need anything, he'll sort it out, Oh and his Ma says if you need an exorcism or any spells then it's all free. Laura Dillon still hasn't came back to Derry, she's living away somewhere now. I'm sure she'll be at a few of your shows! :) Looking forward to getting the gang back together again when you're done. Later man!

As if I don't have enough on my plate with an actual gangster, I don't want to be hearing about any of Marty the moon-man's fucking made-up people. It gave me a nice feeling hearing from him, though, there's a part of me that misses the way things used to be. But then again the old way will only hold me back. Actually, where the fuck did Decky get the money for a new car? The sickening feeling is starting to sink in that the best friend I ever had sold me out.

I just text him back:

Thanks for the update.

My ,a and da are arriving for the live show. I don't mind as much my ma being here, but my da wasn't exactly the most supportive of my dreams when I was young. Now he thinks he can just become my number one fan. My ma once entered the fucking dog into a competition, not once did she ever try to get me on stage, but she did like for me to perform in the living room for her all the time. She obviously seen something in me, and I'm actually proud to have them here being proud of me. All week I've been with my voice coach and choreographer, just getting everything right and I swear to God, I think I've nailed it. Every week in the live finals they have a theme, and this week is 'number ones'. I don't mean like a number one, as in a piss, I mean like an actual number one hit single. Louis and my voice coach want me to do 'She's the One' by Robbie Williams and I absolutely love that song. When I sing it, I think of Mandy and all that we've went through to get where I am now. From the first time I seen her when she was going to batter a man dressed up as a cow, I knew she was the one. I'm sitting with Mike, Sharon and Maggie having a cup of tea and chatting about tonight's show, Mike seems to be the most nervous:

'I actually feel sick about tonight, like physically sick.'

Mickey Doc

Maggie holds his hand:

'You're going to nail it, Mike. You're bound to be nervous, we all are.'

Then Sharon joins in:

'Every time I think about it, I feel like I'm going to throw up, and I'd say everybody is like that at this moment.'

I've never seen Mike as down in the dumps before. He just nods:

'I know, guys, and thanks, but it's just those harmonies … I keep fucking them up in practice and I'm scared I'll do it on live TV. My daughters and my wife are here and I really don't want to let them down, they're all dead proud.'

I feel so sorry for him, so I try my hand at cheering him up:

'Don't even think about your performance anymore, you'll get that no bother, overthinking it will kill it. You'll be going out and doing the opening performance with everybody here, along with Sam Smith and One Republic. It's the thought of the big crowd and live TV that's freaking you out, just get yourself through the opening song and you'll ease your way into it.'

He's smiling again, thank fuck:

'Jesus, Mickey, for a guy that's renowned for being pretty brainless and mixing up words, you really do talk sense sometimes!'

Everybody laughs and nods, including me, it seems to have lifted the mood a bit:

'I don't know much about anything, actually … I don't know anything really … but for some reason I know this game. Now, let's go get ready to blow this place up …'

Everybody is just staring at me.

'… Er… I mean let's go get ready to blow the roof off this place!'

Mike puts his hand on my shoulder:

'And the real Mickey Doc is back!'

My ma and da are in the room with me. I've done the collaboration with the other contestants, Sam Smith and One Republic. It went class and everybody nailed it. It gave Mike a great boost, too, he actually said to me straight after, while we were still on the stage, that I was totally right. My ma and da seem a bit different with me, in a weird sort of way. They keep smiling at me and asking me if I need anything and telling me how proud they are. It's nice, but it's like they can't really find anything to talk to me about. My da is trying:

Mickey Doc

'So, what's the craic with that interview, then, where you shit yourself?'

My ma punches him in the arm. Obviously, he wasn't allowed to mention that.

'Sorry …'

He's scratching his head, he does that when he's nervous:

'Did you hear about Tina Fleming that works in the bookie's?'

'Naw, I didn't hear.'

'She was smoking in the bookie's on Wednesday morning when she opened up, ended up nearly burning the whole place down. There was five fire engines there, blocked up the whole street, too.'

Then my ma jumps in:

'Five fire engines? There was not! She set fire to a bin, it was hardly the great inferno now, was it?'

'Aye, but they sent out engines because it was a built-up area.'

'You haven't told him who put it out, though!'

'I was getting to that if you'd let me finish my story.'

'Maybe if you told the story right, then I wouldn't interrupt!'

'You know wee Jim, from down the end of the road? The man can hardly lift one leg in front of the other, but he managed to lift a fire extinguisher and put the thing out. Had his photo in the paper and all!'

I can't help but laugh. I laugh way more than I should for such a crap story, but it's not the story, it's more the fact that I'm sitting backstage at a packed arena, there's people running around panicking all over the place and I'm sitting listening to my ma and da tell a story about how wee Jimmy from down the road put out a fire in a bin in the bookie's. My ma and da laugh, too, purely out of nerves I'd say. We're laughing away for a few minutes when Nigel from the production team comes through the door:

'Mr and Mrs Doherty, I'll have to kindly ask you to follow me to your seats. Thank you.'

My ma is just looking at me and smiling. My da stands up first:

'No bother hi, are you going to show us where we're sitting, I've got lost twice in here already?'

'Of course, Mr Doherty. Somebody will be along then to bring you refreshments.'

'A pint of Harp, please and thank you.'

'We don't sell Harp. Mr Doherty.'

Mickey Doc

'Just a wee whiskey then. For the nerves.'

'Certainly, sir. Follow me.'

My da follows Nigel out the door, then it's just me and my ma. She stands up:

'Do you remember when you used to sing in the living room, Mickey?'

She's got tears in her eyes, so do I now. The whole emotion of everything is coming out.

'Aye, I remember ma, you were the only one I'd perform in front of, now ... I'm going out to thousands, mad isn't it?'

'Well, there was three other people you'd perform for too.'

'Who?'

'Remember Alice, Joe and Tommy?'

I say the names back:

'Alice, Joe and Tommy.'

They were the three who took care of me in the pub the night of my christening. They used to visit me all the time after that, I was the only baby any of them would have, but I completely forgot about singing for them.

'They used to love listening to you sing, it used to make their day … no matter how tough things were for them, the three of them would leave singing the songs that you'd sung to them, God rest their souls.'

I'm crying, laughing and smiling all at once. My ma gives me a hug, then goes to leave as soon as Nigel comes back to the door, then turns back:

'When you go out there, Mickey, look up. Your three biggest fans will be watching you from above.'

****

I use the next ten minutes on my own to get my head straight and go over a few vocal exercises. I'm ready. I'm just waiting on the call. It can't be long now. Then it comes, Nigel arrives with his clipboard and he's chatting away in his headpiece:

'Okay, I have Mickey in position, awaiting instruction …'

He holds his hand to the earpiece, obviously listening

'… You ready, Mick?'

'Born ready.'

'… and we're going in 3 …2 …1…'

'Ladies and gentleman, please welcome to the stage … Mickey Doc!'

I walk out on to the stage and the place goes absolutely crazy, it's almost deafening. There's lights flashing cameras moving all over the place. The four judges are sitting behind their desk, but I don't look at them at first, I look up to the skies and hope that my three angels are proud.

****

Okay, I'm not really what you would call a reader. The last full book I read was a copy of Britney Spears's life story, and even at that, I just looked at the pictures. But, the next chapter in my book is newspaper headlines from my rollercoaster ride through the X-Factor live finals.

CHAPTER 19.

Newspapers- 16th October 2014

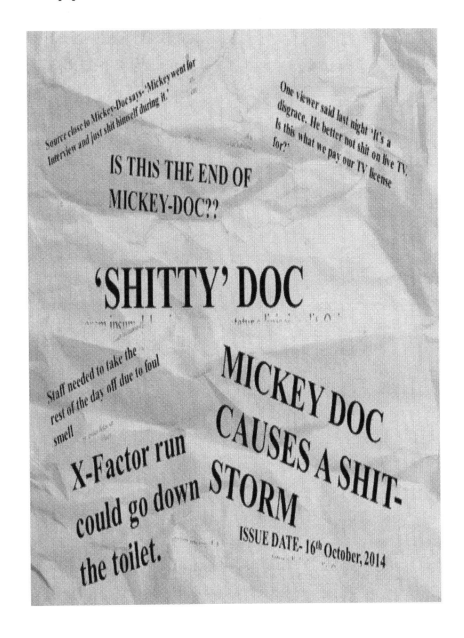

Newspapers- 20th October 2014

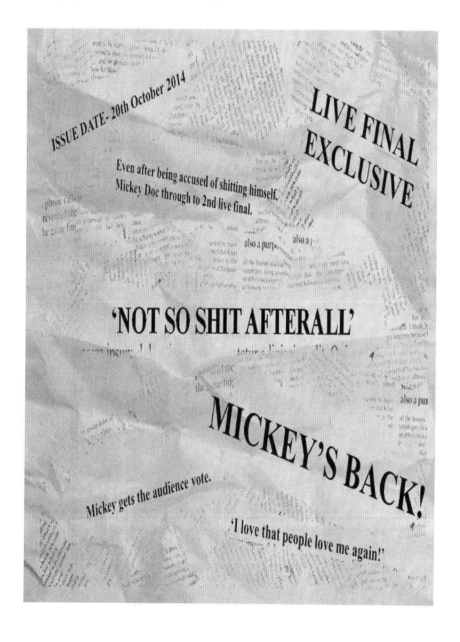

Newspapers- 27th October 2014

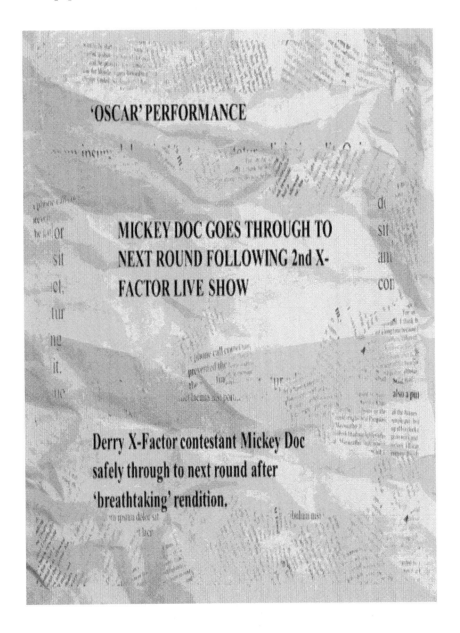

'OSCAR' PERFORMANCE

MICKEY DOC GOES THROUGH TO NEXT ROUND FOLLOWING 2nd X-FACTOR LIVE SHOW

Derry X-Factor contestant Mickey Doc safely through to next round after 'breathtaking' rendition.

Newspapers- 3rd November 2014

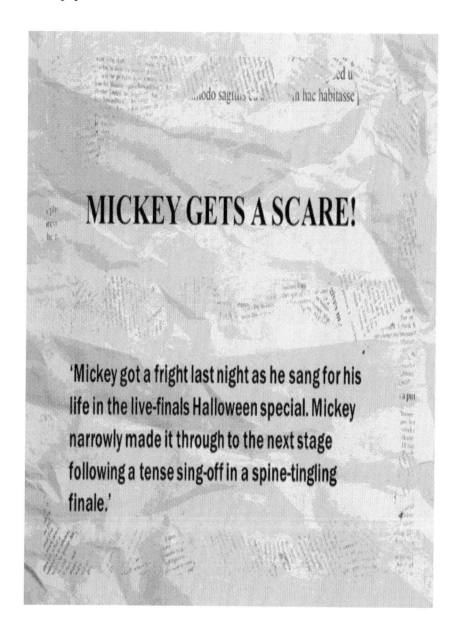

Newspapers- 10th November 2014

Newspapers- 13th November 2014

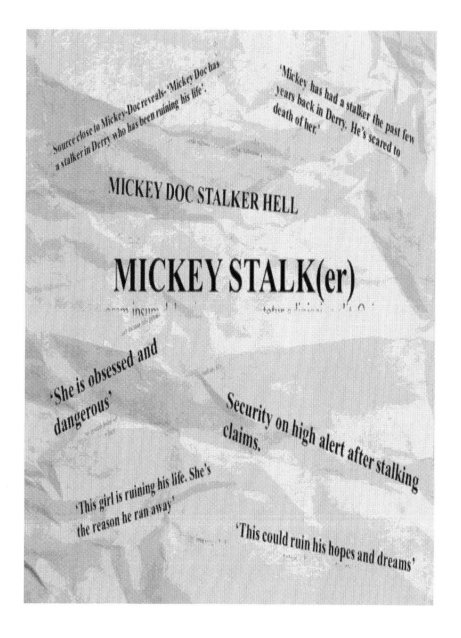

Newspapers- 24th November 2014

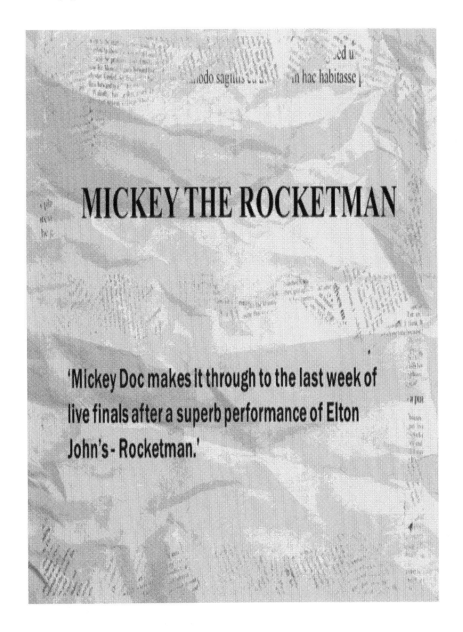

Newspapers- 30th November 2014

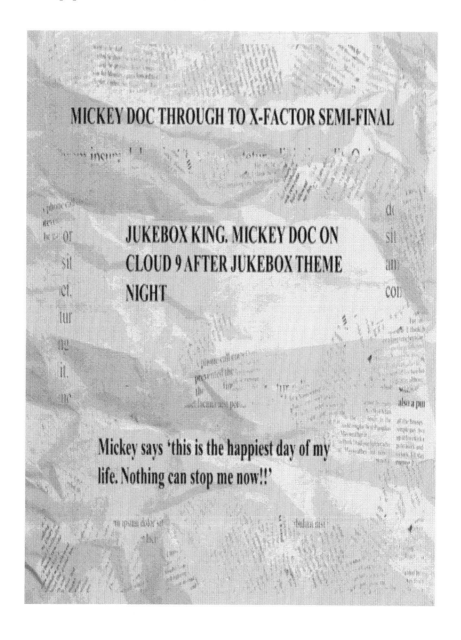

Newspapers- 1st December 2014

CHAPTER 20.

This whole thing has really been a rollercoaster. Not an actual one, like at the amusements, I just mean that I've had loads of ups, which have been the best moments in my life, but I've also had lots of downs that have left me feeling sick in my stomach. The main downers I've had have definitely been the bad newspaper stories about me. First, there was the one about me shitting at that interview in Derry. People thought I'd be eliminated because of it, that people would look at me as a joke and I wouldn't get much further, but I proved them wrong. Then there was the story about Laura Dillon being my stalker. I mean, she was like a stalker in some ways, actually in most ways she was an actual stalker, but I know her and I always knew it was never out of badness that she done those things. I wanted to put out a press release to explain the story and tell the world that she's actually a nice person and the term 'stalker' was way too strong for her. I wanted to say that she was actually my friend and the person who got me on to the X-Factor in the first place, by getting me an application pack and she's the one person who always believed in me, even if I did treat her badly. I couldn't do this, though, firstly because the X-Factor executives thought it would be best if I had a stalker. They said it would raise my profile and make me seem like a genuine star. The second reason why I couldn't tell the world the real story about Laura is that Mandy would go absolutely bonkers.

Things have been good between us lately, and I couldn't afford to lose both her and our baby. I'll do absolutely anything she wants. Mandy is four-and-a-half-months pregnant now, and is due on April 31st. I haven't seen much of her to be honest, she still thinks people should see me as a single bloke until the end of the show, and I'm still not allowed to tell anybody that I'm going to be a daddy. I feel like I'm going to burst. I can't wait to become a father and I want to tell the whole world about it, I want to shout it from the rooftops that Mandy is my girl and she's carrying my baby. There's a chance she might be at the show tonight, the semi-final, if she can make it, she says she has important business to be taking care of whatever the hell that means? Probably doing her nails or baby shopping. I have a seat reserved for her anyway. I'm keeping her away from my ma and da, though. They're both coming over and they said they're bringing a few of their friends for the craic. I just don't want them to be sitting with Mandy, as anything could happen there.

Then there was the latest newspaper story that said about Decky being gay, or more to the point: it said that I stopped being his friend because he was gay, which wasn't what happened at all. Like who would have thought that newspapers would print lies?? Mandy's explanation for the whole thing is that Decky and the lads sold their stories to the newspaper because they wanted to make money for themselves, and they were jealous of my success. I really don't think they would do something like that, but it's the only explanation there is for the whole thing. I hate the fact that people think I would fall out with somebody because they're gay, I would never do a thing like that. I fell out with him because, well it seems a bit silly now, but I fell out with him because he was taking away from my story. It should have been all about me and my getting accepted for the X-Factor, but instead it was all about Decky being gay. I couldn't care less if people said I got annoyed over small things and get a bit jealous, that's just the way I am, but I hate people saying I'm homophobic. I'd love to talk to him so he knows that's not true. Actually, he knows me better than anybody, so he knows it's not true! I think I'm beginning to lose my mind, well, whatever bit I have anyway. That newspaper story could have ruined everything for me on the X-Factor, and it nearly did. I owe everything to Phil and Mike, they saved me as soon as the article came out. Even though it's only me, Mike, Phil and Passive X left in the show and about to compete in the semi-finals, Mike and Phil both went on TV to support me and tell people that the story wasn't true. Phil ism of course, gay himself and Mike has a twin brother who is gay, and they both told the world what really happened and what type of a person I am. They basically said I was amazing and loads of other great stuff. Within an hour, social media had exploded and I was back to being a good guy. For some reason everybody else in the world seemed to already know that newspapers can tell lies. I must have been the only person who wasn't told? Even though I shouldn't be, I've had my ma tell me about how the lads are getting on back home. Marty has his mobile shop up and running and apparently it's doing really well, which is amazing because he is a complete and utter moon-man! This is the same guy that told me he owns half of Alan Sugar's fortune because of a mix-up at the banks. As I said, the fella is a bit loop the lou. I already knew about Stevie getting set up in his da's new company. I always said his oul' boy would get himself back on his feet, even though he has always been a dick to me. Still, it's good to see Stevie doing well, he's a good guy and one of my best friends, even though we're not technically speaking? Word on the street is that Decky is about to sign for Derry City football club, and even though all the crap that has went on since I came to England, I'm still the happiest person in the world for him and I really hope he plays for them. Hopefully, when this is all over and I get things sorted out I'll be able to hang out with the lads again from time to time. I'm sure if Mandy gave them a chance, she'd really like them and I'm sure if the lads could learn about the nice things she does for me, like keeping Knuckles off my back by paying him, then they'd see her differently. Everything is just so up in the air at the moment and I'm missing both Mandy AND the lads. My ma said, too, that my cousin, George the priest-boy, has been saying extra prayers for my soul and has talked to the bishop about me. I just hope the bishop texts a few votes my way when they're needed.

The Live Finals have been some of the most amazing nights of my entire life. When I look back on them now, they are like a dream. I only ended up in the bottom two once out of all the nights, and that scared the hell out of me. It was Week 4 and it was a Halloween theme night. I had been out the night before and got absolutely pissed. Louis almost killed me the next day when he seen me, he said that I'm in danger of throwing everything away, and that I would only have myself to blame. I had to sing-off against Belle from the girls category, then I had to wait until the following night to see if I had been voted off or not. I was so scared and annoyed with myself that I could have blown my chances, but, luckily for me, Belle ended up with the least votes and was sent home. I feel so sorry for anybody that gets sent home, but I can tell you I was more than relieved it wasn't me. My favourite night out of all the live finals was Week 8 where the theme was jukebox. They had to explain to me what a jukebox was after I put my hand up to say I didn't know any Jukebox songs. Turns out a jukebox is an olden days machine for playing music. I don't know why they couldn't have just called it an iPod box? The reason why this night stands out so much is because that's the night I finally got to meet my all-time favourite artists: Little Mix. I've met some of the biggest names in the music industry through this show, but Little Mix take the biscuit. Not only are those girls some of the best talents this world has ever seen, but they are also some of the most nicest and most gorgeous people ever. We chatted for about an hour, plus they helped me get my song ready for the show. I had to do the whole rehearsal sitting down, because if I stood up they'd notice I was pitching a tent. I dedicated that night to the Little Mix girls.

It feels mad in the house now that there's so few of us left, it's so quiet. At the start the place was bursting at the seams with people … and that's saying something, because it's a mansion! Now it's just me, Mike, Phil and the lads from Passive X. Because me and Mike were in the same category, we've been mates from the start. Phil and the Passive X lads both came from different categories, but we are as close now as I have been with anybody here. I thought things might be a bit strange between me and Phil after the whole homophobic lies thing, but he has been like a brother to me. We're all getting our bags packed because nobody will be staying in the house tonight, we're all staying in a hotel close to the arena, then we have the results show tomorrow night, I just hope I'm not involved. Me and Mike are both in our room when he throws a hat at me:

'Here, mate, meant to give this to ya yesterday, my missus bought it for you.'

I catch the hat and it's the most ridiculous thing I've ever seen. Somebody obviously knitted it, because it's like something my granny used to give me at Christmas:

'Aw, nice one, man, tell her I love it!'

'Glad you like it, mate, she wants you to wear it on the show tonight!'

'Really? Erm ... aye ... I'll see if I have anything with me that will go with it?'

'That would be great, she stayed up all night knitting that for you!'

The hat is brown, yellow and blue. I'm pretty sure the holes in it aren't supposed to be there and there's bit of wool hanging out of the top. I put the hat on just as Phil comes into the room. He sees me and right away starts giving it loads:

'Oh. My. God! Mickey Doc, that has to be the nicest piece of clothing I've ever seen you wear! Where did you get that and how much did it cost?'

I'm not sure if he's being serious or taking the hand out of me:

'Mike's missus, Trish, made it for me.'

He turns to Mike:

'Seriously? And can I ask you why your darling wife hasn't made me such a beautiful piece of head covering?'

'Well, mate, she said she was going to knit one for you too but she spent so much time on Mickey's that she didn't have time to make yours.'

'Oohh, well now I'm even more jealous!'

Phil turns to me then:

'I'm assuming that you'll be wearing this fine piece of craftsmanship on the show tonight?'

Mickey Doc

Mike butts in:

'That's why the missus made it, she'd be gutted if he didn't wear it!'

'Of course, I'm going to wear it!'

I look at the hat again, trying to figure out if I'm looking at it wrong or something. I hold it upside down and turn it inside out but it still looks like the ugliest thing I've ever seen. Then the two of them burst out laughing. Phil can hardly talk he's laughing that much:

'Aw, Mickey mate …. Your…. Your face when I gave you … when I gave you the hat!'

They are actually bent over laughing and I'm not really sure what the joke is? Why are they laughing at the hat his wife made? After almost five minutes of them laughing, Phil finally gets his breath back and tells me:

'We found it in the street …'

He can't finish his sentence 'cause he's laughing too much again, so Mike takes over:

'We found it on the street and we thought we'd see if you'd wear it tonight!'

The two of them high-five each other, then Phil says:

'Aw, Mickey darling, you are the most innocent of people I've ever met!'

****

There's a limo sent for us to bring us to the arena. It's only 9am in the morning, but we'll be spending the full day there rehearsing and doing interviews. We all feel really comfortable in Wembley Arena now, because we've spent so much time there throughout the live shows. The first thing we see when we get there is the amount of people milling about. There's press photographers waiting to get photos and there's hundreds of fans waiting to get a glimpse of their heroes. I love signing my autograph, I even bring pictures of me and a packet of markers, just in case somebody needs something signed. Some people don't even need paper for me to sign: I've signed arms, arses, boobs, legs, hands, heads, feet – one man even asked me to sign his you-know-what, but I moved on to the next person as quick as I could. Next thing I knew he was being arrested for getting his lad out in a public place. The seven of us, me, Mike, Phil and the Passive X lads spend about 20 minutes signing autographs and posing for photos on the way in, until one of the production team, Nigel, sends out a few security staff to bring us in. Thank God, too, because it's absolutely freezing out and they reckon it's going to snow. None of the judges are here yet, they normally arrive much later in the day, but all the rest of the production team are here. I head to my changing room to sort myself out before we start, and as I'm heading there, my phone beeps. My heart jumps when I see that it's from Knuckles:

It's me, Mandy, Some dick stole my fuckin phone again! I swear to God if I get the cunt I'll kill em! I'm heading down to London this afternoon. Oh and get another ticket, Knuckles is coming with me.

I text back:

Sure, no prob. Can't wait to see you. And Knuckles too.

I just wrote the last bit 'cause I know he'll be reading it as soon as he gets a chance. He better not be planning on threatening me again, not on a night like this. The first thing I'll be doing as soon as it's all over is paying him off. Maybe then I can get Mandy to stop hanging about with him. I have a feeling she's just keeping in with him so he doesn't do anything nasty to me, which is kinda nice. Although she never tells me she loves me, or likes me for that matter, it's the wee things like this that make me know she cares without her having to say the words.

I open the door of my changing room and the first thing I notice is the Christmas lights and the Christmas tree in the corner. It's now the 6th of

December and the first time I've actually thought about Christmas, and the first time this year I've got a bit of the Christmas spirit. The room looks unreal, there's little decorations hanging all over the place and there's even Christmas music playing softly in the background. My Christmas spirit couldn't have come at a better time, because tonight's theme is Christmas songs. I'll be performing Stay Now by East 17 for my first song, then my second song will be Run by a Northern Ireland band called Snow Patrol? I still call it Leona Lewis' song, though, obviously she made it what it is. I'm sitting in my chair in front of the huge mirror that has lights all around it, I'm not fixing my hair or any of the things I usually do, I'm just sitting looking at myself and thinking. Of course, I'm not really known for thinking, but this time I'm just sitting thinking about how far I've come. This time last year I was in a job I hated. Now, I know I always said I hated my job, but this time last year it would have been Christmas, too, and I can tell you the worst place in the world to be at Christmas time is working in a shop. Every Christmas I used to say 'I won't be working here next year', but I just couldn't get a way out and my ma would never let me quit. I wonder if my old boss, Barry, watches the show? It must be killing him to see me on the TV being famous while he's still stacking turkeys. Then I start thinking about how things will be this time next year. I think I'll definitely be living in England with Mandy and our baby. Our baby. This time next year I'll be playing Santa Clause and giving he/she all the best presents that money can buy. I'm just staring at the mirror for ages when there's a knock on the door:

'Hello? Come in!'

It's Emma, one of the girls from the production team. She's lovely and always smiling:

'Hi, Mickey, sorry to disturb you, I hope you like what we've done with the place?'

'Did you do this? I love it, it's so Christmassy!'

'Well I can't take all the credit, there was a few of us working on them.'

'It's class, it got me right into the Christmas spirit!'

'Brilliant, glad you like it. Are you ready to come with me now for the sound and positioning checks? Then you're over to Yvie for the voice coaching, then another run-through with the choreographers and a few interviews.'

She's reading from her clipboard. The production team ALWAYS have a clipboard on them!

'Oh, and we picked up your parents and your friends from the airport. We brought them to the hotel. They're all staying in your hotel.'

'That's grand. I hope they didn't melt anybody's head on the way there.'

'Your parents are lovely, and your friends seem nice too.'

I burst out laughing:

'They're my ma's friends, Emma!'

'Oh, they seem quite young.'

'Don't be telling them that, they'll get a big head!'

She laughs:

'Okay, I won't. I told them that with your busy schedule today there's a chance you won't see them till after the show.'

'Aye I told them that anyway, suits me grand!'

'Lovely. Now, are we ready to go?

'Hold on a minute till I fix my hair.'

****

When she said I have a busy schedule, she really meant it. As soon as I'm done with one thing, I'm being led to another. I hardly get a chance to see Mike, Phil and the Passive X lads. Every time we pass each other and get chatting, we're being hurried along to somewhere else. You really notice the lack of contestants at this stage. At the start of the live shows you were with people all the time and doing the same things. Now everything is timed so the three of us are at different places at different times. All this running around makes the day absolutely fly in, and before I know it I'm back in my changing room and getting ready for the 2014 X-Factor semi-final. Obviously, there's only four acts left, and we'll all be singing against each other. In a twist this year, one act will be automatically voted through tonight by the judges, while the rest of the contestants have to wait till the results show tomorrow night to see if they get enough public votes to make it to the final. One act will be going home tomorrow night, I just really hope it's not me.

My clothes are all laid out for me on a table. I pick them up and start to put them on when I notice something drop out of the jacket. I jump at first 'cause I thought it was a rat, but then I notice it's the hat that Mike and Phil tried to get me to wear. There's a note inside saying 'Good luck, mate, from Phil and Mike'. I can't wipe the smile off my face as I whip out my phone and take a picture of me wearing the hat with a caption underneath saying 'Gud luck 2night… nd gud luck trying to luk as gud as me!' I do my usual voice exercises, sit-ups, push-ups, poses in the mirror, then I go over my song one more time. Just as I'm

finished, Emma arrives back at my door:

'Hey, Mickey, looking great dude!'

'Thanks hi, I always try to look my best!'

'We're almost ready for you now, do we need to go over anything?'

'Nope, I'm as ready as I'll always be!'

I get up to leave, but Emma is looking at me funny as I go out the door:

'Isn't there anything else?'

'Erm… thank you for everything?'

'You're welcome, Mickey, but I wasn't fishing for a compliment. I was

wondering when you're going to get rid of that hat.'

'Fuck!'

I chuck the hat through the door and head out to the wings to await my

call.

****

I can hear Simon, Mel B, Cheryl and Louis talking about Mike's

performance. He absolutely smashed it! They're all singing his praises and telling him how amazing he was. It's a crazy feeling, you want to see your mates do well, but at the same time they could get a place and I could end up on the first plane back to Derry on Monday morning. I get rid of that thought from my head right away, and get into the zone. I know that my ma and da are out there in that arena waiting for me to come out. I also know that Mandy and our baby are here too and it'll be the first time our baby gets to hear me sing. I try not to think about Knuckles being there too. Mike leaves the stage from the other side and I know my time is getting near. Nigel is standing with his clipboard and listening away into his earpiece, waiting for somebody else to tell him when it's my time. I can hear Dermott O'Leary talking and I know it's only a matter of seconds:

'Ladies and gentleman, it's time for your second act of the evening. With two acts remaining in the contest, this judge must think that he's going to be having a happy Christmas this year... it's Louis Walshe!'

Then it's over to Louis:

'I can't tell you how excited I am to see this next act perform tonight, he has been something special right from the start and I know he'll be just as special tonight with a Christmas classic. Ladies and gentlemen, please put your hands together, all the way from Ireland... Mickey Doc!'

The crowd go absolutely nuts! I feel like I'm in total control as I've rehearsed this a million times. I totally nail the performance and the judges love it. It's all over in a second and before I know it I'm being swept back to my changing room to get ready for my next performance. The blood is racing through my body and I just want to get back on that stage again and do what I do best... sing.

I'm back in the room for what feels like hours, when Emma comes calling for me again. We hardly even speak this time because tensions are so high in the whole arena. This is what it's all about. Next, I'm standing beside Nigel again and waiting on him to let me on. I feel like a caged lion about to be set free. Dermott does his bit, then Louis takes over again to introduce me. This is it, this is the song that is going to get me to the final, this is my time. This is Mickey Doc time. I sing my way through the song, making every high note and nailing every move. The crowd love it and I can see by the faces of the judges that they love it too. Mel B is waiting on the audience to calm down before she speaks, but that's not happening so she has to shout:

'Mickey Doc... waaaaaooohhhhhh!! You just continue to do what you do and you get better every week. All through this show you've had controversy and bad press, but you never let it stop you from being you.

And that's what we love, Mickey, we love you and your fantastic voice!'

'Thank you, Mel, I really appreciate that.'

Cheryl is next to speak:

'Aw, I just love your voice, man. You can reach notes without even trying and there's some notes you hit that I don't even know where they came from. I've said from the start you're one of the favourites for the whole show and there's nothing since that has made me change my opinion.'

'Thank you, Cheryl, thank you so much.'

Then its Simons turn:

'There was a few times throughout the contest that I didn't share Cheryl's favourite tag for you…'

The crowd start booing

'… But, Mickey, what I like about you is you're resilient. You never give up, you've been focused on your dream from day one and even though your name became a bit of a joke, you still came out here every week and gave it your very best and that's all we can ask for. Tonight I thought you were incredible, you should be very happy with that performance.'

'Thanks, Simon, I've loved every minute of it here!'

Simon gives me one of his trademark winks, then it's my mentor, Louis who speaks:

'Mickey, Mickey, Mickey! Your hard work throughout has been something else and you've always made it easy for me to coach you. Words can't describe how proud I am of you tonight, your performances throughout and especially your performances tonight have been out of this world and you're such a great guy too! You're already a superstar and I think there's a lot more of Mickey Doc for us to see in the future!'

'Thank you, Louis, thank you very much for everything.'

I'm back in my changing room. I feel like screaming, laughing and crying all in one go. I don't get a chance to do anything, though 'cause I'm straight back out the door again and back towards the stage. I meet Mike, Phil and the Passive X lads on the way because we're all going back out together to find out who gets the safe vote and will be the first person through to the 2014 X-Factor final. We all hug each other and chat excitedly about what went on tonight. Everybody put in great performances and nobody knows whose name will be called out. The seven of us are brought out on to the stage and we all put our arms around each other to await the judges' verdict. Then it's over to Dermott:

'Okay … I have, in this envelope, the name of the act who will automatically qualify for the 2014 X-Factor final, as voted by the judges. If the judges cannot agree and we have a draw, then all four acts will be fighting it out for the public vote. Ladies and gentlemen … the first act to go through to the Live Final…. Is …. we have a name … Mickey Doc!'

****

I can't explain how good it feels to not have to worry about the results show tomorrow night. I think I may even have some drinks tonight to celebrate. I get back to my hotel room and all my clothes are put away and hung up. I'm not sure if this is a service from the hotel or if my ma has got my key. Just as I'm about to go into the bathroom, there's a knock on the door. I walk over to answer it and get a really bad feeling in my stomach. I open the door.

It's Knuckles. He pushes me through the door and walks on in, closing the door behind him.

CHAPTER 21.

'That was some fookin' performance, Mickey son, that was some fookin' performance!'

'Thanks very much, Knuckles.'

I'm lying on my back, shaking like a leaf and looking up at him. He's staring into my eyes the whole time, and he's giving me a scary stare that I've never seen before. He's dressed in a nice pair of jeans, and a shirt, but he still looks like an absolute scumbag.

He's standing above me, looking down into my eyes:

'Aren't you going to get up off the floor when you have a guest? That's very bad manners, Mickey son, very bad manners.'

I go to get up, but he uses his foot to push me back down again

'You fookin owe me ...'

'...You fookin' owe me big time.'

'I don't have your money yet, Knuckles. I'm fucking broke till this whole thing is over, I swear to God we get fuck-all for doing this. After this is over, I'll be making good money, amazing money. Just give me till then.'

He just stares at me for about a minute and says:

'You see, when we was watching you out there tonight, I thought, this guy is good. A twat … but good at singing, know what I mean?'

I just nod.

'And then, when we saw that you got through to the final, I thought "this is interesting". My business brain started ticking over and I thought I could offer you a little proposition. And when I say "offer", you don't really have a choice in the mater, old son.'

He presses his foot on to my chest and I can hardly breathe:

'What … what is it? I can hardly breathe.'

He takes his foot off my chest and lifts me with one hand onto the bed. His face is like a man possessed. I've never been as scared in my life. He just stares at me for about 40 seconds, then says:

'I want you to make a cock-up in the final. I want you to go out and sing, but I don't want you to win. Got it?'

'How can I go out and try not to win?'

'Because, Mickey, not only will I beat your stupid-looking face to a pulp with my own bare hands, I'll also make sure the police connect you with the fingerprints they found when they was investigating a warehouse robbery in Manchester a few months back. Ring any bells?'

'You can't do that!'

'Oh, but I can, old son. There isn't a shred of evidence that links myself or my boys to that robbery. All the pigs have is a single set of fingerprints that they can't match to anyone … not unless I can help them with their enquiries. Now, the only way I'll help you out of this is if you help me. I could make big money on a little betting scam, all you have to do is make sure you don't win. Simples. And another thing: I don't want you going near Mandy ever again.'

'Where is she? She'll never let you get away with this.'

He starts laughing, it's a really long and sickening laugh. He even ends up slobbering all over himself and he just wipes away the slabbers with his hand and starts shouting:

'Mandy? You really fink, mate, that Mandy gives a flying fuck about you? She done you real good, I'll give her that, she done you real good, son. See, Mickey, our plan from the start was a little bit like yourself, mate. Simple. Mandy met a little plaything, which I was a bit pissed off about, so I thought I'll show this little prick …'

I'm assuming he's talking about me here.

'I told her she can keep her new toy. I've known of others before, Mickey. You ain't her first toy. With the others, though, I always made sure they ended up in hospital. My trick was to focus my kicks between their legs …'

He grits his teeth and makes a kicking motion with his leg, which makes my hands automatically move over my nuts.

'I called this "removing the batteries from her toys".'

He stares straight into my eyes and gives me an evil smile that makes the hairs stand on the back of my neck. Then goes on:

'But I had different plans for you, Mickey old son. Get a bit of use out of you before I get rid of you. I thought, this guy is dumb as fuck, I'll use him.'

Next thing there's a knock on the door. Knuckles just stares at me and I'm too afraid to speak.

Knuckles whispers:

'You expecting anybody?'

'Aye, I'm expecting loads of people, to be honest. I'd say that's my ma and da with their friends, though. They know I'm in here.'

'Lovely, I'm going to meet whatever it was that produced somefhing as ugly as you.'

My mind is racing, but I can't get past the fact this bloke is calling me ugly. Like, seriously, you have no idea how ugly this bloke is and he has the cheek to call ME ugly. I don't say anything, though. I'm too scared and it's really not the time.'

'I want you to bring them in, introduce me as a friend, then, I leave. But the business proposition still stands. You cross me and you're fucked.'

The door knocks again, this time harder. I brush myself off, then walk over to the door. I really hope it's my ma and da so I can get rid of this psycho. I open the door and my ma and da both start hugging me and telling me how proud they are. Then they notice Knuckles, he's just standing there with a big smile on his face. My da is standing at the door, holding it open. My ma is still looking at Knuckles when he says:

'Aren't you going to introduce me to your family, Michael?'

'Mum, dad, this is my mate, Knuckles.'

He puts out his hand to my mum:

'Call me Kevin, Missus Doherty, Knuckles is just a little nickname we have.'

'Hello, love, nice to meet ye. Are you a part of the show too?'

'No, no. I just thought I'd be the first to congratulate young Michael here on a job well done. I'm hoping I can work with him myself very soon in my own business.'

My ma is standing smiling like a total gack.

My da doesn't even speak to Knuckles, he just talks to me:

'Mickey, son, there's a few friends here to see you.'

'Da gone tell your friends I'll see them after, I've a few things to sort out here first,'

'It's YOUR friends I have with me, Mickey. They have a few things they need to tell you.'

'What? Who?'

I end up getting an even bigger fright than when Knuckles had me pinned to the ground with his size 14 boots. In through the door walks Stevie, Marty then Decky. I'm standing staring at them when I get an even bigger surprise. Laura Dillon.

I just about manage to say something:

'What? What's going on? I didn't know you were all here?'

Decky is the first to speak. They're not smiling or congratulating me, they look like something bad has happened:

'Mickey we found out some stuff that you need to know ...'

He's staring straight at Knuckles. Actually, all the lads are staring straight at Knuckles.

'... well, when I say 'we', it was Laura that found out stuff.'

I'm just standing staring and trying to make out if I'm dreaming or not. I manage to speak:

'What? What is it?'

All of a sudden, Knuckles makes his way towards the door. He's staring at Decky like he wants to pull his head straight off his shoulders, but Decky is meeting his stare and isn't flinching.

Knuckles says while still staring at Decky:

'Why don't I leave you to sort out whatever you have to sort out with your little friends here and I'll talk to you later, Mickey old son.'

'Alright, no bother Knuckles!'

I feel a huge relief when I see that Knuckles is about to leave. That is until Marty, the fucking looper, stands in front of him and says:

'I think you'd better stay for this too, big lad.'

I can see from the look on my ma's face that she's in the same boat as me. We seem to be the only two people in the room who don't have a fucking notion what's going on. Knuckles doesn't seem too sure either, but he knows something is going down. He stares at Marty, then Decky, then Stevie and says:

'Okay, I'll join your little party if you really want me here. Watch you all kiss and make up and say how much you fackin' love each other. Let's all love each other, eh?'

Knuckles is laughing and walks back into the centre of the room. He does it in sort of like slow motion, like he doesn't give a fuck what's going on. My ma is looking at my da as if to say 'what's happening here?'

Decky starts talking again:

'As I was saying ... Laura found out a few things about what's been going on over here, and she brought them to us. We thought we'd come over and tell you everything so you don't get into any more trouble than you're already in.'

Laura starts talking:

'You know the way I was away there for a while, Mickey?'

Mickey Doc

'Aye...'

'Well, ever since that one you call your girlfriend threatened to kill me AND you in the café, I thought I'd start digging a little. I don't like the term 'stalker', Mickey, but I do know how to follow somebody without them knowing ...'

I can definitely vouch for that.

'... so I decided to follow that conniving little so and so...'

That's when I interrupt:

'Houl' on a minute, Laura, just 'cause you're jealous about what me and Mandy have, there's no point you coming here making up stories. She's my girlfriend and the mother of my soon to be born baby!'

'What??'

That was my ma, this wasn't how I wanted her to find out.

'It's alright ma, we're happy!'

My da puts his arms around my ma and tells her to keep quiet a minute. Then Laura starts up again, she looks real calm:

'As I was saying, I decided to follow her and see what I could see. Turns out I can see a lot when I go to Manchester ... and see who she really is...'

Knuckles is starting to get very annoyed, he's standing twitching. Laura continues:

'... I also know who that excuse for a human being is that's standing beside you.'

She's staring straight at Knuckles. Everybody seems to be staring right at Knuckles. They obviously don't have a clue exactly how dangerous he is. Then he speaks:

'Listen little girl, you better watch what comes out of your mouth, because some things can't be put back in, no matter how hard I try to force them.'

Laura doesn't seem to give a fuck, she doesn't even flinch, just keeps staring at him and talking:

'You see, I got my hands on a whole lot of information, I found out just how much trouble you got yourself in, Mickey, and with whom. Knuckles and Mandy have been taking you for a ride for a while now.'

Knuckles pulls out his phone. It must only ring once because he speaks almost straight away:

'Come up to his room, now.'

Then he just hangs up and puts his phone back in his pocket. My ma is asking my da what's going on and he just keeps telling her it's alright.

I can't even speak anymore, although I want to ask a million questions.

Laura starts talking again:

'Firstly, the newspaper stories. That was Mandy.'

I finally find a voice:

'Don't be trying to tell me that Mandy done that, you're talking shite now, Laura.'

There's another knock at the door. As cool as you like, Knuckles walks past everybody and opens it. It's Mandy. She gets the shock of her life when she sees who all's in the room:

'What the fook is going on in here?'

She doesn't even look at me, she's just trying to take in who's there as she walks across the room with Knuckles walking behind her. I call her name and put out my arms, but she just totally blanks me and stands with Knuckles. I say her name again and more words come out:

'Mandy … what's going on?'

'You fookin' tell me, Mickey? You got your folks here, you got your mates who sold you down the river here, and you got that psycho stalker here. Now you tell me what the fook's going on, Mickey?'

'I don't have a clue, I swear to God, I didn't even know these were coming!'

Mandy has her eyes glued to Laura Dillon:

'Didn't I warn you before about stalking my man?'

Laura meets her stare:

'Your man? I know who your man is and I know who you are. You sold the stories to the paper, you let Mickey think he was your boyfriend, you got him to take a loan out from your gang boss, who coincidently is also your boyfriend, you got him involved in a robbery …'

'… You should also be more careful of where you leave your phone. Didn't even learn your lesson after I took the first one.'

Mandy makes an attempt to get at Laura, but Knuckles holds her back:

'Wait. Not yet.'

At the same time my ma passes out and my da catches her. He sits her down on the chair. I feel like my whole life is crumbling around me on what was supposed to be the happiest day of my life. I can't move, I can't take it all in.

Laura keeps going:

'... you've been fleecing him from the day you met him, and you're planning to extort money from him again.'

Mandy is obviously in shock, too, but Knuckles steps forward and starts laughing:

'You stupid little Irish cants, if you had even the slightest fookin' idea of who you're messing with, you would not be standing talking like that ...'

Marty of all people interrupts him! He's standing holding the door open, only he can see out the door because everybody else is in the room, then he says:

'Don't you worry your wee baldy head, big man, I know exactly who you are!'

I can't believe he just said that. I honestly cannot believe those words just came out of his mouth. I look over at him and shake my head as if to say 'this isn't an imaginary thing in your head now Marty, this is real life!

I think Knuckles gets a shock by his bravery too:

'What? What the fook did you just say to me? Nobody, and I mean nobody speaks to me like that!'

Knuckles starts walking across the room towards Marty, there isn't anybody in the room who could stop him doing what he's about to do. Marty is staring at him, then, out of nowhere, a strange man walks into the room and Knuckles stops, probably not able to keep up with what's going on either.

Cool as you like, Marty starts talking again:

'Knuckles, I believe you might already know my mate, Sean?'

There's a few cogs starting to spin in my head when I hear the name, but nothing's happening, they're just making noises. Knuckles is still playing it cool:

'Yeah, I know Sean. This has nothing to do with him, though, I say it's nothing to do with him, son.'

Marty isn't giving up that easy:

'Sean is a personal friend of mine who's from down the road from me, and owes me a wee favour, so to speak.'

The penny finally drops! He's Marty's imaginary gangster friend, the witch's son. But he's not imaginary, he's real!

I'm looking at Mandy, and I can see by her face that she knows who Sean is, too. Knuckles turns to Sean:

Mickey Doc

'This is just a bit of business between me and some people here, Sean. You know yourself, mate, sometimes these things have to be turned up a crank or two?'

Sean is only a wee fart with a shaved head and a few tattoos on his arm, but Knuckles looks a bit worried for the first time. Probably first time ever. Sean fixes his collar, then, turns to Knuckles and talks to him, only he's not really talking towards him, he's talking at the floor beside his feet:

'When wee Marty here came looking for me about helping out a friend, I thought 'that's not really my scene', know what I mean? And then he reminded me that I owe him a wee favour so I thought I'd look into it. Then I heard your name, and I knew I heard that name somewhere before. Knuckles. Then it hit me. I have a few things going on everywhere, a bit here, a bit there, a bit abroad, a bit in... say, Manchester. Then I figured out where I heard the name. It seems some man who fits your name and your description stole some goods from me a few months ago? £20.000 worth of goods I might add. Now, that sort of money doesn't really interest me, I could lose that in a casino in one night after a few J.Ds, but what does worry me is the fact that some dickhead thinks he could steal from me.'

Knuckles looks to be shitting them now:

'Hold on, old son, I had no idea those warehouses were yours!'

'Knuckles, I don't really care if you knew or not, that's besides the point. The point is that you stole a substantial amount of money from me … and I want it back.'

Everybody in the room is standing with their mouths open, this is some serious, serious shit going down between the two of them.

'Fook, mate, I'll get you the money tonight, I swear to God if I'd known it was yours I wouldn't have touched it! We're cool, man, it's just a misunderstanding.'

Sean hasn't taken his eyes off the ground the whole time, he won't even look at Knuckles:

'You're right, you'll get me my money tonight. And whatever you've got going on here, I want it stopped now, or I'll put a stop to it.'

'This was all just a misunderstanding, mate, me and Mickey and the boys are good.'

'Don't treat me like a fucking dickhead. Tell the lad whatever it is you want from him is gone.'

Knuckles turns to me and I can see the fear in his eyes:

'That debt you owe me Mickey, it's gone.'

'That's grand, Knuckles.'

'And the other arrangement we came to earlier, that's gone now, too.'

Sean, who I must add, *still* hasn't taken his eyes off the carpet, says:

'Now get out of my sight, I'll send the boys around in an hour to collect.'

Knuckles just nods and heads straight out the door. Mandy can't believe what's going on and neither can I to be honest. This is all just far too much to take in. Mandy turns to me and says:

'I need to talk to you, Mickey. Alone.'

Laura speaks up again:

'Not a chance.'

'Laura, she's the mother of my child!'

'No she's not. Mickey, I didn't want to have to tell you like this but Knuckles is Mandy's boyfriend. She has been his girlfriend for years. She met you by chance when she was out hustling the X-Factor crowd, then she started playing you, getting a few quid out of you, mostly for kicks. She's a professional con-artist, Mickey. Seems her loving boyfriend got a bit jealous she had a new plaything and decided to take it out on you.'

I think I can hear the very moment my heart breaks in two. I can feel the tears running down my cheeks.

'I'm not a daddy?'

Mandy can't even look at me when she says:

'No.'

All of a sudden, my ma is up on her feet again and running towards Mandy. I've never seen her move as fast in my life! In one swoop she catches Mandy by the hair and trails her towards the door that Marty still has opened. Mandy is like a little ragdoll flying through the air 'cause my ma is strong as fuck and she has a rage on:

'I never liked you from the day and hour I set eyes on you, ye little tramp ye. Aw, I'll tell ye I had you well sized up from the start. You might be able to manipulate the men of my house with them wee perky tits of yours, but you couldn't fool me!'

Just as my ma is about to chuck Mandy out the door, I run over and stop her:

'Please ma, I need to talk to her. Alone.'

My ma keeps her full grip on her hair and turns to me:

'Son, naw, don't be listening to a word this little trollop says!'

Mickey Doc

I put my hand on my ma's arm, the one that's removing Mandy scalp from her head:

'Please ma, I need to talk to her.'

My ma lets go and Mandy falls straight to the ground, then bounces up and walks back across the room again, rubbing her head.

Everybody is staring at me now:

'Please, everybody, just get out of my room and let me talk to Mandy alone for a minute.'

Everybody looks shocked, but they all turn to leave.

Mandy takes a breath and stares at the floor. I can see that none of the rest want to leave but they do it anyway. My ma is last to go, and peeks her head back in through the door:

'If you need anything, son, we'll be just next door.'

Then the door closes and it's just me and Mandy. She's sitting on the bed now, rubbing her scalp and lifting bits of hair my ma ripped out:

'Your mum's a strong fookin' woman!'

'Tell me about it.'

I sit beside her on the bed and she puts her hand on my hand, then looks into my eyes with those eyes I fall in love with every time I see them:

'This is all fucked up, Mickey. Things were never supposed to be this way. Knuckles, he … he makes me do things, he makes me steal and lie and cheat, and I swear to God, man I'm sick of it. I just want a normal fookin' life, man. That's what I felt when I was around you. Normal. For the first time in my life, I felt normal …'

She's rubbing my hand now.

'… we could still be normal, Mickey. We could fuck off somewhere and be a family like you always wanted, just me you and the baby.'

She lifts my hand and puts it on her belly. She has a bump now, it's not a very big bump, but still a bump.

'Run away with me, Mickey, just you, me and the baby. Fuck everything else. We could walk out on the whole lot and start over somewhere new.'

CHAPTER 22.

I'm just staring at Mandy, like a bear caught in the headlights. Her eyes have always done that to me. I always felt like I could see something in there, like, goodness? Even when I first met her and she was threatening the guy dressed as a cow and kicking him up the arse, I seen something in her eyes. Even when she was staying out all night and pretty much ignoring me, I could still see something good. I move my hand from her belly and put my hands on my knees. Then I realise I'm sitting like Forrest Gump, so I move them down beside me, onto the bed. Ever since I saw that movie I was always paranoid that I was a bit like him.

Mandy has tears in her eyes. I can't stand seeing people cry. Tears are running down my face, but my mouth has dried up. I just about manage to say:

'I can't go with you, Mandy. I'm sorry.'

She's just sitting nodding and staring at the floor. I've never seen her like that before. Then, after about a minute of silence, she wipes her eyes and starts talking:

'See, Mickey, at the start, I was just on for having a bit of a laugh, you know. You seemed like good fun, somebody I could hang out with at the auditions. I liked what I seen in you. You had dreams. Big dreams. I used to have those, too, when I was a kid… '

She starts finding it hard to talk, so I hold her hand. Then she takes a few seconds to *com-post* herself?

'… But I was never allowed to have dreams. I was the daughter of two of the most fucked-up people you've ever met, man. They was always either banged up inside or doing things that was about to get them banged up. I was just somebody they could use for their own personal gain. They didn't give a fuck about me. They taught me how to lie and cheat and get things from people by being cute. They scoffed at my dreams, and told me I would amount to nothing unless I went and took things for myself. They taught me how to be this selfish bitch you see in front of you now.'

And I only thought my parents were fucked up. I've got an awful urge to hug my ma and da right now. I put my other arm around her. I can feel her warm tears soak into my shirt. She's just staring off into the distance as she talks:

'I left home when I was 16. Just got up one day and ran away. I didn't know where I was going. I was on the streets for about a week or so, then, I met Knuckles. He took care of me. Gave me somewhere to stay, fed me, and seemed like he really cared for me. Wasn't long before I was stealing and conning people again. I just thought then that my parents were right all along. This is how the world works and I would never amount to anything. I never had dolls or any sort of toys growing up, Mickey. But I knew I could sing ... and sing well. It was all I ever wanted to do. I had a teacher at school once, Mrs Beasley, who used to tell me I could be anything I wanted to be, and that I had the voice of an angel. I ran home from school the day she told me that and I announced to my parents that I was going to be a singer. They were both drunk as fuck, man. You know what they did? Locked me in my room for six days. Told me that until I stop talking like a fucking idiot, they wouldn't let me out. They weren't a bit shy about using their fists on me. They crushed my innocence. I thought they had crushed my dreams too. When the X-Factor came up, I applied. I didn't know it at the time, but I was indulging the six-year-old me. I told Knuckles ... and myself, that I was going there to do a job. Pick the pockets of some of the absolute wankers who go to those things. '

She squeezes my hand really tight and lets out a breath. She starts crying again as she says:

'But, somewhere inside me, the dreams I had as a little girl were still there ...'

She's still squeezing my hand. I can hardly feel my fingers, but, I'm not going to say anything. She's still staring away, somewhere in the distance.

'... Then I met you, Mickey. You brought out the six-year-old me. You made me feel like things were possible again. For the first time in almost 20 years, I felt like me again.'

The tears are streaming down my face now, almost as fast as the snotters that are coming out of my nose. I reach across the bed and pick up the packet of hankies from the bedside table. I carefully blow my nose and wipe away the tears.

'I knew you liked me, Mandy, I knew the whole time. I could see something in you. I could see the little six-year-old you.'

Then I catch on what I said:

'Fuck, I don't mean that in like a creepy way? I'm not into kids, like.'

She lets out a little laugh, then takes the tissues.

'What I mean is, I always seen past your toughness. I always knew inside, that wasn't really you.'

'It's hard to shake off the habits of a lifetime, Mickey. The more I got to know you, the more I knew I wanted you. The more I wanted you, the more I hurt you.'

'You hurt me a lot, Mandy. You cut me off from my friends, you sold stories, personal things, to the newspapers about me. You told me ...'

I choke a little bit, then come out with it:

'You told me I was going to be a daddy.'

'I fucked up, man, that's what I do. Look, I know I can't make things better between us, I just want you to know that I'm sorry. I'm sorry for everything.'

She reaches into her handbag , pulls out a brown paper bag and places it on my lap.

'Knuckles knew that I had feelings for you. Real feelings. He wanted to use you, then get you locked up in prison. He knows me better than I know myself. He knew that I was going to try to go straight with you. He thought that if you didn't turn up for the X-Factor final, then I wouldn't want anything to do with you. He was wrong.'

My brain is going a hundred miles an hour right now. Normally it's just ticking over at a tail's pace, but, now there's loads going on and it's making my head sore.

'What's in the bag?'

'Open it and see.'

I open the bag and there's bundles of money. I look at Mandy and my hands are shaking:

'There must be hundreds in here.'

'Thousands, Mickey. £9,860 to be exact.'

'Where did ... where did you get it?'

'There was more than that, but I had to give it to Knuckles. This is the bits I've taken for myself. Sort of a little 'starting again fund'. When Knuckles lent you the six grand, he made me take money from your account and give it back to him. It was a win/win for him. He was getting his money back, plus he'd still hold a debt over you. Then there was the money from the newspapers.'

I feel my body stiffen up. Those stories could have ended my X-Factor dream and I accused my friends in the wrong over them. Mandy puts her arm around me, kisses me on the cheek, and says:

'I'm giving this money to you, Mickey. It's rightfully yours and you should have it. I have the price of a flight to Spain where I'm going to stay with one of my foster families who have retired out there. They're nice. Probably nicer than I ever deserved ...'

Mickey Doc

She stands up from the bed and pauses. Then, still looking straight in front of her, she pulls an envelope from her bag:

'This has my contact details and address for Spain. Maybe, when the whole X-Factor thing is over, you could come out to me? There's a plane ticket inside the envelope.'

I go to speak, but she puts her fingers over my lips. The kinda way they do it in the movies:

'Don't answer now, Mickey. Think about it.'

She bends over and kisses the top of my head. I try to get up from the bed, but my legs won't allow me. She reaches out her hand, softly dries a tear from my cheek, turns, and walks out the door. I'm left just staring at the plane ticket in my hand.

It isn't long before my ma and dad come into my room. I quickly stick the envelope under the duvet and just run over to hug the two of them. My ma is dabbing at her eyes so her make-up won't run . My da is trying to be tough by not crying, but then it all starts coming out. The three of us are just stood in the middle of the room, crying and hugging. We're stood like that for at least ten minutes and nobody says a word.

My ma is the first to break the hug. She takes my head in her hands and looks me straight in the face:

'We love you, son. It wasn't easy for your da and me having a kid. We had never planned it. But, we done our best.'

My da is standing nodding away. I look at the both of them:

'I don't think I realised before just how good of a job you done.'

Next thing, the lads are coming in through the door. It's high-fives and hugs all around. Finally, people are getting a chance to congratulate me on getting through to the final of the X-Factor. I figure now is as good a time as any to order some drink to the room. Just as I'm about to lift the phone, I see Sean walking into the room. And as if the fella hasn't done enough for me, he has two gigantic bottles of champagne in his hands. He leaves them on the table and walks over to me, looking at the ground the whole time:

'Mickey, I just want to say, congratulations on getting through to the final. It's always great to see a fellow Derry man do well for himself.'

I look around the room at everybody who is there. My ma and da, Decky. Marty and Stevie. I take a deep breath and soak it all in. These are the people who are always there for me, through thick and thin. I can't help feeling emotional and start crying again. Sean puts his arm around me and says:

'You've been through a lot, kid. An awful lot. And you still made it to the final. That shows balls in my book.'

That feels so good to hear.

Sean then shakes the hand of everybody in the room before leaving. Such a seriously sound bloke. It's not long then before my ma and da head off. My ma says she's still feeling a bit faint over the whole thing and needs a lie-down. Doesn't stop her refilling her champagne glass, though, before she walks out the door, with my da behind her actually high-fiving my mates. I definitely have a newfound love for them tonight, but, they're still a pair of dicks. I do a quick scan of the room, but there's no sign of Laura. I hope she isn't hiding behind the curtains or something. Marty then comes over and puts his arm around me and looks straight at the side of my face. I don't look around at him, 'cause I know he's about to start gloating 'cause he was right about Sean. Actually, wasn't even that he was right, just that he wasn't lying for a change. I think he surprised himself. He looks pretty drunk too. Must have been knocking it back since he got here:

'So, Mickey … Mickey Doc … Mickey , Mickey Doc. Ye didn't believe me about my mate, Sean, did you?'

'I don't believe half the things you tell me, man. Are you half-tubed?'

'A little bit, aye. Brought the van over with me to pick up some cheap booze and fags. Thought I'd sample the goods before I start selling them.'

'You have the van with you?'

'Aye, me and Stevie came over in her. Marty's Mobile Shop. I'm going to change the face of retail in Derry.'

'You should try changing your own face first, man. No offence. Hi, so what's the craic then with Sean's ma. Is she actually a witch?'

I'm loving having my mates back.

'Well, she goes under the name 'holistic healer', but that's just a front. She's definitely a fucking witch man.'

Stevie and Decky then come over. Both of them are actually looking pretty pissed too. I didn't really notice before.

'Have you two been helping him with testing his illegal booze?'

I don't think I've ever seen Decky as drunk:

'Well we couldn't have Marty here testing it on his own now, could we? Plus, a little bit of Dutch courage was called for.'

Marty goes to high-five Decky and misses, falling straight through a wooden coffee table. We all break down laughing and I swear to God this is the best I've felt in a long, long time. Decky then pulls an envelope from his pocket and my heart sinks. I didn't want anybody to know about Mandy's offer.

'I forgot to give you this, man. It's a letter from Laura. She had to rush off.'

Thank fuck, it's not Mandy's envelope. I look at Decky for a few seconds before saying:

'You know I didn't fall out with you, man, because you're gay?'

'I never thought that for a second, Mickey. You'll always be like a brother to me.'

'I just wished you'd have told me earlier.'

'I thought about it many's a time, man. I just couldn't bring myself to tell people. Even you.'

We both give each other a huge hug.

I look at Steve and he looks better than he has ever done. Obviously, I don't mean that in a gay way. I feel like I should tell him:

'You look better than you have ever done, Stevie. Congratulations on the new job.'

'Thanks, man, things are going great. I wouldn't be here if it wasn't for you guys helping to so sort things out. Thank you, Mickey. Thanks for everything.'

Stevie then picks me up and gives me a massive hug. My feet are lifted off the ground. He has definitely been working out. He sets me back down again.

'I'm going to go now, lads. I have to be back at the office in the morning, me and my da have a huge meeting with some investors.'

He rubs my head and says goodbye to the lads before heading out the door, holding his two middle fingers in the air as he walks out.

****

I take Laura's envelope and go across to the desk at the other end of the room, sit down and open the letter.

Dear Mickey,

I'm sorry I couldn't stick around. I hope your chat with Mandy went well and you told her where to go. I wouldn't be surprised if you didn't, though. I know what you're like. But, that's your choice to make. You're on your own now, I've done what I had to do and saved you.

Mickey Doc

The next time you see me, Mickey. You'll be calling me 'Sister.' (Calm down, this doesn't mean I'm your actual sister. It means I'm going to become a nun.) I met your little cousin, George, after mass a few months back and it was him that first alerted me to the fact you were in serious trouble. He told me that if he could, he would go to England and help you himself. I'd been contemplating becoming a nun for a while and all of a sudden I had this kind of epiphany, that this was my first calling from God, to help Mickey Doc in his time of need. George was really supportive and arranged for me to stay in a convent in Manchester. When I wasn't playing detective, I was praying and discussing my future with the other nuns. This all feels right. I feel happy and content for once.

I know you're out of danger now, I can feel it. Whatever happens in the final, remember, you are always loved, Mickey, and keep those that are dear to you close by.

George also sends his love. He says to tell you that he's proud to call you his big cousin.

We are all proud of you, Mickey.

Take care and best of luck in the final. You won't need it though, you're the best.

Laura. Xxx

I'm just staring at the letter. I have so many questions, like, what does a nun do? Isn't a nun a priest's wife? Is she planning to marry George? Is that legal? I decide it's best to leave all those questions for tomorrow and find out if Marty has any more of that booze that needs testing. I think I need to get pissed.

****

The last week has been like a world-wind, between interviews, photo-shoots and getting myself ready for the actual final. I'm standing on the X-Factor stage. It's just me and Passive X left. Phil had got through to the finals, but he was voted out last night. I can't help but think of the incredible people I have in my life, from the ones I knew since I was a child, to the ones I met here at the X-Factor. All of them are in the audience right now, awaiting the final verdict. Well, except one, but I'd like to think she's cheering me on from rainy Spain. The only people I can make out are my ma and da. I bought my ma a present during the week. A new puppy. She was absolutely fucking delighted and cried when I gave it to her. She's waving at me now and blowing kisses. I blow a kiss back at her. The arena falls silent as Dermot O'Leary starts talking:

'Britain you have voted on the matter of the winner of the X-Factor 2014 …'

He looks around at me and the Passive X lads:

'… Good luck to Passive X, and good luck to Mickey.'

This is it. This is what it has all been about. Not just the past year but my entire life. I'm shaking like a leaf.

There's a really long pause. I'm imagining the three people who came up with my name, Tommy, Alice and Joe, watching from heaven and saying my name for the first time.

''And the winner of the 2014 X-Factor is…'

…'MICKEY DOC!'

CHAPTER 23.

Marty has just dropped me off. As the X-Factor winner, I could've got myself a limo, but, I didn't want all the fuss. I've been doing so much promo work since the final, I'm so glad to finally get some time to myself. Marty beeps the horn of his ugly-looking mobile shop and waves me goodbye. I take the envelope from my pocket and walk into the airport. Vivo la Spain-ya.

The End.

Printed in Poland
by Amazon Fulfillment
Poland Sp. z o.o., Wrocław